A Curious Death

Jason Vail

A Curious Death

A CURIOUS DEATH

Copyright 2022, by Jason Vail

All rights reserved, including the right to reproduce this book or portions thereof in any form.

A Hawk Publishing book.

Cover design by Ashley Barber.

ISBN: 9798412229133

Hawk Publishing
Tallahassee, FL 32312

ALSO BY JASON VAIL

The Attebrook Family Saga

The Outlaws
The Poisoned Cup

Stephen Attebrook Mysteries

The Wayward Apprentice
Baynard's List
The Dreadful Penance
The Girl in the Ice
Saint Milburgha's Bones
Bad Money
The Bear Wagon
Murder at Broadstowe Manor
The Burned Man
The Corpse at Windsor Bridge
Missing

Lone Star Rising Stories

Lone Star Rising: Voyage of the Wasp
Lone Star Rising: T.S. Wasp and the Heart of Texas

Viking Tales

Snorri's Gold
Saga of the Lost Ship

Martial Arts

Medieval and Renaissance Dagger Combat

A Curious Death

A Curious Death

A Curious Death

March 1264
to
April 1264

A Curious Death

Chapter 1

"He's dead! Oh, God, he's dead! Help me!" A woman's shrill cry cut through the hum of conversation in the Oxford bathhouse known as the Castle Keep.

There was a moment of stunned silence, followed by shouts of alarm. Feet pounded on the dirt floors between the curtained alcoves containing the bathtubs, the figures fleetingly visible between breaks in the curtain.

Stephen Attebrook, nearly asleep from the lulling warmth of his own bath, raised his head at the cries of alarm. The fact that a man was dead nearby, while once a matter of professional concern when Stephen had been a county coroner, was not enough to drive him from the comfort of the bath. He had been on the road for four days from Ludlow in answer to King Henry's call for men to honor their feudal obligations and gather at Oxford in preparation for the war with the rebellious barons under Simon de Montfort, and he was dirty and dead tired. Until this moment, the water's heat made it feel as if he was melting. The thought of rising from that pleasurable warmth to address a corpse was appalling. But a woman's plea for help was something he could not ignore.

He stood up, cascading water over the sides of the tub.

Gilbert Wistwode, Stephen's companion in the tub, stared at him aghast, sputtering from the wave that had struck him in the face. He rubbed water from his jovial round face with a stubby-fingered hand which then moved on to pat what remained of his hair, a fringe of brown and grey about a dome as bare as an upturned cooking pot. Guessing what Stephen intended, he hugged Stephen about one muscular thigh to restrain him.

"What are you doing?" Stephen asked.

"Saving you from yourself! I know what you have in mind! Leave well enough alone! Let others deal with it. It's not our business anymore." Gilbert had been the coroner's clerk when Stephen took over as deputy, and they had examined many a death together. Now that Stephen was no longer a coroner and Gilbert a coroner's clerk, they had no business getting involved in the investigations of unnatural deaths. But somehow that had not stopped them from doing so.

"Do you know how ridiculous you look?" Stephen said.

"It doesn't matter," Gilbert said. "No one can see."

Stephen peeled Gilbert's fingers apart and freed himself. He stepped out of the tub.

"You're going to regret this," Gilbert said. "I have a bad feeling."

"Nothing will come of it," Stephen said.

He wrapped his cloak around his nakedness and left the alcove to see what the disturbance was about.

A crowd had gathered at an alcove two spaces away where the curtain had been pulled back and there was a great puddle that many feet were already churning into mud. The press of bodies screened what had provoked the disturbance. Stephen edged around the crowd to the other side for a better view.

As he reached the other side, where his view was not as obstructed, one of the men in the crowd stared down at Stephen's stub of a left foot, which was missing from the arch forward. The man's eyebrows rose.

"What are you looking at?" Stephen growled.

The man looked Stephen up and down, taking the measure of Stephen's six feet in height and broad shoulders, which could mean trouble better off avoided. "Nothing," the man said.

Stephen almost said, "what happened?" as a peace offering, but what happened seemed pretty clear from the tableau in the alcove. Someone had tipped the tub on its side, which explained the great puddle. Half in and out of the barrel was the dead man, naked as bathers always were. He was a handsome fellow, barely into his twenties, slim but muscular as Stephen was himself. The corpse's brown hair was sodden from submersion in the tub, which was unusual in itself since people did not usually dunk their heads; tub water was not changed between clients and was usually dirty by the end of the day. The thin lips were a ghastly slate color and the skin of

A Curious Death

his face had that waxy yellow appearance so characteristic of death. There were mottled bruises all about the neck, shoulders, arms and torso. Some looked fresh, but some were old and yellowing.

Stephen squatted by a young woman who held the dead man's shoulders and head in her lap. Calling her a woman might be stretching things. She was, in fact, probably fourteen or fifteen, her face unlined and with the smoothness of youth. Her head scarf had come undone and mousy brown hair tumbled about her face and got into her eyes. She brushed the rampant tresses away with a thin, muddy hand. Her dress rested on thin shoulders and was too big for her, resembling a sack.

Mud from the spilled water oozed between Stephen's remaining toes. He shifted and something sharp jabbed the underside of his good foot. He lifted the foot and saw a roundish object stuck to the bottom. He plucked it loose; it was a button with some muddy threads attached. He almost flung it away, but its shine suggested it was made of silver, which meant it was as good as money. Money was in short supply in the Attebrook household at the moment. He closed his fist about the button.

Questions surged into his mind but he could not ask them and be heard over the uproar of many voices talking at once. He barked for silence. He had a good command voice, honed by years of leading soldiers, and it worked as well with these ordinary people as it did with hard men. The crowd fell silent.

"Did you find him?" Stephen asked the woman.

The woman nodded.

"Tell me about it," Stephen said with the same voice of authority, although this direction was issued more gently.

He was so intent on the young woman that he hardly noticed Gilbert edge into the alcove, cloak clutched about his shoulders, his pallid round belly fleetingly visible. Gilbert edged aside a pale woman with a face covered with freckles and strands of red hair showing from beneath her head scarf who was standing at the back by a pile of clothing. Gilbert knelt and retrieved a clay cup from the ground. He sniffed the cup even though it had to be empty; Gilbert was a connoisseur of wine and Stephen wondered if he was absurdly curious about the vintage. A clay pitcher, its outside white enamel with red dragons painted on it, rested on the side table near where the tub had stood. Gilbert sniffed the pitcher as well.

The woman gulped. "When I came in to check on whether he needed anything, he was in the tub."

"All in. Head too?" Stephen said.

The woman nodded. "Sunk to the bottom, all curled up, like. I tried to pull him out, but he's too big. Bill helped me tip over the tub." She pointed to a burly man with a nose bent as though someone had stamped on it. "We got him out then. But it was too late, as you can see ..." Her voice trailed off with a note of helplessness.

"Looks like a drowning," a man in the crowd said. "I've seen the like before."

"How could a grown man drown in a bathtub?" another asked.

This was a good question, since bathtubs were only deep enough to submerge someone up his shoulders when he was sitting down. The question reignited the loud babble.

How, indeed?

Stephen was about to pursue the question when the crowd parted to admit three men with red badges on their coats indicating that they were local bailiffs.

"All right, everyone," one of the bailiffs ordered. "Clear off. The coroner and the jury are on the way. You're not to interfere, hear?"

The crowd reluctantly began to withdraw, it being a crime to interfere with the work of coroner and jury. The satisfaction of curiosity was not worth a night in the stocks.

Stephen was slow to step away, however.

"I said, clear off!" the bailiff snapped at Stephen and the woman with bright red hair at the rear of the alcove.

"Right, sorry," Stephen said.

A Curious Death

The freckled woman by the pile of clothes gathered them up and hurried around Stephen, who withdrew and splashed back to his alcove, where Gilbert waited.

Stephen washed his feet and got dressed, as Gilbert did the same.

Gilbert sniffed the air as he put on his boots. "Is that mince pie I smell? I wouldn't mind a bit of that." He eyed Stephen. "You owe me, you know, after dragging me on this wild goose chase."

Stephen sighed. Gilbert was right, of course. Stephen owed Gilbert a great deal for coming with him to the muster at Oxford, where he had no reason to be.

"I'll get you one on the way out," he said.

He and Gilbert ambled into the amber light of a setting sun just now peeking from beneath dissipating storm clouds, and turned toward Oxford's south gate, a pair of pies steaming in their hands

"What did you think of the vintage?" Stephen asked before he bit into his pie.

"Of the pie? Oh, you mean the wine," Gilbert said, after he gulped down a mouthful of pie. "Very curious."

"How so?"

"It smelled of chamomile and lavender — and something else I could not identify. An odd assortment of spices to flavor the wine." People often put spices in wine to blunt the harshness of a bad vintage or to hide the fact it had gone off.

"You certainly have a discriminating nose," Stephen said.

"The odor was strong enough to knock out a horse. There's something else as well. The pitcher was empty and you noticed that puddle."

"It was as big as a pond. How could I not?"

"Not that one. There was a smaller puddle by the side table."

"Oh. Missed it. You sniffed that one, too?"

"Yes. Well, the dirt, anyway." Gilbert rubbed his fingers together. "It smelled of chamomile and lavender and that mystery spice. Same as the pitcher."

"Someone poured out the wine?" Stephen asked.

"Your mind is working today," Gilbert said.

"Perhaps our victim didn't like the spices."

"If you don't like the wine, you send it back. You don't pour it out. You still have to pay for it then."

"It's odd that a man drowns in a bathtub," Stephen said, echoing a sentiment he'd heard earlier.

"Yes, it is. And with a crowd all about." Gilbert kicked a loose stone which bounced down the road and splashed into a puddle. "Two oddities, one big, one small."

Curiosity about these oddities tickled at Stephen's mind, but he thrust such thoughts aside as Gilbert changed the subject to ask what they should do for supper, since a single small mince pie was not enough for Gilbert's prodigious appetite — proper meals being a matter of critical importance.

After all, the curious death in the tub was none of their business.

A Curious Death

Chapter 2

The army camp was in fields beyond Oxford's North Gate by the king's house on Saint Giles Street, one of his many palaces scattered about the country.

The gathering of an army was as much a social event as it was a military one, and the evenings were usually taken up by carousing as men renewed acquaintances with those they may not have seen in some time.

Stephen left Gilbert in their tent with Wymar, a strongly built lad of sixteen who had been a groom at Stephen's manor, Priors Halton but had come along as Stephen's squire, and spent the evening circulating among the throng in search of old friends and acquaintances, enjoying many a toast by a fire and an exchange of lies about exploits they had undertaken. So, it was long after midnight when he finally staggered back to his tent. It was not easy finding the tent in the dark given how many tents occupied the fields, and he fell twice getting there, once over a tent stake and another time over a drunk who had collapsed between two tents heedless of the obstacle he presented in the pitch dark.

Consequently, Stephen was still asleep more than three hours after dawn, and would have slept longer if Wymar hadn't prodded his foot.

"My lord," Wyman said. "You have a visitor."

"Who is it?" Stephen inquired without opening his eyes, resenting both Wymar and this unidentified visitor.

"I did not get his name, my lord," Wymar said.

"What kind of a squire are you, if you can't do a simple thing like ask a man's name?"

Wymar was not moved by this accusation of dereliction of duty. "He says he has come from the earl of Arundel. The earl would like to see you. As soon as convenient. I think he means right now. It's not good manners to leave an earl waiting, is it?"

"That bastard can wait until hell freezes over, as far as I'm concerned," Stephen growled. They were neighbors of a sort. Percival FitzAllan's principal castle, Clun, lay only eighteen miles from Priors Halton. But they were bitter enemies. FitzAllan had not forgiven Stephen for his part, though it was only rumored, in the burning of his castle at Bucknell and for marrying Ida when she had been given to him as a ward; the wardship being a source of income that FitzAllan had lost.

But Stephen sat up and rubbed his face. His tongue felt as though a herd of horses had trampled across it and he desperately needed a drink. "Did this emissary say what the earl wanted?"

Wymar did not have a chance to reply, for the tent flap stirred and a voice said, "Your pardon, Sir Stephen. I can speak better for myself." The emissary, a grizzled man of more than forty but wearing a fashionable blue coat with silver buttons shaped to look like the heads of bears, bowed. "Ernald de Helleston, at your service."

Stephen knew the name, as he did the names of all the gentle families in the vicinity of Ludlow. Helleston held Hopton Castle and manor from FitzAllan, which made him a neighbor and enemy as well. "I don't think we've met."

Helleston smiled. "We've met. You just don't remember. I was at Clun when you stayed there."

The reference to "staying" at Clun was a euphemism. Stephen and Gilbert had been imprisoned there in a converted pigsty in the castle's middle bailey on charges of battery and inciting a riot. They got away when the Welsh partly overran the castle and set the middle bailey on fire.

"Ah," Stephen said cautiously. "Sorry if I don't recall you. It was such a busy time. What does his lordship want?"

"Your help."

"Your help!" Gilbert said as he hurried after Stephen. "Your help! He wants your help to put your head in a noose, most likely!"

"I imagine FitzAllan would be happy to have your head as well," Stephen said. He scanned about for the possibility of ambush as he followed Helleston through the forest of tents

A Curious Death

toward the king's palace, where apparently the earl of Arundel, as a valued ally, enjoyed a roof over his head rather than a leaky tent. Ambush seemed a remote chance, though, especially in broad daylight, but he wanted to be mentally prepared just in case. "He was happy to have it once."

"I daresay!" Gilbert panted. As far as they knew, the charges still stood, although FitzAllan hadn't done anything about them. "But you are the bigger fish."

"I doubt this is a ruse to do us harm," Stephen said with more confidence than he felt. He would rather settle into a den of poisonous snakes than a chamber with FitzAllan. "I am Leonor's man now, which means I am Edward's. And Edward won't have us fighting among ourselves when there's Montfort's people to deal with. I heard him say so."

Leonor was Lord Edward's wife and daughter-in-law to King Henry. She had granted Stephen the manor of Priors Halton for services he had rendered at Windsor in the affair of her chaplain's suicide.

"You have more faith in the forbearance of outraged magnates than I do," Gilbert said. "They tend to do what pleases them and damn the consequences."

"If you're worried about it, go back."

"As if I'd leave you to face death alone."

Stephen smiled thinly. "I think it's best for your health and peace of mind that you remain outside."

The king's palace was a big stone building, long and narrow and brilliantly whitewashed, housing bedchambers and a vaulting central hall. Helleston crossed the hall to the central fire, where Lord Edward, his uncle Richard, and several other high-born men were seated. Percival FitzAllan was among them. He must have been watching the door, because he rose and retreated to a corner, where someone had placed three chairs, two facing one. FitzAllan settled into one and motioned Stephen to take the chair opposite him.

A young man of eighteen or nineteen clad in a cleric's robes and with a familiar look about him occupied the third chair beside FitzAllan. He had carefully combed brown hair that fell about a high and broad forehead and was not clipped in the manner of a monk or priest. Flecks of what might someday become a moustache adorned his upper lip. The long fingers of his hands in his lap clasped and unclasped, as if he was troubled by something, although this did not show on his face, which was bland. He brought one arm out from the slit in his robes and smoothed his hair, revealing golden buttons on the sleeve of his blue undercoat. FitzAllan glanced at the boy, but did not introduce him.

"My lord," Stephen said warily as Helleston backed out of earshot. "You asked to see me."

FitzAllan nodded. He normally favored highly colored clothes, in rich reds, blues and golden yellows. But today he was clad brown and black, the sort of thing men wore when arming for battle. He was more than ten years older than Stephen with close-cropped red hair greying at the temples adorning a head that looked like a block of stone balanced on massive, muscular shoulders. His thick wrists, ordinarily adorned with silver bracelets, were bare, but his hands, oddly slender and feminine looking, still sported emerald and ruby rings. His face, more lined than it had been in January the last time Stephen had seen him, was distracted, despondent. There was no sign of the menace, anger or duplicity that Stephen had been expecting.

"Thank you for coming," FitzAllan said. He paused and steepled his hands beneath his chin as if uncertain what to say next.

"We've certainly had our differences," FitzAllan said.

"Enough for you to want my death or ruin," Stephen said.

"Yes," FitzAllan said heavily. "And you deserve it, too."

He took a deep breath and went on. "Be that as it may, I need a favor."

"From me?" Stephen could not keep the surprise and disbelief out of his voice.

"Yes. There has been a death in my family," FitzAllan said. "My dearest sister's eldest son died yesterday."

A Curious Death

"I see," Stephen said, for now there was no doubt what was coming. He had once been a deputy coroner, and later coroner, for a part of his county. But he lost that post, and its stipend, during the present political turmoil. He regretted the loss of the stipend, but not the loss of the position. He had never liked the coroner's main business, the sad inquiry into the manner and means of people's deaths. Yet, for some reason people kept expecting him to be eager to continue that work on a private basis.

FitzAllan did not go on, and Stephen filled the silence with a question. "What was his name?"

"Miles de Dinesley," FitzAllan said. "He was a son to me, better than the real ones."

The young man beside FitzAllan snapped, "He died in a whorehouse! Drowned in a bathtub! Or so they say!"

"This is Miles' brother, Serlo," FitzAllan said. "As you can see, he is greatly affected by his brother's death."

"Drowned in a bathtub?" Stephen asked. This had to be the death he and Gilbert had seen yesterday evening.

"The damned coroner thinks so!" FitzAllan broke in. "Incompetent wretch! A misadventure! An accident! The result of too much drink!"

"And you think otherwise," Stephen said.

"The lad didn't drink anything but small ale. Wine made him sick. Yet that imbecile of a coroner concluded he was drunk on wine!"

"Did you communicate this fact to the coroner and the jury?" Stephen asked.

"Of course, I did!" FitzAllan exclaimed harshly. "As soon as I heard the verdict last evening!"

"And the coroner refuses to amend the verdict?"

"Yes, that useless swine! No proof that anyone else was involved, he says!"

"Yet, you suspect murder."

FitzAllan fixed Stephen with narrowed, furious eyes. "A sober man does not drown in a tub without help."

"It is curious," Stephen said.

"Curious!" FitzAllan spat.

"And you want me to make a private inquiry into the matter," Stephen said. "To determine if there is error in the coroner's conclusion."

"I know your reputation and I saw your work at Windsor," FitzAllan said, a reference to the inquiry Stephen had conducted into the drowning of the chaplain Giles de Twet in the River Thames. "I would have you give me the same service."

"Such inquiries are often difficult, expensive and fraught with danger. Why would I do that, given our history?"

"I will cover your expenses. That's the normal thing to do, correct?"

Stephen nodded.

"And," FitzAllan went on, "if you are successful in finding the killer, I will speak to Lord Edward about arranging the return of Hafton Manor to you."

A Curious Death

Chapter 3

"He promised to return Hafton Manor!" Gilbert burst out, astonished, as they made their way to the king's chapel, where Dinesley's body had been laid out. A funeral Mass would take place later in the day with burial immediately afterward.

"Yes, if we are successful at identifying a killer," Stephen said. "A long shot even if there was a killer." A very long shot, indeed. Odds were, Miles de Dinesley drowned in his bath without help. There was no evidence to indicate otherwise. If there had been, the coroner and the jury should have discovered it.

Yet more than anything, Stephen wanted to get his hands on Hafton Manor. It was where he had been born and grew up. It had been held by his brother William, and upon William's death, should have come to Stephen as the closest surviving male relative. But William's widow connived with FitzAllan to forge a will that showed William had adopted Ida, his step-daughter, as his heir so that Ida would take possession. Ida became a king's ward given to FitzAllan, who had intended to marry her to a retainer. To avoid that marriage, Ida and Stephen had pretended to wed. In punishment for marrying without the king's or FitzAllan's permission, Lord Edward had seized Hafton. He subsequently granted the manor to FitzAllan. Even a remote chance of regaining Hafton was a gamble he could not shirk.

"A very long shot," Stephen muttered, voicing his thoughts, misgivings and greed.

"To be sure." Gilbert rubbed his ample belly. "Well, at least it gives one something to do besides loll about playing dice and getting drunk."

"I do not loll about playing dice and getting drunk."

"I was thinking of Wymar. We can put him to work on this, too."

"I don't know. He's got enough to do keeping the armor and tack clean."

Many chapels of the rich were built into the hall so that the patron did not have far to go or to expose himself to inclement weather for spiritual sustenance, but this one was a freestanding stone building set in a grove of cherry trees. Modest and boxy, which meant it was very old, it could easily be mistaken for a small limewashed house instead of a chapel.

Stephen paused on the porch, his hand on the doorhandle. What came next was perhaps the most unpleasant aspect of the job. He took a deep breath and entered.

There was no one in the chapel, which was a relief, since Stephen wouldn't have to order out the occupants, who often relished the spectacle of his examination of the dead. Their eagerness and reluctance to go always irked him. Death itself was indignity enough without having people reveling in it.

He was also pleased to find that the chapel's tall, narrow windows admitted enough light to see. There had been times when he had been forced to view a body outside in the open air where it was impossible to keep spectators away.

As it was a small chapel, Stephen required only five paces to reach the coffin set before the altar. He and Gilbert stood over it for a few moments while Gilbert said a silent prayer, as he often did before this ugly work.

"And God forgive us for what we are about to do," Gilbert finished in Latin.

Stephen remained still after the prayer.

"You want *me* to get him out?" Gilbert asked when Stephen did not move. "By myself?"

Stephen did not answer this question but glanced back to the door at a shuffling sound, and saw Miles' brother, Serlo, enter the chapel. "You can go," Stephen said.

Serlo flinched at the commanding tone. "You are in no position to give me orders," he said.

"I'm not?" Stephen inquired.

Serlo said "I am the son of William de Dinesley."

"So?" Stephen said, unimpressed. He had never heard of the Dinesley family.

"He is the baron of Hockesford," Serlo said.

A Curious Death

"Oh," Stephen said, still unimpressed, although it made sense that FitzAllan's sister would have married well; no struggling merchant for her, as was the case with many gentry women whose families could not make marriages in the upper classes. Such a marriage made Serlo a lordling; people of that ilk were often prickly about their position and easily offended. Yet Stephen didn't care what this boy thought of him.

"I want to find out how Miles died as much as my uncle," Serlo said.

"Suit yourself, but you may not like what has to be done," Stephen said. "At least, he hasn't begun to smell yet."

He lifted the coffin lid, which wasn't nailed down.

The body within was wrapped in a linen shroud.

"You get the feet," Stephen said to Gilbert as he bent to grab hold of the corpse's shoulders.

There was a brief struggle as they lifted the body out; it was flaccid in the strange way of corpses, as if its bones had dissolved, that made it ungainly. The shroud slipped off as they laid it on the rushes covering the ground; it had not been sewn, the usual practice, and the body was naked except for braise concealing his private parts — a sign that FitzAllan expected Stephen to accept his offer? Ordinarily, a corpse was dressed in his best, but they would have had to cut away those clothes to conduct their examination.

"What is the point of this?" Serlo gasped.

Stephen looked up. "FitzAllan didn't tell you?"

"No."

"This is how we work. Murder always leaves its mark upon a body. If you look hard enough, you'll find it — assuming it's there."

"Almost always," Gilbert murmured. "If it was poison, it may not have."

"Right," Stephen said, remembering the empty pitcher and cup. "The wine."

"As we have seen before," Gilbert said. Not long ago, they had investigated the death of magnate who had been given drugged wine which put him to sleep so he could be hanged in a way that suggested suicide. This death could be similar.

"But Miles never drank wine," Stephen said.

"There is that problem," Gilbert said. "Someone in that alcove ordered wine. If it wasn't for Miles, who was it for?"

"A mystery visitor," Stephen said. "Perhaps our suspect? If this is, in fact, murder?"

"No doubt," Gilbert replied.

They bent to the examination. Laid out full length in the bright morning light of the chapel, Miles de Dinesley's body confirmed Stephen's first impressions. He was tall and muscular without being heavy, handsome with a pointed chin and high cheekbones and broad, pale forehead. There were bruises upon his arms, chest, and legs, some of them new, but many old and yellowing. Stephen smoothed back the dead man's brown hair and fingered the skull for depressions characteristic of a skull fracture or for cuts to rule out a blow on the head. There were none. Nor were there any marks on the neck that indicated strangulation, apart from the purplish hue at the back, which often formed on corpses; sometimes that hue mimicked the folds of the clothing worn by the deceased. Stephen had once seen a corpse with a perfect impression of the man's belt upon the mottled skin.

They turned the body over and looked at the back, where, as expected, there was more bruises old and new and more of that purplish reddish color and here and there lighter seams that probably came from folds in the linen shroud.

There was one thing that was out of the ordinary. A narrow line of scraped skin ran across the back from shoulder to shoulder. It looked like a fresh injury; flecks of blood were visible here and there in the scrape.

"What to make of that?" Gilbert asked about the scrape.

"Rubbed his neck on the rim of the tub?" Stephen said. He had suffered something similar in his own tub.

"Very curious," Gilbert said. "No sign of an obvious wound, except for those bruises, and I don't know what to make of those."

A Curious Death

"He was a wrestler, I think," Stephen said. He drew back a curtain of hair and pointed to one of Miles' ears, which had a peculiar swollen shape. He poked the ear. Instead of being soft and yielding, it was hard.

"I used to get bruises like that when I wrestled, but I avoided the problem of the ear, which is common." Stephen turned to Serlo. "Was he a wrestler?"

"Yes, He was quite good, too," Serlo said stiffly, as if he disapproved of wrestling, which was odd, since for the knightly class, wrestling was considered as important a foundation for knighthood as the ability to manage a horse.

"How good?" Stephen asked.

"He often wrestled — as a gamble."

Stephen nodded. Common wrestlers fought for prizes, but those in the upper classes, if they sought profit, did so as a gambling matter. "Won more than he lost?"

"He never lost. Not so far as I know."

"Very fit looking," Stephen mused.

"As befits a wrestler," Gilbert added.

They exchanged glances.

"Hard to imagine someone drowning him in his bath," Stephen said.

"Quite," Gilbert said.

"I think we're done," Stephen said. "Let's get him wrapped up."

Stephen laid out the linen wrap. They turned the body to brush off straws from the rushes adhering to the skin. As Stephen plucked loose straw from Dinesley's hair, he saw something that made him pause. He parted the dead man's hair at the back of his neck and bent close.

"Look here," he said to Gilbert.

Gilbert stooped by Stephen to see what Stephen was pointing to.

"A wound of some kind?" Gilbert asked.

It was a little slit about an inch long at the base of the skull. Stephen pried back the edges. Flesh the color of chicken meat could be seen with some difficulty within the wound. He wormed his little finger into the slit. It was customary for coroners to use a measuring stick to determine the depth of a death wound, but Stephen had left his back in Ludlow since he had not imagined he'd ever have a need for it. Thus, a finger would have to do. Gritting his teeth at the unpleasantness, he wormed the tip of his little finger into the wound.

The sounds of retching filled the little chapel — Serlo de Dinesley was throwing up behind them.

Stephen glanced back at Serlo. He retracted his finger.

"How deep does it go?" Gilbert asked after a pause.

"Hard to say," Stephen said. "My finger hit bone. So, at least as far as that. It probably severed the spine. Enough to kill him, surely." He wiped the finger on the linen shroud.

"Murder after all," Gilbert said. "And we almost missed it."

"As the local coroner apparently did."

"These people are such bumpkins," Gilbert murmured, although they both knew that this discovery had happened only by chance. Even a close examination of the body could have missed it — certainly, they almost had.

They placed the body onto the wrap, but as Gilbert started to cover the face and cinch the sides, Stephen gripped his hand to stop him.

"What is it?" Gilbert asked.

"There's something else . . ." Stephen mused.

The death wound had been deftly and accurately applied — too deftly for the killer to have simply slammed the blade home. Too much chance of missing. Stephen peeled back Miles lips. There were fresh abrasions on the inside of the bottom lip.

"That explains it," Stephen murmured.

"You've lost me," Gilbert said. "What explains what?"

Stephen held the lower lip down so Gilbert could see the scrapes on the inside of the lip. "Someone grasped him from behind along the jaw and plunged the blade home," he said.

"What made you think of that?"

A Curious Death

"Because somebody tried the same trick on me in Spain. He didn't reckon on my mail coat, which stopped the blade."

"He didn't aim for your neck?"

"No. Lower down. On the back. Anyway, his grip on my face left my mouth cut rather as you see here."

"Ah-ha!" Gilbert said. "Which also explains that long scrape along his shoulders! He was held momentarily against the lip of the barrel, his head clasped tightly, and stabbed to death."

"That's the size of it, I think," Stephen agreed. "Help me wrap him up."

Stephen lifted the body by himself as he would a very large and ungainly baby, to avoid the problem of unraveling the wrap, and, with a great grunt, pitched the dead man back into his coffin. The corpse landed with a loud thud and the head knocked against the coffin floor, sounding like two pieces of wood striking together. Stephen smoothed out a few places where the linen had come loose. Then they replaced the coffin lid.

"So, murder you said," Serlo gasped, wiping vomit from his chin with the back of his hand. His face was the color of fresh dough.

"I'm afraid so," Stephen said. "Not a drowning after all."

He walked into the sunlight with visions of Hafton Manor dancing in his head.

Chapter 4

"What will we do now?" Serlo asked as the three men emerged from the chapel into the fresh morning air.

"There's only one thing to do, right off," Stephen said, concerned about Serlo's use of "we." He didn't want the young man tagging along while they conducted the tedious business of an investigation, to witness one failure after another and maybe the failure of the entire enterprise and be in a position to criticize the effort as incompetent. But perhaps he would grow bored and leave them to it; boredom was a common affliction of people of his class. "We need to question the people at the bathhouse."

Serlo was quiet for a moment. "Why?"

"Miles had a visitor before he died," Stephen said, feeling as though he was lecturing a particularly stupid pupil. "We need to find out if anyone saw him."

"Or her," Gilbert interjected.

"Or her," Stephen said in agreement.

"I . . . see," Serlo said. He stopped dead.

"Something the matter?" Stephen asked.

"I'm studying for the priesthood," Serlo said. "It's not fitting that I be seen in . . . that place."

"At which college?" Gilbert asked innocently. As someone who had come close to becoming a priest, he had a natural interest in the activities of a like-minded fellow.

Serlo turned to Gilbert as if surprised he had been addressed by such a lowly person, especially since the question had not been accompanied by the required token of respect, "sir." Even crotchety old men who could barely stand were expected to address youths like Serlo as "sir."

"Balliol College," he said.

"Balliol . . ." Gilbert said. "I don't think I've heard of it."

"It's new," Serlo said. "Just a year old."

"You don't look like a student for the priesthood," Stephen said.

Serlo shrugged. "Because I haven't the proper haircut? I haven't taken orders yet." He frowned. "Since I cannot be

A Curious Death

seen in a house of ill repute, I'll leave you to it. You can report your findings to me rather than bothering my uncle. He's very busy, with the war and all. He's very close to Lord Edward, as you know. In the thick of the planning."

"I've heard there is a war," Stephen said.

"Good for you." Serlo turned on his heel and marched toward the king's palace.

After a few steps, he turned around. "There is something that might have some bearing on our inquiry. My brother had trouble keeping his dick in his drawers." He looked in the direction of Oxford Castle. Its great stone keep on the towering motte could be seen in the distance. "He was deputy constable at the castle, and he dallied with many women in the town. Not only ones who took coin up front. There is one who claims he got her with child. Anne Buckerel is her name. Her family were very upset about it. Demanded compensation. They were refused, of course."

"And this is important, why?" Stephen asked.

"Her brother has a vicious temper. He's known to get in fights and he's quick with a dagger," Serlo said. "Adam Buckerel. Ask around about him. You'll see."

Stephen and Gilbert had already turned down Saint Giles Street toward Oxford when it occurred to him that there was something he should do before he went to the bathhouse.

He spun on his heel, catching Gilbert by surprise, and marched back to the king's palace.

"What is going on?" Gilbert gasped and he trotted up. "Have you had a thought?"

"Half a thought," Stephen muttered.

"That's comforting," Gilbert said as he slowed to a jog, since Stephen was striding fast toward the palace. Gilbert could not walk as fast as Stephen, having legs that were much shorter. "Half a thought's better than none at all. What about?"

"Don't you think we should tell FitzAllan that his suspicions were right?"

"Yes, I suppose he would be flattered to know that the facts concur with his judgment."

"Well born men do like being right," Stephen said.

At the palace, Stephen went in and looked about for FitzAllan, who was standing at a table with Lord Edward, his uncle Duke Richard, his father King Henry, and half a dozen other magnates who had brought their warbands to Oxford in answer to the king's call to the feudal host.

Had the group been headed by Lord Edward, Stephen would have marched straight up and stated his need to see FitzAllan. Edward knew him, and while the prince did not seem to have a great liking for Stephen, they were on speaking terms; besides, owing to Stephen's possession of Priors Halton Manor, he was Princess Leonor's man, which made him one of Edward's. A feudal dependent was always able to approach his lord. The king was another creature entirely. So, he stood back and waited.

Stephen was appalled to see that he was witnessing a strategy conference for the coming conflict with the rebellious barons led by Simon de Montfort — here, in the middle of a crowded hall, where all sorts of people could overhear it. One faction argued for a march on London when the full army had gathered and either force a decisive battle with the rebels or capture the city. A second faction suggested a march around London and Montfort's army directly to Dover to secure the king's links with the Continent. A third faction supported picking off garrisons of rebel supporters in the north, such as at Northampton and Nottingham, to isolate Montfort and to leave no enemies at the king's back when he finally went south to confront his brother-in-law.

About the participants, servants came and went, some leaving pitchers of wine on the conference table and carrying away the empties, others tending the hearth fire, still others sweeping the floor nearby; one tossed morsels to a pair of greyhounds under the table which noisily consumed them.

A Curious Death

And that was only the servants. A bevy of high-born women had their heads together in what on the surface appeared to be a sewing circle, but little attention was being given to the sewing, for their ears were cocked toward the discussions. Women liked to know what was going on, and often seemed better informed than the men. A few male hangers-on were also in earshot, including Serlo de Dinesley, who nursed a cup of wine, his lips stained red from it, his face unusually pale. After what he'd seen in the chapel, it was no wonder he needed refreshment.

A young girl in a shimmering blue satin overgown with pearls on her sleeves who was about Serlo's age stood behind him. She put a hand on his shoulder and squeezed. Serlo looked back at her, smiled and patted her hand. The girl withdrew to the sewing circle, and Serlo returned his attention to the magnates about the table.

At last, the conference broke up and the great men stood about while servants hastened to refill their wine cups.

Edward's restless eyes fastened on Stephen. Those eyes, such a startling blue, narrowed in thought. His fingers tapped on the tabletop, where a map of southern England had been spread out.

Stephen stepped up to the table and bowed. "My lord."

"Attebrook," Edward said. "What is it? Can't you see we're busy here?"

"If you would grant me a word in private, my lord," Stephen said.

King Henry looked up at the mention of Stephen's name. The king was a curious man. Handsome in an ordinary way, he had not inherited the Plantagenet stockiness of his father King John. Instead, he was short and slender. His greying brown hair was well combed and secured with a gold ribbon in the absence of his kingly circlet. His brown beard, flecked with grey, was square cut at the chin and his moustaches were long and curled about the sides of his small mouth.

"Attebrook?" the king said. "Is this the fellow who helped you with the death of your chaplain?"

"One and the same," Edward said. "He was also useful at Gloucester."

The king smiled at Stephen, who was taken aback at this attention. "We need good men like you, Attebrook. Thank you for coming."

"Of course, your grace," Stephen said.

"Attebrook here has some matter he wants to get off his chest. No doubt about his manor," Edward said. "Spit it out, man, and be done with it."

Stephen glanced around, not at those about the table, but at the servants, women and hangers-on in earshot. He couldn't say what needed to be said in front of others.

The king had been watching this. He laid a hand on Edward's arm. "My son, we can spare you for a few moments. See what troubles your man."

Stephen and Edward walked through tall grass toward the orchard surrounding the king's chapel, where Miles de Dinesley lay awaiting his funeral mass and burial.

"What is it, Attebrook?" Edward asked testily. "I can ill afford this interruption."

They stopped and faced each other. Edward was a tall man, but only a few inches taller than Stephen, who stood six feet in his bare stockings. So, they were eye to eye.

"There is a spy in your midst," Stephen said.

"A spy?" Edward asked with scorn and disbelief. "How could you know that?"

"I have an acquaintance on the barons' side," Stephen said. "She told me."

"A rumor. The world is full of rumors."

"I believe her," Stephen said. "She told me you want to march on Northampton."

Edward was quiet. "We have discussed many possible things to do," he said carefully.

Stephen took a stab in the dark. "But you are in favor of Northampton."

A Curious Death

Edward looked surprised by this guess. "I am. So?"

"So, you will let all the others have their say, and you will persuade the king to go to Northampton."

Edward gripped his hands behind his back. He strode a few paces in one direction, then turned about and came back to Stephen's side. "Who is this woman? What is her name?"

"I'd rather not say, my lord." Her name was Margaret de Thottenham and she was an agent for Simon de Montfort's master spy, Nigel FitzSimmons, and Stephen's on-and-off lover.

"Protecting her, are you?" Edward asked.

"I am." Stephen added, not really believing it, "She may be useful in the future — to us, if she can be brought around."

"How can I judge what you say if I do not know its source?"

Edward was right about that, but Stephen couldn't bring himself to speak Margaret's name. People were terrible about keeping secrets, and if he gave her away, the enemy would learn eventually, and her life would be worth nothing.

"You'll have to trust me," Stephen said.

Edward scowled. He didn't like being disobeyed or kept in the dark. "I'm not sure trusting you is wise. You have a reputation for being tricky."

"That may be, my lord, but I get results."

After a pause, Edward nodded. "All right. So, how do we catch this spy? He could be anyone. Damn it, the whole town in probably riven with spies. Most of the miserable university students were for Montfort, you know."

"So, we must assume," Stephen said. "Therefore, catching one spy won't solve your problem."

"What exactly is my problem?"

"Keeping your intentions secret until it is too late for the enemy to do anything about them."

Edward folded his arms. "Spies have to send their reports to their masters. Why not simply have all the roads guarded and catch the messengers?"

"Because you can't be sure that you will get them all. If I were FitzSimmons, I'll have arranged for many different routes out of Oxford for my agents' reports."

"FitzSimmons?" Edward asked.

"Yes, Nigel FitzSimmons. He is Montfort's master spy."

"I know him," Edward said, startled. "I had no idea. Imagine, a gentleman stooping so low as to play at that. So, I assume you have a plan that does not require bagging messengers."

"You should make it appear that you agree with those who argue for an advance on Rochester and Dover so that everyone thinks that's where you'll go. The spies will send that message to their superiors. And when it comes time to move, you go north and catch them by surprise."

"What was that about?" FitzAllan asked when Stephen and Edward returned to the hall.

"A personal matter," Stephen said.

FitzAllan didn't like this answer. He sensed it was a lie, and he didn't appreciate people keeping secrets from him any more than Edward did.

But before he could vent his displeasure, Stephen said, "Did Serlo tell you?"

FitzAllan had not been prepared for such a change of subject. "Tell me, what?"

"What we found when we examined Miles' body."

FitzAllan looked taken even further aback. "He did not. There hasn't been time. What did you find?"

"Your suspicions were correct. Miles was murdered. A dagger thrust at the base of the skull. The coroner missed the wound during his examination," Stephen added. "You will have to ask the coroner to reexamine the body and recall the jury to consider this new evidence."

FitzAllan looked grim. "Elias de Fanecurt — that useless wretch. You will fetch him straightaway and show him what you found."

A Curious Death

In the end, Stephen didn't have to suffer the humiliation of summoning Fanecurt himself. Fanecurt was staying at his townhouse, according to Ernald de Helleston, who instructed one of his retainers to deliver the message.

Fanecurt arrived at the king's house two hours later. He came through the doorway of the hall three rapid strides ahead of the young man sent to fetch him, and paused to look around.

"That's our fellow," Helleston remarked, pouring himself some wine from the pitcher on the side table. "This will be a pleasure," he added, swigging hard from the cup.

"You know him?" Stephen asked.

"We've had words. Saying he's a man of overweening pride is praise."

Fanecurt caught sight of FitzAllan and stamped across the room. He was a short man, no taller than Gilbert, the top of whose head only reached Stephen's shoulder, but where Gilbert was inclined to roundness, he was broad and stocky. One arm had a woodcutter's great muscled forearm and thick fingers, but his left arm, held against his chest, was withered, the hand hanging limp and covered by a glove. The sight of that withered arm made Stephen's heart lurch with sympathy, and he was grateful that his own damaged foot was not on view for all to see.

"My lord," Fanecurt said when he halted before FitzAllan. "You wanted to see me." His tone was stiff and formal.

"Thank you for coming," FitzAllan said although he was no more known for cordiality than Fanecurt apparently was.

"Your man said this was about Dinesley."

"Yes, my nephew," FitzAllan said, as if Fanecurt needed to be reminded of the family connection. "There has been a development."

Fanecurt blinked and looked confused. "A development?"

"It seems Miles didn't drown after all."

"Of course, he drowned. I examined him myself."

"Closely?" FitzAllan said.

"Of course, closely."

"Well, it seems you missed something."

"I am sure I did not."

FitzAllan gestured to Stephen across the fire. "My associate here, Stephen Attebrook," an ironic reference not lost on Stephen who fought to keep his face straight at being introduced as FitzAllan's friend when they were anything but, "examined Miles' at my request."

"Why would he do that?" Fanecurt asked, suddenly cautious.

"Sir Stephen was once a coroner himself," FitzAllan said. "He has some skill in the investigation of suspicious deaths. I wanted a second opinion. It is impossible that Miles could have drunk wine, fallen asleep and drowned."

"That's how it appeared," Fanecurt said.

"So you say. But Sir Stephen found something you missed."

Fanecurt heard the indictment of incompetence in FitzAllan's tone and drew himself up. "What did I miss, sir?"

"Someone stabbed Miles at the base of the skull with a dagger." FitzAllan rose. "Come. See for yourself."

FitzAllan led Fanecurt to the chapel behind the king's house, followed by Stephen, Helleston, Serlo de Dinesley, the pretty young gentlewoman whom Stephen had seen Serlo with earlier, and two servants.

At the chapel door, FitzAllan touched the woman's arm. "Ysabelle, this will be unpleasant."

"Uncle," Ysabelle said, "I am made of sterner stuff than you know. I would see my betrothed one last time."

"And we will make sure this time that no insult is done to his body," Serlo said.

"All right, then," FitzAllan said. "If you must." He stood aside so Ysabelle could enter.

A Curious Death

The chapel smelled as dusty and damp as it had when Stephen and Gilbert conducted their examination. But it was dimmer, owing to an overcast that had settled over the town. So, the servants lit candles to provide illumination.

When they had done that, Stephen and Serlo held the candles while the servants unboxed the coffin and lay Miles de Dinesley upon the ground.

Stephen unwrapped the linen cover from Dinesley's head, rolled the body on its side and lifted Miles' long hair. He held a candle close to the wound as Fanecurt bent over to see it. When Fanecurt said nothing, Stephen widened the wound with a finger and thumb.

Fanecurt removed a small stick with black inch marks painted upon it from his pouch. He inserted the stick into the wound.

Ysabelle gasped and buried her head against Serlo's chest as he put his arms protectively around her.

"Stop that!" Serlo shouted over Ysabelle's head.

This objection did nothing to deter Fanecurt, who withdrew the stick and stood up. "I see," he said.

Fanecurt sneered. "How do we know that man —" he pointed at Stephen, "— didn't make this wound to please you?"

"There are reasons to dislike Attebrook, but he is not a liar!" FitzAllan thundered. "And I would not expect him to desecrate a corpse!"

Fanecurt tapped his thigh with the measuring stick while he locked eyes with FitzAllan. At last, he said, "I shall have to summon the jury to reconsider its verdict." His voice was flat, and quavered with what seemed like repressed fury.

"Very good," FitzAllan snapped.

FitzAllan's face was rigid with fury when he returned to the yard. Was this his way of dealing with grief? People handled the death of someone they loved very differently. Some cried, some shouted and tore their clothes, some banged about breaking things, some bottled up their feelings as FitzAllan seemed to be doing. Stephen had seen such reactions and more during his sad tenure as a coroner.

"You know, my lord," Stephen said awkwardly, since dealing with grief and bereavement was not something he was very good at, "the jury will probably be sent to inquire further. They may find evidence of Miles' killer."

"I don't trust Fanecurt or his niggling jury," FitzAllan said. "My offer still stands. Spare no effort or expense — do you hear? No effort or expense! I will not tolerate failure!"

They went on a few more paces when FitzAllan stopped.

"When you find out who did this, tell no one," he said. "No one but me. Do you hear?"

"I understand, my lord."

A Curious Death

Chapter 5

The bathhouse where Miles died, the Castle Keep, lay south of Oxford on a stream that powered a flour mill owned by the Dominican friars and provided water for four bathhouses on the stream's north bank.

These four bathhouses, tall and narrow like bricks laid upon their sides, stood alone on a path emptying into the road from Oxford's Little Gate to the Dominican friary, which was reached by a bridge only a few paces from the first bathhouse.

The Castle Keep was the second one from the road. Its main building was a long and tall timber hall with the usual hearth in the middle of the floor. The interior walls were painted with hunting and battle scenes as befitted its not altogether successful attempt to appeal to the knightly and gentry class, but it was doubtful the denizens paid much attention to them, for they were preoccupied with drink, gambling games, and the interplay between the male patrons and the whores who circulated among the tables encouraging the patrons to drink and to sample their talents in the chambers above or in the bathing alcoves at the rear.

A door at the back led to these alcoves, which were in another long and narrow timber building extending through the rear garden to the river. This structure held eight alcoves, each with a large wooden tub that looked like a massive wine barrel, four on a side separated by embroidered curtains, with a passage down the middle to a back door.

When Gilbert and Stephen arrived, it was late morning, and the hall was empty apart from six women at a table by the back door enjoying an early dinner.

"Good morning," Stephen said as he came around the smoldering hearth; with no customers at the moment the owner did not spare expensive wood to heat the place.

"Find out what they want, Hilde," said one of the women at the table.

"What will you fellows have?" asked Hilde, the freckled woman Stephen remembered seeing in Dinesley's alcove. A thick thread of red hair had come loose from her head scarf and hung behind her ear. "Too early for hot water, but wine? An early dinner? One of the girls?"

"None of that, thanks," Stephen said. "I am making a private inquiry into the death of Miles de Dinesley, and I wondered if you might answer a few questions."

"Ach!" Hilde snorted. "Dinesley! Why bother? The bastard drowned. Though how he managed it is anyone's guess."

"Not that we care," one of the others said.

"What if I told you it wasn't drowning. It was murder," Stephen said.

"Ah!" said a third whore. "Got what was coming to him at last!"

"How do you know better than our coroner?" Hilde asked.

Stephen told the women briefly of his examination and findings.

"Well, can you beat that?" Hilde said. "Wonder how they pulled it off with nobody seeing?"

"None of you went back there last afternoon?" Stephen asked.

Hilde looked at the other girls. "Some of us might have done. To take care of a client or two. But nobody saw anything that looked to be murder."

"You might not know what you saw. Did any of you see anyone come or go to Dinesley's alcove? Such as someone carrying a pitcher of wine?"

Hilde shook her head. "No. Not a thing. Don't know why anyone would take wine to him. Dinesley never touched the stuff. He said it made him sick. He could barely tolerate ale. Why?"

"A pitcher that had once held wine and a single cup were found in his alcove," Stephen said. "I'm curious how they got there."

"Why, someone carried them there, of course!" one of the whores laughed, to the merriment of the others.

"Yes," Stephen said. "But who?"

A Curious Death

Hilde waved a hand as if batting away a troublesome fly. "We're all too busy to notice such things. I'm sure you understand."

"Is there anyone else who might have seen anything?" Stephen asked. "Some other staff?"

"Well, there's Gillian and Midge," Hilde said. "They serve the back. And the boys."

"The boys?" Stephen asked, puzzled at the reference.

"The boys who fill the tubs. They're in and out all the time."

"This Gillian and Midge," Gilbert said, "where are they?"

Hilde shrugged. "Don't know. Could be anywhere. They never show up until the afternoon."

"I see," Gilbert said. "That is most helpful." Which, of course, it wasn't.

"Are the boys anywhere about?" Stephen asked.

Hilde hooked a thumb over her shoulder. "They're out back, heating the water."

The only way "out back" was through the bath chamber, where a rear doorway opened to the yard.

There were six men in the yard splitting wood tumbling from a massive woodpile that obscured any view of the bathhouse hall, and tending two large cauldrons over a big fire.

One of the men leaned on his long iron poker and said, "If you boys are looking for the privy, it's over there." He pointed with the poker to a pit by the mill stream.

"No, we're here to see you," Stephen said.

The effect of this seemingly simple statement was not what he had expected. Instead of boredom or polite curiosity, all the men's faces went hard and hostile.

"You here from Hughie?" one of them asked.

"I don't know anyone named Hughie," Stephen said. "We've other business with you."

The man with the poker pointed his poker at Gilbert. "Nah, they aren't. Hughie wouldn't send out a wad of dough like that to collect yer debts, Alfie."

"Are you referring to me?" Gilbert said, drawing himself up, a not altogether intimidating exercise, since the top of his head came no higher that Stephen's shoulder and the accompanying scowl made him look like a bulldog with indigestion.

"You're the only wad of dough in sight," the fire tender said.

"I am a fighting fit wad of dough, I'll have you know," Gilbert said.

"Down, Gilbert!" Stephen said, who was surprised that Gilbert would react this way. "No, we're here about the dead man in the tub."

"That fellow Dinesley," Alfie asked.

"That's the one. You have any others die on you?" Stephen said.

"That's the only one this week," one of the others said.

"The wages of drink!" one of the men laughed. "Passed out and drowned."

"Even lords aren't immune to folly," said the lead fire tender.

"We're not sure it was folly," Stephen said.

"Not folly?" the fire tender said. He poked the fire, and added two logs to it. "What was it then?"

"Murder," Stephen said.

"Get on!"

"Someone stabbed him in the neck."

"How did the coroner miss that?" one of the fire tenders asked.

"The wound was under the man's hair at the base of his skull," Stephen said. "Not easy to see."

"And you found it?"

"I did."

There was a moment of uneasy silence.

"We had nothing to do with it," another fire tender said.

"I'm not saying any of you did," Stephen said. "But I want to know if any of you saw anything — anyone at all going in or about Dinesley's alcove."

A Curious Death

There was another moment of uneasy silence, punctuated by the shuffling of feet.

One of the men raised a hand.

"And you are?" Stephen asked.

"Name's Alex." He was a thin man with sunken cheeks and crooked teeth. "I didn't think nothing of it. Still don't, really."

"What was it?" Stephen asked.

"Just two men come out of the dead man's alcove."

"Two men," Stephen repeated. "What did they look like?"

"Can't say really," Alex said. "Didn't get a good look. Didn't pay them much mind. I was busy, see? Lugging in a pair of buckets. Them damned things are heavy."

"You must have noticed something," Stephen said.

Alex shrugged. "One was big, the other small."

"And their faces, did you see their faces?"

"They was cloaked and hooded against yesterday's bad weather. And when they came out, they turned away and headed back toward the hall. So, all I saw was their backs."

Stephen considered this for a moment. "How long was this before the body was found?"

"A quarter hour? Half an hour?" Alex said. "I don't know."

"And you saw no one else go in or out?"

"The only other person I saw in there was Midge, just doing her job, tending to people, you know, fetching their drinks, towels, alerting us to the need for more hot water, stuff like that. She's not one of the girls, just so you know."

"But I suppose you were in and out. You weren't inside all the time."

"Of course not. The water doesn't fetch itself."

Stephen let out a breath. This was something but not much.

"Any of you," Stephen said, directing his attention to the other men, "see anyone go in or out of the dead man's alcove?"

The question was greeted by a chorus of, "No . . . no . . ."

"You wouldn't happen to remember who was in the alcoves near Dinesley, would you?" Stephen asked, casting a question into the dark and hoping for a good answer. But all he provoked was a round of shaking heads.

Then Stephen thought of one other thing to ask Alex. "Are you sure both people were men? Could the smaller person have been a woman?"

Alex pulled his chin. "You know, it could have been. It was hard to tell, now that I think on it."

A Curious Death

Chapter 6

The whores were at work when Stephen and Gilbert returned to the hall. Two were occupied with early clients in different corners, while Hilde was at the bar, where Richard the barman was cleaning cups in a bucket and setting them out on a shelf.

"You sure there's nothing we can do for you but flap our gums?" Hilde asked as Stephen started past her.

Stephen was glad she was still here. The interview with the fire tenders troubled him. He had not taken seriously what Serlo de Dinesley had said about the Buckerels, but he was forced to do so now.

"Do you know an Anne Buckerel?" he asked.

"Anne?" Hilde said. He eyebrows rose and fell. "Heard of her. She's Adam's sister."

"I take it, then, that you're acquainted with Adam Buckerel."

"Hilde's well acquainted with Adam, and so am I," Richard said.

"Oh?" Stephen said.

"Adam and his father are wine merchants," Hilde said. "The house buys from them. Adam's in charge of deliveries."

"He comes every Monday, regular as the rain," Richard said.

"So, he was here yesterday?" Stephen asked.

"Course, he was," Richard said. "Left us with four hogsheads. And we were lucky to get that, with the army in town. We'll be out of it in a matter of days, too, with the way things are going."

"When was he here?" Stephen said.

"The afternoon. He almost always turns up in the afternoon. Wish it were earlier."

"Does he ever stop for a drink?"

Richard smiled. "Well, we have to test the wares, you know. Even though I trust the Buckerels. Unlike some, they never deliver piss water. But you never know, eh? Even the best wine merchants have stuff that goes off."

"It pays to be careful about things like that," Gilbert said.

"And what of yesterday?" Stephen asked doggedly.

"I checked the stuff," Richard said. "Same as I always do."

"Each barrel," Gilbert said.

"Of course, each barrel."

"Free drinks for the staff," Gilbert said to Stephen. "That's why he was so thorough."

"Now, what would you know of it?" Richard said, offended.

"I run an inn," Gilbert said.

"Then what are you doing here and not tending to your business?" Richard said.

"Solving a murder and saving the kingdom," Gilbert said.

"Who'd have thought you were so important," Richard said. "I'd never have guessed from the look of you."

"Well, I'm helping him." Gilbert gestured to Stephen. "He's the important one."

"So, Buckerel stayed for a drink," Stephen said. "Did he do more than supply your samples? Such as ask for spiced wine?"

"Adam don't like spiced wine," Richard said. "He thinks it's sacrilege to desecrate good wine like that."

"But people do that all the time. Especially if the wine's gone off. So you must have some."

Richard shrugged. "The cooks prepare a bit every day. Some people like it."

"Did anyone order spiced wine yesterday?"

"All I remember is one of the students called for a jug," Richard said.

"Do you recall his name?"

"No. He comes in now and then, but not so much that we're on a first name basis."

"Was this student wearing a heavy black cloak by any chance?"

"He could have done. I don't know. It was busy, you know. Hard to recall every order."

A Curious Death

"Did you have your eye on Buckerel the whole time he was here?" Gilbert asked.

"Course not."

"Could he have slipped back to the tub room?"

"Could have, sure. But what reason would he have?"

"Did he ever ask you anything about Dinesley, like whether he was there, where he could be found?" Stephen said.

"Never mentioned Dinesley," Richard said.

"Did he say anything to you about Dinesley?" Stephen asked Hilde.

"He's never said a word to me about Dinesley," Hilde said.

"Not once?"

"Not ever," Hilde said.

"How long before Dinesley was found did you and Buckerel test the consignment?" Stephen asked, turning back to Richard.

Richard frowned. "I don't know. An hour? Half an hour?"

"Where can we find Buckerel?" Gilbert asked.

"Buckerel's shop is on the High Street, between All Saints and Saint Mary's," Richard said.

The Buckerels' shop was not hard to spot. It was the only one in High Street between the two churches with a barrel suspended from a post jutting out above the first-floor window. That floor itself projected outwards on pillars, forming a porch beneath the overhang. In the center, a stone-paved incline rather than a set of stone stairs ran down to what had to be a cellar, a common feature for storing wine at cool temperatures so it did not turn so readily.

They could hear voices in the cellar, and a young man with the look of a squire was holding two horses by the entrance.

"Are you sure we must hasten in?" Gilbert asked. He gazed across the street at a tavern, where people were lining up at the windows for meat pies. The wind brought the aroma to them, and he licked his lips, fingers tapping on his ample stomach as if to a tune only he could hear.

One of the horses dropped a load of manure almost at Gilbert's feet and would have covered his legs if he had not danced out of the way.

The squire sniggered at Gilbert's awkward dance and protests he had been violated. "Got your feet a bit dirty, eh, fat boy?"

"Mind your manners or I'll wipe your face in that shite," Stephen barked.

"He's with you?" the squire asked, not terribly phased by the threat. "Sir?"

"He is," Stephen said.

The squire looked into the cellar, which probably held his lord. Just when it seemed that he might tell Stephen to stuff it, he reconsidered, perhaps because Stephen was slapping a palm with his gloves, the prelude to flinging them at his feet with a challenge to fight. "Sorry. Sir."

"Good," Stephen said, relieved, because he really didn't want to have to fight a duel, and angry with himself for having lost his temper so easily. To Gilbert, he said, "You go get us a couple of pies. I'll wait for Buckerel here."

He did not have to wait long. Two men climbed the slope to the street. One of them was a landed gentleman, identifiable by his thigh-high red riding boots and whip. The other man, a merchant, wore a bright blue coat with brass buttons so polished they could have been mistaken for gold and a shiny brass wine barrel pin on his floppy green hat.

"One tun of the red and one of the German to Lord Edward at the king's house, Buckerel," said the man in the red riding boots. "The rest to the castle. This afternoon, before supper."

"Of course, my lord," said Buckerel, a man in his fifties with a weather-beaten and age-lined face and thus not the

A Curious Death

Buckerel that Stephen wanted to speak to. "I'll have the lot delivered straightaway."

The lord gave Stephen the up-and-down with an expression that said, "I've seen you before but I'm damned if I can remember where." And it was at this point that Stephen recognized him: Sir Michael de Lasingby, who had been pointed out to him that afternoon at the army camp as the king's quartermaster.

Lasingby said to Buckerel, "Good. See it done. And I'll not be responsible for any breakage, do you hear?"

"Yes, my lord," Buckerel said.

Lasingby nodded to Stephen, and stalked to his horse.

"Damned robbery — a shilling a gallon, more than twice the usual price. Can you imagine," he said to the squire as he took the reins of his horse. "Taking advantage, that's what it is."

He and the squire mounted, and they turned down High Street toward Oxford Castle.

"If you've come to place an order, I've been cleaned out," Buckerel said to Stephen. The merchant sighed. "Don't know when I'll be able to restock, either, what with the damned war. Can't get anything up from London. We've been embargoed."

When Stephen did not take his leave or display disappointment at the lack of wine, Buckerel said, "Is there something you want?"

"Is your son, Adam, about?"

"No. He is making deliveries."

Stephen probably should have kept his mouth shut then, but he blurted, "Can I speak to your daughter, in that case?"

"Which one?" Buckerel asked, immediately suspicious. "I have several."

"Anne."

"What about?" Buckerel asked as sharply as could be expected from a protective father.

"About Anne's relationship with Miles de Dinesley."

A number of expressions played across Buckerel's face: anxiety, worry, fear and anger; anxiety and anger predominated but were quickly replaced with bluster.

"They've sent a new boy, eh? I've paid!" he exclaimed, leaning his face to less than a hand's breadth from Stephen. "I've paid everything you've demanded! I'm cleaned out, hear? Not a penny more!"

No sooner had Buckerel uttered these words than he looked aghast at the outburst, as if he had spoken some blasphemy like denying the Trinity. He glanced around to see if anyone had heard or apprehended. No one seemed to have noticed, but he stumbled back toward the door of his shop.

Stephen followed him. "Who are 'they'?"

This brought Buckerel up. "You're not with them?"

"No," Stephen said. "I am from the earl of Arundel. He's asked me to look into Dinesley's death."

Buckerel took a breath, let it out. "Come inside. The street's no place to discuss these things."

Stephen followed Buckerel through the shop at the front of the house and down a passageway to the hall.

There were two women servants tending the fire and a pot hanging over it. Buckerel sent them away. He took a seat on a bench and motioned Stephen to take a seat on a bench across the fire from him.

"Dinesley drowned," Buckerel said. "What is there for Arundel to look into?"

"Dinesley was murdered," Stephen said.

"How would you know?"

"It has been my business to investigate such things."

"And you know better than our coroner?" Buckerel asked.

"He missed the signs," Stephen said.

"That is unlike him," Buckerel said.

"Perhaps he was in a hurry. It was late in the day."

"And what would Anne have to do with such a thing?"

49

A Curious Death

"A woman was seen leaving Dinesley's alcove at the bathhouse shortly before his body was discovered."

"And you think it was her?" Buckerel said this forcefully, scornfully. Yet the indignation seemed over done, and Stephen sensed something in his voice that suggested he was worried.

"I don't know. Perhaps it was. Perhaps it wasn't," Stephen said. "I want to hear what she says about it."

"I don't see why my Anne would be involved in something as sordid as murder," Buckerel said.

"Revenge for her ill treatment," Stephen said.

"You would know about that, coming from Arundel," Buckerel said heavily.

"It's true, then."

Buckerel's hands clasped each other in his lap. "I suppose that soon the whole town will know of her disgrace. I won't have to pay those bastards anything."

"So, someone is blackmailing you over that secret," Stephen guessed.

"They are," Buckerel said.

"Any idea who?" Stephen asked.

Buckerel shrugged bitterly. "One of the student gangs. Don't know which one. Their representatives come masked and hooded, so I can't tell who they are."

"Student gangs?" Stephen asked.

"Yes," Buckerel said. "There are several of them. Hooligans, the lot of them."

"Was Dinesley mixed up in this?" Stephen asked.

"He's dead. How would he be mixed up in anything?" Buckerel said. "I take that back. He was a charming bastard, a self-important shite. He used women and threw them aside when he was done with them. If you suspect Anne, there are at least a score ahead of her with resentments of their own."

"Nevertheless, I must have words with Anne," Stephen said.

"She isn't here."

"Where can I find her?"

Buckerel's lips moved slightly as if he was debating with himself whether to answer. "You'll find her at her mistress' house."

"She doesn't live here?" Stephen asked in another flash of cleverness.

"She lives with her master and mistress," Buckerel said. "The man's name is Ralph de Leke. He's a mercer. You'll find his shop on Northgate Street.

Buckerel's fingers drummed on the arm of his bench. "You'll say nothing about Anne's condition? If it gets out, she'll lose all chance of finding a decent husband."

"I have no interest in your family secret," Stephen said. "Now, about your son, Adam, when will he return?"

"When his business is done," Buckerel said and stood up. "Now, we're finished here. Get out."

A Curious Death

Chapter 7

Stephen joined Gilbert at the tavern, where the smaller man fidgeted at the delay in his ability to attack his meat pie. Traipsing around town was torture enough, but being denied any dinner on top of that was not something he was prepared to endure, if it could be helped.

At last, however, the moment had come, and they sat by an open window, watching High Street traffic and enjoying beef meat pies.

Stephen ate his slowly, eyes on the Buckerel house. He half expected Buckerel to emerge and hurry toward the Leke house to warn Anne what she might expect from an unexpected visitor. But the only person to show himself from the Buckerel shop was a servant who hurried eastward down High Street instead of west, where Northgate Street lay. Watching that man draw down High Street, Stephen realized with a jolt that if Buckerel did send a warning to Anne, the messenger wouldn't leave through the front door. No, the messenger would use a back way to avoid being seen. He should have thought of that right away, and he was angry with himself for not having done so.

"Hurry up with that," Stephen said abruptly to Gilbert.

"Hurry? It's a delicious pie. I want to savor it," Gilbert said, swirling one of the last bits of meat, pastry and sauce in his mouth.

"Savor it on the way to Leke's shop."

"Why?"

"I want you to question Anne Buckerel."

"Me? Alone?"

"Too much for you?"

"No," Gilbert said slowly, lifting the last spoonful to his lips. "But you're not coming? You're leaving her to me?"

"I'm going to keep watch here for Adam. He's the bigger fish, anyway. We know he was at the bathhouse shortly before Dinesley died."

"I haven't finished!"

"Take it with you. Quit stalling and get going."

"My, we're testy this afternoon. I wonder why."

Leke's shop stood six houses from Oxford's North Gate under a sign displaying a bolt of bright blue cloth within a gold border. It was a jaunty and attractive sign that Gilbert remembered seeing on their way through Oxford only this morning.

The house and shop were large and imposing, one of the few in town with a stone ground floor and timber and plaster uppers, the timbers a fresh black and the plaster between them a shining white that almost hurt the eyes to look at.

Such prosperity was to be expected in a mercer, whose chief business was trade in silk, a fabric that only the rich and well-connected could afford.

Gilbert paused at the door to compose himself for this trial of his diplomatic and persuasive abilities, breathed deeply and entered the shop.

The first thing that struck him was a peculiar, though pleasant odor. It took a moment to place it, then he realized it was incense burning in a bowl by a window, a whisp of smoke trailing into the air. This Levantine innovation, brought back by crusaders in the Holy Land, was not often seen, but was prized since it covered up the often pungent odors permeating houses. The wood of the walls, floors and counters was a dark, stained oak, full of dignity. All about the shop rolls and swaths of many-colored silks were on display, along with samples of orfrays, embroidered silk stoles used by bishops and wealthy priests or sometimes hung up in houses as decoration.

No man was in the shop. Instead, an elderly woman with a long face, commanding presence and graceful demeanor stood by a stack of green, yellow and red silks as a wealthy merchant's wife inspected them with, one expected, a mind for purchase. Gilbert was pushing forty or so he thought (he wasn't exactly sure), but this elderly woman was old enough to be his mother, and was just as intimidating.

A Curious Death

The merchant's wife made her decision. "I shall have twenty yards each of the blue and the red, if you please, Mistress de Leke," she said. Money passed to Mistress de Leke, arrangements were made for delivery and the wife departed.

Mistress de Leke turned to Gilbert. Her eyes measured his worn and stained travel clothing with an air that suggested he had no place here.

"How may I help you?" she asked stiffly in a tone that implied she would rather not and that he should just go away.

"Ah-ha ... ah-hem," Gilbert began. "Would it ... er ... be possible to speak with Mistress Buckerel?"

Mistress de Leke's nose rose toward the ceiling. "What possible business could you have with one of my maids? Who are you, anyway?"

"My name is Gilbert Wistwode."

"Wistwode ..." Mistress de Leke uttered the word as if it was foreign or some kind of nasty disease, although it was a good, stout English name, if not a common one. "What is your business with her?"

"She may have information that may help an inquiry I've been asked to undertake."

"Information? Inquiry?" Mistress de Leke the elder sounded doubtful. "What sort of inquiry?"

It wasn't until this moment that Gilbert realized that speaking of the nature of the inquiry to this formidable woman could suggest a connection with Miles de Dinesley that the Dinesley family was keen to avoid and which Stephen at least had promised to keep secret.

Perhaps there was another way. "Did she have any occasion to leave the house yesterday?"

"No," Mistress del Leke stated with severe finality. "She is suffering from her women's time and was so yesterday. She has been confined to her chamber until it is over."

"What of the other maids?" Gilbert asked. "Surely a woman in your station will have more than one? Can they confirm this? May I speak to them?"

"This is ridiculous. What are you playing at?" Mistress de Leke slapped the counter in emphasis, a substantial ring on one finger knocking loudly. "Are you accusing Mistress Buckerel of … something untoward?"

"No! No!" Gilbert exclaimed. Trapped and a bit frightened by Mistress de Leke, his first thought burst from his lips: "She may have been a witness to an assault! I merely wanted to ask if she saw anything!"

"Where was this assault?" Mistress de Leke was taller than Gilbert and leaned forward to emphasize this question.

"On the road to the Black Friar's Priory!"

Mistress de Leke drew back. She loomed over Gilbert, resembling a furious dragon about to spit fire. He could see in her eyes that she understood the implication of the statement. There was nothing on the road to the priory but the bathhouses. Women of good reputation never ventured to one of them alone.

"Mistress Buckerel did not leave the house yesterday," Mistress de Leke said. "Of that I can assure you."

"Oh, good, oh, good," Gilbert said.

"Martin!" Mistress de Leke called into the back of the house. "There's trouble! Please show this unpleasant little man the door!"

"Oh, no need," Gilbert said, scuttling toward the door.

He almost made it, too, before a foot caught him in the bum and hastened his exit to the street.

Gilbert wore a downcast expression when he slouched into the tavern.

He sank onto a bench across from Stephen and signaled a servant to fetch him a cup, which he filled from the pitcher on the table.

"Careful," Stephen said, as Gilbert upended the cup and consumed its entire contents in one lengthy series of gulps. "It's pretty strong."

A Curious Death

"I need strong," Gilbert gasped as he set down the cup. "Stronger the better."

"Things did not go smoothly?" Stephen asked.

"You are not allowed to gloat."

"Ah. I see no bruises, although now that I look at you, your coat is soiled."

"I stumbled and fell."

"Hmm. Were you helped?"

Gilbert's eyes flicked back and forth. "A little."

"They threw you out?" Stephen asked incredulously. "You? The great diplomat?"

"I *said*, you are not allowed to gloat."

"I am not gloating. I am merely teasing the story out of you." Stephen sampled his ale. "All right. Did you get to speak to Mistress Buckerel?"

"I got to speak to Mistress de Leke," Gilbert said, looking appreciative as Stephen refilled his cup. "The girl's mistress. Anne's employed as a maid."

"I rather gathered that from her father."

"Poor girl, being in that woman's employ. A real harpy."

"I take it this means that you didn't get to speak to Anne."

Gilbert rubbed his insulted bottom, which still smarted. "No. But Mistress Leke swears Anne did not leave the house Monday."

"She could be lying."

"Could be. But to what end?"

"None that I can see — at the moment," Stephen said. He sipped his ale and glanced over Gilbert's shoulder at the Buckerel house, where nothing was happening. People in Ludlow thought Stephen's work in finding out things and solving deaths was thrilling stuff. While it had involved moments of risking death — something not thrilling when it was happening — more often it involved tiresome plodding and a lot of dull moments when you didn't have a clue what you would do next or whether you'd solve the problem. This was one of those moments. He wished he was back at his manor of Priors Halton with Ida, dealing with the myriad problems of rebuilding it from the wreckage left when rebel raiders burned the manor house and village to the ground a few weeks ago. At least there the way forward was clear. And he missed Ida. Odd, that.

The afternoon wore on. They finished the pitcher and ordered another. This one Stephen insisted they drink more slowly, mainly to make it last, although after an hour or so they began to draw looks from the barman and servants. It was unusual for two men to while away hours at a time. Most people had work to do in the afternoons. Men without work were a source of suspicion.

Stephen had long gotten to the point where he pretended to drink rather than actually drinking. Gilbert, for his part, was not masquerading, although he did sip rather than gulp.

There wasn't much to talk about, but Gilbert did his best to fill the silence with reminiscences of his time as a monk. He had been a copyist at the priory at Greater Wenlock and was very proud of his work, which apparently, to hear him tell it, was well-received: the priory made much hard coin copying religious and other works for various religious establishments all about the country.

"It's getting harder for them," Gilbert remarked, staring into the depths of his cup. "You know, with all the secular scribes popping up."

"I thought there was so much of a demand for books now that the religious houses couldn't keep up," Stephen said.

"That's true — but the competition! It cuts into the priory's revenue. The king should make a law forbidding secular scribes!" Gilbert's eyes stared into the distance over Stephen's shoulder. "One of my best works I made while I was very young, just a new brother — Saint Augustine's Confessions."

"The whole book? I assume it had illustrations. You did those, too?"

A Curious Death

"Just the lettering. It was such a fine thing when it was done. I thought the priory would keep it in our private collection, but the prior sold it to Saint Andrews Priory at Northampton. God's blood, I hated to part with it. It hurt so much to hand it over. At least, I got a journey out of it."

"A journey?" Stephen asked, mainly to be polite, not because he was really interested.

"I got to see Northampton and all the country in between," Gilbert fondly recalled. "Not sights I'd ordinarily get to see. Northampton is a fine, big town." Although Gilbert was rather well traveled now, having been to London and even the mouth of the Thames, most ordinary people didn't get more than twenty or thirty miles from the place where they were born, so a journey to Northampton was a treat to be remembered and savored.

"So I've heard," Stephen said.

"You've never been there?"

"No. Haven't had the opportunity," Stephen replied, thinking that if Lord Edward's plan for the campaign went forward, he would have an opportunity indeed. But he could not share this knowledge with Gilbert.

"I got in trouble, there, though," Gilbert added sadly.

"You? In trouble? Hmmph. It must have had to do with your stomach. What did you do, raid the pantry after hours?"

"No, nothing so criminal. Me and a couple of postulates slipped out a sally port and collected a few apples in an orchard just outside the wall. The caretaker caught us, though. I got a whipping for it."

"It was well deserved, I'm sure." Stephen was about to move on to another topic more interesting than filched apples when a question floated up from the dark mire of his mind. "This sally port? Was it on the priory grounds?"

"It opened into the cellar of the guest house. It was very old. Apparently, they just built the house right over it. It was forgotten and not used, except by brothers in on the secret who wanted some fresh apples."

"Did you get to eat any of the stolen apples?"

"They weren't stolen. They were recovered. Just lying about on the ground."

"Well?"

"Not a one."

A Curious Death

Chapter 8

Shadows stretched across the street as sundown approached, and a cold wind sighed through the window, stirring the wisps of hair on Gilbert's head, which rested on his forearms. One of the servants went out to the street and began closing the shutters against the chill.

Stephen reached across the table and prodded Gilbert with a finger.

Gilbert's snoring stopped and he jerked up his head. He looked about wildly and over his shoulder at the Buckerel house. "Is he here? Did you see him?"

"It's getting late," he said. "Time to go."

"Go? Go?" Gilbert asked. "He isn't here?"

"No, I'm afraid we've wasted the day."

Gilbert rubbed his face. "I feel sick."

"No wonder, after you drank so much. I warned you it was strong ale."

"Can we stay for supper?" Gilbert asked.

"How can you mention food and throwing up in practically the same breath?"

"Because I'm hungry?"

"You can remain, if you like. I need to save money. Getting you drunk is a costly business."

Stephen rose and went out to the street.

He waited for Gilbert to join him and they went down High Street, turned the corner at Saint Martin's Church, and continued up Northgate Street to the gate and out into the suburbs along Saint Giles Street. Gilbert dragged his feet, looking disconsolate at the prospect of old bread and cheese for supper, for that's all they had left in their baggage; Gilbert and Wymar had polished off the dried beef the day before they reached Oxford. But at least he did not complain. Stephen was in an irate mood and complaints would not have gone down well.

When they reached their tent, Wymar rose from the fire in their tent circle. "There you are, my lord," he said. "The earl of Arundel sent his compliments and requests your presence at supper."

"And not me?" Gilbert asked, aggrieved.

"Not you," Wymar said.

"At the king's house?" Stephen asked.

"That's right, sir. I think if you hurry, you may still make it in time," Wymar said. "They were getting a late start, I heard. On account of Lord Edward, who had a late audience with the king."

"Old bread and cheese," Gilbert muttered as Stephen turned toward the king's house.

"It was your idea to finish the beef," Wymar said accusingly.

"You helped!" Gilbert said.

Wymar let Gilbert's dismay at a meager supper linger a few moments, then added, "Never fear. We've got rations from the army! Oat porridge!"

"Delightful," Gilbert grunted. "Do I look like a horse?" Englishmen generally reckoned that oats were not fit for people, unless they were Scots. He added with some hope, "Is it hot?"

"Get your bowl and we'll go see," Wymar said.

Supper was getting underway as Stephen entered the hall of the king's house. He looked across the great room and spotted Percival FitzAllan at a table set at a right angle from Lord Edward's at the back, where a hearth fire burned high to provide heat.

Stephen made his way to the table. FitzAllan, in conversation with a cleric at his left hand, waved him to a seat across from the earl. Two of the earl's household knights moved apart to make room for him. It was a good place to sit, for the hearth fire toasted his back.

"Wine or ale, Attebrook?" asked Serlo de Dinesley, who was on the earl's right hand. His dull clerical robes had disappeared, replaced by a peacock's finery, a silver-buttoned

A Curious Death

coat of blazing red and green, the rest of the display concealed by the table.

"Ale," Stephen said. He'd had plenty to drink this afternoon and was feeling sleepy. Wine would knock him out or drive away his senses, and he had the feeling he needed all the wits he could muster. A servant hurried to comply with Serlo's wave for attention.

The first course was white bread with a honey topping on the crust and clam soup. Stephen sipped his soup with his eyes on FitzAllan. He wondered why the earl would summon him to supper and offer Stephen a seat at the earl's table. As a small landholder and a knight, he might have been entitled to sit at one of the lower tables where the food was less elegant than this close to Edward's high carved chair.

At last, FitzAllan fixed Stephen with a stare that, while not hostile, was not filled with affection.

"Any progress, Attebrook?" FitzAllan snapped.

This abrupt question, issued out of the blue, caused heads to snap around or come up. People seemed eager to learn what he had been asked to do.

"Not much, my lord," Stephen said slowly, his spoon sinking into the soup. He gave a brief account of the day, leaving out the part where he spent the entire afternoon outside Buckerel's shop waiting for Adam Buckerel. No sense in making himself look the fool for doing so before this audience.

FitzAllan received this report with a disappointed grunt. "That's all you've done, eh? I rather expected more."

"I've done what I could today. Perhaps tomorrow there will be a breakthrough."

"Tomorrow," FitzAllan spat, anger and disappointment in his voice. "Yes, tomorrow. . . . About that — Lord Edward wishes to speak with you after supper. It seems he has a greater need for you than I do."

Supper, being a lesser meal than dinner, had fewer courses and was over while it was still light. Servants took down the tables and stacked them against a wall, while everyone in the hall mingled about the fire. Musicians began gathering in the walkway over the hall entrance, tuning their lutes and warming up with scales while a pair of drummers beat softly; the effect was a jarring clamor.

Stephen was by the fire, watching the coals, nursing a cup of ale and wondering when it would be a good time to approach Lord Edward when someone came up behind him.

"Attebrook," Lord Edward said over Stephen's shoulder. "Don't turn around. Smile and nod."

Stephen did not turn, smiled and nodded.

"We should speak privately," Edward said. "Come to my chambers in an hour. Use the back stairway."

"One hour, my lord," Stephen said.

"Good," Edward said, and drifted away.

The music was still playing to a fairly large crowd when Stephen slipped out of the hall. There was a guard at the back stairway, which rose to the first floor from the pantry. However, the guard did not stop Stephen and merely nodded as he went up behind a servant bearing a tray with a pitcher and cups.

The servant went down the passageway where he knocked on the door, then entered.

Stephen stopped by a guard leaning against the wall by one of the doors.

"Is that the Lord Edward's chamber?" Stephen asked.

"No." The guard straightened up and hooked a thumb at the door at his side. "This is it. You Attebrook?"

Stephen nodded.

The guard knocked on the door. Stephen heard Edward's deep voice call out, "Come!"

The guard opened the door for Stephen and shut it behind him.

A Curious Death

Edward was seated at a small table. A candle burned at each end of the table, illuminating a map between them.

Edward turned from the map. "I've done what you suggested. I've made it seem that I have acquiesced to the suggestion that we go south."

"But you have not changed your mind about Northampton."

"No."

"And the king is with you?"

Edward nodded. "It's ultimately his decision." He stood up and began to pace to a shuttered window and back to the lighted table. "Have you ever been to Northampton?"

"No, sir," Stephen said.

"It is a well-defended town. And its castle is strong." Edward smirked without humor. "The defenses were kept up, unlike what you can find in many other places, where people let the walls fall to ruin." He thumped his chest. "We! We are responsible for Northampton's fine state. My father!"

"And it has a large, well-armed garrison."

"It has," Edward said bitterly. "The town opened its gates to Montfort. After all my father had done for that miserable place."

"And yet, you propose to attack it, this walled town with its large garrison." Stephen wondered if Edward's insistence in an attack on Northampton was more fueled by anger at the town burghers' betrayal than by strategic concerns. But, of course, Stephen could not speak these doubts. "I suppose you have a plan."

"Have you ever taken a walled town or a castle?"

"I have been part of forces that did so."

"How did you do it?"

"Twice by escalade, once by trickery."

Edward smiled again without humor. "Trickery? As Gloucester was taken?" he asked, referring to the recent struggle in the Marches, where rebel forces loyal to Montfort gained entry to Gloucester pretending to be Welsh wool merchants. Once admitted to the gate tower, they had drawn weapons, subdued the watch and admitted the enemy army.

"Something like that," Stephen said. "We were disguised as pilgrims."

Edward drummed fingers on the table. "I need something similar. The king won't approve an attack that involves a direct assault on the walls if that can be avoided. Such assaults can be costly. We can't afford to lose the men."

"They can be costly," Stephen agreed, with a sense of foreboding.

Edward looked Stephen in the eye. "I've heard you're skilled at slipping in and out of places, and I've seen you're good at finding out things. What I want now, what I most need, is for you to ride to Northampton straightway and find me another way in that doesn't involve ladders and climbing."

A Curious Death

Chapter 9

Gilbert put his hand on Stephen's shoulder. "Are you sure about this?"

"Get it over with," Stephen growled. He cast an eye toward the tent flap, where Wymar had stuck his head in. "Get your arse out of here!"

"Yessir!" Wymar piped. He ducked out. The tent flap fell closed.

"And keep an eye out!" Stephen shouted at Wymar. "Let no one in!"

"If I know that boy, he'll be charging for people to peep under the tent flap," Gilbert said. "Especially if she's young and wears a skirt." He swirled the shaving lather in its bowl with his fingers.

"You don't have to look so amused at this," Stephen growled.

"It's not that bad once it's done," Gilbert said. "You won't notice a thing, except for the wind on your naked head."

Stephen looked sullen. This had been his idea, but that didn't mean he had to like it.

Gilbert put down the bowl and wiped his fingers on a towel. "Now, first things first," he said, picking up a pair of shears. He fingered the hair on Stephen's head. Then he applied the shears, first cutting off most of Stephen's long hair, which fell to his shoulders, leaving the remaining hair in a rough bowl shape, and then cropping a circle about the top and back of Stephen's head.

When he had cleared out the brush down to a fair, though uneven, stubble, he set down the shears and took up the bowl. He applied the slather to the cleared spot. Stephen shivered at its cold, clammy touch as well as an unexpected chill on the back of his neck, which was now exposed to the elements in a way it had not been since he could remember.

"You had to do this once a month, did you?" Stephen said through gritted teeth.

"Prior's orders," Gilbert said with more cheeriness than the solemn situation warranted.

Done with his application of cream, Gilbert bent over Stephen's pate with a straight razor.

Stephen did not hold his head still, which required Gilbert to grasp his chin. Stephen moaned through closed lips.

"Hold still," Gilbert said. "You've been shaved before. You know what to do."

"Yes, but never on the top of my head. Why do monks do this?"

"You know, I'm not sure. Custom. To set themselves off from the common people?"

Gilbert proved remarkably dexterous at shaving and within a short time he produced a tonsure on the top of Stephen's head.

"There we go!" he said with some relish as he gave Stephen a mirror and held a second over Stephen's head so he could see the results of Gilbert's work.

The white skin of Stephen's crown looked like black-stubbled snow against the jet black of his hair. Only a circlet of black hair remained about his head. He shivered at the sight.

Wymar rattled the tent flap. "The underchamberlain's here!"

"A moment!" Stephen called back. He fumbled for a knit hat, which he pulled over this head so the underchamberlain, a servant at the king's house, would not see his humiliation. That there were long locks of his hair on the floor about his stool escaped his attention.

But he avoided questions about the fallen locks by pushing through the tent flap to confront the underchamberlain.

The underchamberlain held out a folded garment — a friar's black cloak and a white woolen tunic, the ordinary wear of a Dominican friar.

Stephen accepted the cloak and tunic. The tunic was stained: grass and some dark, uncertain substance.

67

A Curious Death

"It could use a washing, sir, but you said you were in a hurry," the underchamberlain said.

"Lice?"

"No, sir. We did check for that."

"Good," Stephen said, although he wasn't sure he should trust the claim.

Stephen started to turn away, expecting the underchamberlain to make his retreat. But the man remained where he was.

"If you don't mind my asking, sir," the underchamberlain said, "But why do you need a friar's robes?"

"Why does anyone need friar's robes?" Stephen said. "I've found my vocation."

"No!" the underchamberlain gasped. "What am I to tell Lord Edward?"

"Tell him nothing. It's a secret. You can keep a secret, can't you?"

"Of course, sir!" the underchamberlain exclaimed, and hurried off in the direction of the king's house.

"Do you think he'll say anything?" Wymar asked.

"Of course, he will," Gilbert grumbled.

Stephen rolled up the robe and pushed it into his satchel. Then he belted on his sword and shouldered his bow case. "Time to go, I suppose."

Gilbert crossed his arms. "I'd say be careful, but you never are. Whatever you do, don't make Ida a widow."

Stephen glanced at Wymar, who was ignorant about the true state of his and Ida's relationship. "I'm just going for a look around. There's little danger in that."

"Look around where?" Wymar asked.

"None of your business. And if you tell anyone about what you've seen and heard here, I'll cut off your lips and feed them to the pigs," Stephen said.

Wymar blinked. Stephen had never spoken to him like that.

"I'm serious," Stephen repeated to drive the point home.

Wymar gulped. "I understand, sir."

"Oh, one more thing," Stephen said. He fished into his pouch and removed the button he had stepped on at the Castle Keep. He held the button out to Gilbert. "I just remembered. I found this at the bathhouse in Dinesley's alcove. I don't know if it's important or not. But hold on to it for me, will you? I don't want it to get lost."

The guide took Stephen by back roads and little-known tracks as far as the village of Kislingbury, which he informed Stephen was only three miles and a bit from Northampton.

"You take the road north out of the village," the guide said as he turned his horse to depart. "About a quarter mile after you cross a stream, you'll come to a good road. Follow it east to Northampton. Good luck to you!"

The guide spurred his horse and cantered off to the south, eager to be away. For this was rebel country — except for one lonely house.

This house lay not far from the south end of the village, where the guide had deposited Stephen. He walked his mare down the road leading to this house and in a few moments arrived at a stone manor house sitting behind a low wall and moat, that was filled with lilies and lily pads, frogbit, water mint, and water forget-me-nots that had not flowered yet.

Stephen crossed the bridge and passed through the gatehouse, where no porter was on duty to pester him with questions about why he was here. It was quiet and deserted in the yard, except for a pig rooting in a refuse pile. The pig regarded Stephen with suspicion, but when it became clear that Stephen was not interested in her, she returned to her work.

He tethered the mare to the railing of the stairway and climbed up to the door at the first floor. He heard the murmur of women's voices through the open windows. The door was open as well to admit the pleasant afternoon breeze and a circle of women were knitting by the hearth fire.

A Curious Death

Stephen knocked on the doorframe to draw the ladies' attention.

One of the women put down her knitting and came to the door. "May I help you?" she asked in a musical voice. She did not add the usual "sir" since Stephen was not dressed as a gentryman. He had his old worn coat on, his patched stockings, and a bow in a canvas case over his shoulder.

"I'm looking for Hugh Picot, my lady," Stephen said. "Is this his house?"

"It is," the woman said. "But my lord is ill, and not receiving anyone. Can I help you?"

"You're the lady of the house?" Stephen asked.

"I am. Mabile Picot. And you are?"

"I am Stephen le Pondere, my lady," he said. Le Pondere meant someone who lived by a pond, close enough to his actual name, and he felt rather clever at having thought to use it.

"And what is your business Master le Pondere?"

Stephen hesitated. He wondered if she knew the password and the secret work that Picot had been doing for the king's faction. If she didn't, he would have to make other plans. But he decided she did. Gentry wives usually knew about their husband's dealings, and this one, secret work for the crown, was a potentially deadly business that affected the whole family.

"*Tour foys prest*," he murmured. Always ready.

Lady Mabile blinked. This was not an answer she had been expecting. She stepped out the door to the landing at the top of the stairs.

"What will you require of us?" she asked in a low, anxious voice.

"Nothing much, my lady," Stephen said. "A place for my horse and things for a few days — while I am gone."

Lady Mabile nodded. She pointed toward a long low building across the yard. "You can stable your horse there. Your things will be safe enough in the loft." She paused and asked, "Will you be with us long?"

"Only long enough to put up the horse."

Stephen had almost finished rubbing down and feeding the horse when Lady Mabile entered the stable.

"I think it would be best if you were not seen leaving the house," Lady Mabile said.

"A good suggestion," Stephen said, putting down the brush. He picked up his satchel and removed the black friar's robe. He intended to change when Lady Mabile left.

Lady Mabile stared at the robe. "I did not take you for a friar."

Stephen smiled and removed his knit hat. He rubbed the shaven spot at the top of his head. "Well, I am."

"Yet you travel as an ordinary man. A man who carries a sword and a warbow. I thought clerics were prohibited such things."

"The exigencies of war," he said. "One day I am one man, the next another."

"Is it coming here, the war? We hear that the king has assembled his army at Oxford." War was something for bystanders to fear — looting, pillage, rape and kidnap for ransom were often practiced on them regardless of their allegiances.

"I don't know the king's mind, my lady. I just do as I am bid."

Lady Mabile put two long fingers to surprisingly sensual lips. "You do not have the look or manners of a friar. Be careful that you do not give yourself away in whatever you are up to." She added, "There is a footbridge at the rear of the house. Go that way. No one will see you."

A Curious Death

Chapter 10

Stephen had ridden out of the army's encampment at Oxford before the morning sun had cleared the tops of the trees to the east and it was a golden half-orb searing through the distant bare branches.

Gilbert watched him go, filled with foreboding and worry. He had no confidence that Stephen's disguise as a Dominican friar would fool anyone. Not only did Stephen not look the part of a humble, wandering friar — he looked like he would fit in any bishop's household as a valued subordinate — but he did not act the part. His carriage and manners were all wrong. They screamed, gentry here! At least, they did to Gilbert's discriminating eye.

Stephen would be caught and hung as a spy, and then what would happen to Ida, Harry, Joan, Christopher and now Harry's son John? Perhaps Ida could maintain the charade of their marriage and so inherit Priors Halton Manor, which could provide a living once it rose from its blackened ruins and was prosperous again. It occurred to Gilbert with a start that Stephen's quarter share of the Broken Shield Inn would also fall to Ida, unless he protested the marriage, which he was not about to do. What seemed like the inevitable prospect of Edith, his wife, and Ida quarrelling over inn management filled Gilbert with horror. For such a small girl, Ida had some strongly held opinions.

Gilbert liked his life to be as tranquil and untroubled as these difficult times allowed, but since Stephen had turned up two years ago, he had been dragged into one harrowing death investigation after another. He had no liking or talent for it, as Stephen did, despite Stephen's haphazard methods. And there was the possibility of sudden and painful death that often accompanied these investigations. He would rather preside over the inn's hall from a comfortable chair by the fireplace while the profits rolled in — although he did greatly miss his employment as coroner's clerk. He had always loved the smell of fresh ink, the deft and careful trimming of the quill to produce its best line, and the light frailness and balance of that quill when he took it up to apply it to parchment. His first love had been bookmaking. But then Edith had come along and swept him off his feet, so the coroner's clerk job had been a Godsend.

Gilbert kept these thoughts to himself, however, as he squatted by the fire, poking the smoldering embers with a stick while Kate, one of the women camp followers, dropped a load of firewood beside him.

"Looks like you've got nothing to do," the woman said. "Have a go at splitting some firewood if you want to eat."

"Dear woman!" Gilbert protested. "Do you take me for a common laborer?"

Kate pushed Gilbert in the shoulder with her foot. It wasn't exactly a kick, but in his precarious squat it was enough to knock him over. "I don't take you for a soldier, so you must be a working man, eh? That's what we've got around here, ain't it? Those who fight, and those who tend to them who do!"

Gilbert picked himself up, greatly disgruntled as much at the prospect of manual labor as at having his revery interrupted.

He spotted Wymar just then slipping out of their tent with Stephen's shield, spare helmet and arming cap. Wymar stepped out of the circle of tents around the campfire and disappeared.

Gilbert shouted, "Wymar! Get back here!"

Wymar, who was as adept at avoiding work as any young man, did not immediately appear. However, after Gilbert called to him a few more times, he returned and excused himself by saying he hadn't heard.

"What is it?" Wymar asked.

"We need some firewood split for breakfast, and, I suppose, for dinner as well," Gilbert announced. "If you fancy eating yourself."

"I have more important things to do," Wymar said, sulkily.

A Curious Death

"What?" Gilbert demanded. "Bashing people over the head with sticks?"

"They aren't sticks. They're practice swords. If I'm to be a squire, I've got to learn to fight, don't I?"

"Indeed, you do," Gilbert said. "You can run along and play with sticks when you've finished. Hurry up. The more time you waste standing there, the longer it's going to take you to get to your game."

"My game," Wymar muttered, reaching for a nearby axe. He was taking this squire charade much too seriously.

Wymar went back to their tent and emerged with a heavy hammer, like that used by blacksmiths. He set a log on end and rested the axe blade on the log.

"This goes faster if you help," Wymar said to Gilbert.

"I? Help?" Gilbert asked, indignant. "How?" He thought Wymar meant that somehow he should swing that axe after all, and, even if he were willing to stoop to manual labor, he was not much good at that sort of thing.

"You hold the axe, while I hit it with the hammer. You'll see."

Gilbert wasn't sure what Wymar meant, but the notion of merely holding an axe did not seem so much like labor.

"All right, then," he said.

He placed the axe edge on top of the log. Wymar adjusted the axe's tilt, and stepped back.

"Whatever you do, don't flinch," Wymar said.

Wymar struck the back edge of the axe with the hammer. The axe acted as a wedge and split the log in two after three blows.

"It's much easier and quicker this way," Wymar said, as he upended another log for splitting.

"So I see," Gilbert said. "Who taught you this trick?"

"Harry," Wymar said. "He has trouble swinging an axe these days, so he had to think of another way to do it."

"Harry's been splitting the firewood?" Gilbert said, astonished. All this time, he had assumed that skinny little

Joan, Harry's wife and keeper of Stephen's townhouse, had done so.

"That's what Joan said when she made me do it."

They were on their third log when Wymar said, "You going to do anything about that Miles fellow?"

"What? The Miles fellow? What do you know about that?"

"Everybody knows that Arundel promised Stephen a manor if he solves the killing. He's not likely to do that wherever he's gone to."

"No, he isn't," Gilbert admitted.

"So, it's up to us," Wymar said.

"*Us?*" Gilbert intoned with emphasis.

"I don't know much about solving murders, but I learn fast," Wymar said.

"I thought you were eager to be off to have your head banged."

"Well, that's important. But helping out our lord is more important, right?"

"He isn't my lord. But yes." Gilbert gazed at the ground and muttered under his breath, "If only I knew what to do!"

Whatever Wymar's urgency about helping Stephen find Dinesley's killer, it did not extend to interrupting his singlestick practice. So, Gilbert had some time on his hands before Wymar came back to think about what steps to take.

He sat on a log near the fire, glancing now and then at Kate and the other women tending the camp, but avoiding their eyes in case they thought of another chore that needed doing, while hoping that a plan to wrap this thing up in a day or two came to mind. No such plan, however, was forthcoming. At least, no plan did that didn't involve a great deal of effort.

One hand wandered to his belt pouch and found the button Stephen had left with him. He examined the button closely. It was dark with tarnish, or what appeared to be

A Curious Death

tarnish. There was a design upon it, but caked dirt made it hard to see. He dipped the button in the bucket of water reserved for washing the used wooden trenchers and bowls to clean it off. The water was cold enough to numb his hands and the button slipped away. Gilbert pulled a sleeve above an elbow and dug into the bucket, fumbling about among the trenchers and bowls.

"Good idea!" Kate called from across the fire. "Those things need washing!"

"I am otherwise occupied," Gilbert muttered.

"Well, when you're done with whatever game you're up to!" Kate replied.

"Fat chance of that," Gilbert said to himself. "I am the hand of justice, and I will not be distracted."

"The hand of what?" Kate called.

"Nothing! Just saying a prayer!"

Gilbert found the button. The dirt had washed away. Even the threads attached to it were now clean and their color, black, could be clearly seen. He turned the button in his hand. A curious design was engraved upon it — a large Crusader's cross in the middle surrounded on the edge by a serpent with an open mouth about to swallow its own tail. It had the look of silver, but it could be simply polished metal. But he was willing to bet it was silver.

Wymar returned an hour later with a cut under his left eye and a cheek beginning to blacken and swell.

"Any idea what to do now?" Wymar asked brightly as he tossed the shield and singlestick into their tent.

"I've solved the whole thing while you were playing," Gilbert said.

"No, you haven't."

"Enough talk. Let's go."

Gilbert knew well enough what he had to do. He just didn't want to do it. He must question Anne Buckerel, but he couldn't face the wrath of her mistress so soon after breakfast.

So, when he and Wymar passed the Leke house on Northgate Street, they kept going to the market, where the town's guildhall sat on the other side of High Street.

There, Gilbert asked three bailiffs lounging under the covered porch where he could find the town coroner.

"Which one?" one of the bailiffs asked, looking bored and scratching his private parts under the skirt of his long shirt.

"There's more than one?" Gilbert responded, surprised.

"Yeah, we've two of the bastards," another bailiff said.

Gilbert shouldn't have been surprised to learn that Oxford had two coroners, although it seemed an excessive number for a single town. After all, Herefordshire once had three coroners, then two, then three again, then one, then two, and now one. Counties were often large and a coroner's duties required a great deal of travel, so it made sense to have more than one, each taking a part of the county.

"I'm looking for the coroner who presided over the inquest into the death of Miles de Dinesley," Gilbert said.

"Ah, that knight who drowned in a barrel," the scratching bailiff said. His hand came out with something between forefinger and thumb, which he flicked away perilously close to Gilbert, who shied involuntarily. This brought a good laugh to the men on porch.

"Yes," Gilbert said, unable to hide his distaste at being the target of random lice. "I believe his name is Elias de Fanecurt."

"That would be right," the lice harvester said. "Should be in the shire hall. It's his day to take appeals." An appeal was a charge of wrongdoing made by the person injured that was taken at a sitting of the county court. One of the coroner's jobs was to record these appeals on the coroner's rolls for presentation later to the king's justices. Where a county had more than one coroner, usually this duty only fell to one of them.

"Where is that, exactly?" Gilbert asked.

A Curious Death

"In the castle, where the devil did you think it was?" the lice-ridden bailiff said as his hand ventured under his shirt again.

"He's clearly not from around here," a second bailiff said.

"Oh, you could tell that from his speech, could you?" his companion on the bench said.

"He does talk funny," the fellow admitted. "Hard to understand. I thought perhaps he was a foreigner, or something."

"You are a credit to the town," the bench mate said sarcastically. "Not jumping to conclusions about a man's background."

"Thank you for your time," Gilbert said and bowed as he backed up, eager to be away before he was the target of any more flying lice or an escalation of insults. "You've been most helpful."

"Glad to be of service," said the bailiff with his hand under his shirt searching for more lice.

The castle sat on a branch of the River Thames at Oxford's western side below where the river parted, forming several meandering channels that flowed about marshy islands. It was a stonewalled oval about one-hundred-fifty yards across at its longest point, the distance from its great motte to the main gate, and surrounded by a deep ditch filled with running river water. The ditch water was as clear as if it had come from a well, and to his amazement Gilbert spotted a pike as long as his leg slither through water grass swaying in the lazy current. The thought of baked pike with apples made his mouth water. All he was likely to get with the army was barley cakes, porridge, moldy cheese, perhaps some watery soup and sour ale. His wife Edith acted as though his journeys with Stephen were pleasure jaunts instead of narrow brushes with death accompanied by a great deal of suffering from poor food, bad bedding if there was any at all, cold wet nights sleeping under trees that afforded no meaningful protection, ornery mounts and constant saddle sores.

The shire hall was a long, tall stone building against the castle's north wall at right angles to the king's hall. There was a large crowd of men and women outside the doorway and listening at the windows to the drone of voices within.

Gilbert had been a coroner's clerk at his fair share of county courts during the days when Stephen's predecessor, Sir Geoffrey Randall, had the duty, and he knew what to expect. It might be hours before he had a chance to speak to Fanecurt. Yet he could think of nothing more productive to do. He had no leads, to speak of. He almost turned away in despair, but instead went in the hall.

He edged his way to the front of the throng until he reached a wooden railing that separated the coroner, his clerks, and the litigants from the crowd.

The proceedings were the usual stuff Gilbert had heard in the past: a claim for assault with a staff; a claim for a stabbing from which the victim had, fortunately, recovered, and who appeared and displayed the wound for all to see as required by the law; a demand for damages for a lost horse which broke a leg in a collision at the market when two men were racing carts down High Street; a man, angry at being stung by his neighbor's bees was charged with setting fire to the hive; a claim for damages to a garden after a sow got into it; several rape claims against men with the army. As usual, Fanecurt ordered the sheriff, who was represented by a deputy, to arrest or attach the appellee to appear either before the King's Bench or at the next county court, depending on the nature of the claim.

This went on for about three hours, as one claimant after another went before the bar to make his or her appeal.

At last, Fanecurt motioned to a bailiff, who announced, "There will be a recess!"

Fanecurt leaned over to talk with his chief clerk, an elderly man with massive eyebrows.

"Is this the dinner break?" Gilbert asked a townsman beside him when he noticed that the crowd was not breaking

A Curious Death

up to enjoy whatever food could be had from vendors in the bailey.

"Sir Elias likes to work through dinner," the townsman said with a hint of disgust.

"Ah," Gilbert said. "He wants to get in all the pleas before nightfall."

"Right."

Otherwise, Gilbert well knew, Fanecurt would have to come back tomorrow to finish.

As Fanecurt wrapped up his conversation with the clerk and rose, Gilbert was struck with an inspiration.

"Can you save my place?" he asked the townsman, and before the fellow could answer, Gilbert was plowing his way as fast as people gave way before him for the door.

He burst through the door into the bailey, nearly knocking down one of the bailiffs attending the door, and ran, which for Gilbert was a rapid waddle, around the corner of the hall.

There before him as he rounded the corner was a privy shed beside a paddock of goats.

Stalking toward it, the maroon skirt of his long coat flapping, was Fanecurt. He entered the privy, pulled down his underdrawers and took a seat on the board stretching across the privy pit, careful that the fur-lined coat did not hang down and get soiled.

Gilbert, judging that it would be impolite to engage in conversation while Fanecurt was occupied in serious business, pretended to be interested in the goats.

Fanecurt hopped off the plank, straightened his clothes with his right hand, the left one being withered. When he headed back toward the hall, Gilbert rushed to intercept him. This wasn't as hard as it might seem, since Fanecurt was no taller than Gilbert. But where Gilbert was shaped like a barrel, Fanecurt was square built, like a hewn block of stone. He dressed soberly, in dark maroon and green of rich wool and linen, except for a flamboyant ring on his right thumb holding a turquoise stone bigger than a giant's thumbnail.

"Sir Elias!" Gilbert gasped. "May I have a word?"

"If it's an appeal, you know I cannot not hear it here!" Fanecurt snapped over his shoulder.

"It's not that!"

"What then? I am a busy man, and you're keeping people waiting! Don't tell me you're a bill collector!"

"It's about that fellow who died at the Castle Keep, Miles de Dinesley."

Fanecurt pulled up and Gilbert threw himself to the side to avoid running him down.

"What is it?" Fanecurt asked impatiently. "Who are you?"

Gilbert was startled that Fanecurt didn't recognize him; after all, they had been together in the king's small chapel when Fanecurt re-examined Dinesley's body. "I'm Gilbert Wistwode, sir. I was once a coroner's clerk, too, and —"

"A coroner's clerk," Fanecurt said, unpleasant apprehension dawning. "I know you now. You are affiliated with Stephen Attebrook."

"Oh, sir, er, yes."

Fanecurt hooked a thumb into his belt and leaned forward so that his jutting nose was close to Gilbert's rather broad one. "I don't like Arundel interfering with my business. I will recall the jury in my own good time!"

Gilbert squinted at the blast in his face for Fanecurt had shouted so loudly, Gilbert's ears rang.

"It's only a small, private inquiry, sir," Gilbert said. "A little thing. Hardly a bother to anyone."

"It is the king's business, and I am the king's representative in the matter," Fanecurt said, his voice several tones lower but still harsh. "I will not tolerate meddling."

"It is hardly meddling. Anyway, earls are earls and they usually get what they want," Gilbert said.

Fanecurt waved a dismissive hand. "Earls aren't above the law, and the law will move in its own due course."

He marched toward the hall.

That seemed to ruin any chance Gilbert had of learning anything useful about the coroner's inquest. He was on his

A Curious Death

way to fetch Wymar from the hall when he passed the bushy-browed clerk heading toward the privy. Gilbert kicked himself mentally as he spun about in pursuit. It was often better to talk to the minions than to the head man. They were usually well informed. As a minion himself he should know that.

"I say!" Gilbert called.

The clerk stopped and looked Gilbert up and down with measuring eyes. "Got off on the wrong foot there, haven't you?"

"You heard?"

"Half the people in the bailey heard."

"He's a bit touchy," Gilbert said.

"He's a proud man, certainly. He doesn't like the earl proving him wrong and then continuing to poke about into the matter. But recent days have been hard on him. His wife died a couple of months back, you see, and he's been distracted."

"Ah. A wife's death can do that," Gilbert murmured, despite himself moved to sympathy for Fanecurt.

"She was young and beautiful," the clerk said. "He loved her dearly. What did you want, anyway?"

"We, or I should say I, wondered if any of the jurors happened to speak to any of the customers at the Castle Keep, and what they might have learned."

The clerk's eyes flicked back to the hall.

"Go see John the archer. He has a shop by the Church of Saint Mary the Virgin. He might be able to tell you something."

Gilbert collected Wymar from the hall and the pair set out toward the main gate. They were halfway there when Gilbert noticed a small crowd emerging from a church to the right at the base of a massive square tower, the tallest such tower in the castle.

The crowd stopped and lined up on either side of the church's entrance and out came two young people, whom

Gilbert recognized as Serlo de Dinesley and Ysabelle de Baresworth. Ysabelle, who wore a garland of flowers in her hair, had her arm linked with Serlo's, where silver buttons arrayed from shoulder to cuff glittered in the morning sunlight. They were smiling broadly. They made their way across the bailey to the king's hall at the foot of the towering motte.

It was a surprise to see Serlo and Ysabelle together like this — they had clearly just been married — for Gilbert understood that Ysabelle had been betrothed to Miles and Serlo destined for a life devoted to the church. For her to marry the brother only the day after Miles' funeral mass and burial seemed, well, unseemly — to say nothing of Serlo's abrupt abandonment of his studies.

Percival FitzAllan, surrounded by his household knights and accompanied by the king's own chaplain who no doubt had performed the wedding service, strolled after the bridal couple to their wedding feast in the king's hall. It was a great honor to have the king's chaplain at hand and to enjoy the celebration in the king's hall, and it was hard to imagine that Serlo or Ysabelle merited such grace. It probably was an attempt to honor FitzAllan and to take away some of the sting from Lord Edward's dispatch of Stephen on his secret mission.

Serlo's marriage was no business of Gilbert's and he was about to turn back toward the gate when Ernald de Helleston separated himself from the tail of the entourage and beckoned to him.

"My lord," Gilbert said. "You wish words with me?"

"Where is Attebrook?" Helleston demanded bluntly.

"I assume that the earl wishes to know?"

"He is concerned about when Attebrook can attend to our problem."

Gilbert knew very well where Stephen was, since Stephen had told him. He did not know why Lord Edward had sent Stephen to *that place*, but it didn't take much work to guess what was on Lord Edward's mind. And Stephen had been very clear that Gilbert was not to give anyone the slightest hint of what was going on.

So, Gilbert said, "I have no idea where Sir Stephen is. On some business for Lord Edward is all I've been told."

"So, you've no idea when he will be back?"

"Haven't a clue, sir."

Helleston was not satisfied with that answer. "The trail is growing cold."

"If it's any comfort to his lordship, we've undertaken to continue Sir Stephen's work while he is away."

"Have you," Helleston said in tones that indicated he did not find that news encouraging. A forefinger wagged from Gilbert to Wymar, not impressed. "The two of you?"

"We can ask questions as well as anyone. That's really what this work involves. The tedious asking of questions until something turns up."

"Do you know what to do?"

"I've assisted Sir Stephen in many inquiries. I hope to stay on the scent while he's away. When he returns, hopefully we will have made progress and he can take things from there."

"You, an innkeeper, and this trumped-up squire?"

Gilbert felt Wymar stirring at the insult, although to Gilbert's relief he had the good sense to remain silent. "Sir, you hurt the squire's feelings. And I would remind you that he is Sir Stephen's choice." There you go, Sir Ernald, insult Wymar and you're insulting Stephen!

"Yes," Helleston said in a voice dripping with disapproval that he did not bother to disguise. "I suppose he is."

To turn the conversation away from this topic, Gilbert said with more brightness than was warranted, "How was the wedding, sir? The bridal couple seem well suited and happy with each other! But I admit I am taken aback by the suddenness of the wedding. I had thought Lady Ysabelle was betrothed to Sir Miles."

Helleston glanced at the last of the wedding party disappearing through the doors of the hall. "She was. But Serlo is the heir now. Their parents desire the alliance of the families, and since Miles is no longer here to play his part, Serlo volunteered. And as to the haste, Miles and the lady were to be married today because we ride to war very soon. Serlo will be taking Miles' place in our ranks, so there seemed no reason to postpone the wedding and every reason to go forward with it."

"Ah, I see," Gilbert said. "If you'll pardon my saying so, Lord Serlo does not seem the warlike type."

An odd expression flitted across Helleston's face. One could have taken it for disgust if one was uncharitable, before it vanished, replaced by a humorless smile.

"He lacks the training for it," Helleston said, "but all that's expected of him now is that he does not run away."

"I am sure he will rise to the occasion and will do his family credit."

"He had better. My lord expects it of him."

The old clerk's directions to the shop of John the Archer were not as precise as Gilbert would have liked, but then directions rarely were. "By the Church of Saint Mary" turned out to cover quite a bit of ground, and the search consumed the dinner hour before an informant directed them to a side street only a few paces from Smith Gate.

Gilbert's stomach was complaining adamantly about the lack of dinner by the time he and Wymar stood outside John the Archer's door. The prudent thing was to ignore his hunger and finish the business with John, but the presence of a tavern and its delicious smells down the street was too tempting to ignore. He would have liked a sit-down meal in a warm tavern — the day had grown cloudy with a blustery wind that blew under the shirt and chilled the backside — but financial circumstances, which included the need to feed Wymar, forced him to economize with a hastily slurped soup in the street outside the tavern's front window. Gilbert found the soup wanting and the bread that came with it so hard that it could not be eaten unless soaked in the soup. But Wymar

A Curious Death

devoured his as if it was the finest meal he'd ever had. It was better than oat porridge, Gilbert reflected.

Having completed this delicious repast, Gilbert wiped his spoon on the hem of his cloak before returning it to his belt pouch, and marched resolutely up the street.

John the Archer's shop was typical of town shops. It was narrow, just over a pole wide at about twenty feet, with a single door opening into a passageway that led through the shop to the rear of the house, where John and his family lived. The place smelled of sawdust and wood chips from the mess on the floor accumulating there as a man with beefy forearms and knobby hands worked with a drawknife on an uncompleted bow stave. Two apprentices behind him were weaving bowstrings. Behind them one rack held completed bowstaves, some of dark wood, one of purple, and others of blond that had to be yew. A good many were light hunting bows but one stack were thick war bows. Another rack held blank staves waiting to be fashioned into weapons.

The man wielding the drawknife paused when Gilbert and Wymar entered.

"Let me guess," said the man, who had to be John the Archer, staring at Gilbert with an appraising eye. "You've not come for my custom."

"I, er, no," Gilbert said.

"Then what are you wasting my time for?"

Gilbert coughed and said in his most diplomatic voice, "It has to do with your work on the coroner's jury, sir."

"Who are you and why do you care?"

After hearing Gilbert's explanation that he was carrying out a private inquiry into Miles de Dinesley's murder, John the Archer sighed.

"So you're the ones bearded old Fannie. I hate to see him humiliated like that," John said.

"Old Fannie?" Gilbert asked, bewildered for a moment. "You mean Sir Elias?"

"Who else?" John said. "He can be a pompous arse sometimes, but Fannie's not a bad sort, really."

"Ah. You heard already," Gilbert said.

"Of course, I heard. You can't keep a thing like that a secret."

"I hope you, at least, harbor no ill feelings," Gilbert said.

John shrugged, and hooked substantial thumbs into his belt. "It was no skin off my back. Not my job to examine the body. I only work with what I'm given or what we find out, same as the other jurors. What are you bothering with me for, though?"

"We wondered if you had had the opportunity to question any of the others in the Castle Keep about the circumstances of Dinesley's death — about what they may have seen or heard."

"Why would I have done that?"

"Isn't it the usual practice to question those nearby to verify the manner of death?"

"Sir Elias didn't think there was a need."

"But now? He hasn't instructed anyone to extend the inquiry, now that we know it was misadventure?"

John shook his head. "I've received no instructions."

"Oh," Gilbert said, deflated. "I seem to have been misled. It was just the clerk — I regret I did not get his name — suggested that you might have spoken to someone who was there and might know something about Sir Miles' death."

John pulled a thick lip as if deciding whether to say anything to this. He had something to say, obviously. Otherwise, he would answer without this obvious extemporization. But why he would hesitate, why he would be reluctant to say anything puzzled Gilbert.

"If you know something, Sir Miles' family would be grateful," Gilbert said.

"He was murdered, then? It isn't just a story to discredit Fannie?" John said at last.

"I saw the wound," Gilbert said. He pointed to the back of his neck in the approximate location.

John shuddered. "That's what they said. A knife in the neck. Nasty way to go."

A Curious Death

He looked at the apprentices, his expression thoughtful.

"You lot," John said suddenly. "Go get your dinner."

That was an order the apprentices were happy to hear, and they rushed out of the shop for the hall.

John waited until the door to the hall banged shut. Then he glanced out of the shop windows to see if anyone was nearby.

"Dinesley's entitled to justice, but not if it endangers peoples' lives," John growled.

"I don't understand," Gilbert said.

"A friend of mine was in the Castle Keep when Dinesley died," John said. "Back among the tubs." His mouth turned down in disapproval of what he was about to say. "Dallying with a woman."

"A woman not his wife," Gilbert guessed.

"A married woman. With a jealous husband."

"Who would resort to violence if the betrayal was known."

"You are a perceptive man," John said.

"I suppose your friend is married himself?"

"He is. But that is of much lesser account."

"It often is," Gilbert murmured, for the transgressions of men were overlooked far more often than those of women.

"I don't know what he saw exactly, except he and his companion heard Dinesley and another man having an argument," John said. "It was rather heated. Threats were made, apparently."

"You don't know of what sort?" Gilbert asked.

"No, I didn't think it was important, given our findings."

"Oh. Of course," Gilbert said.

"I will give you his name — but only if you swear on the altar of Saint Mary the Virgin you will never speak it to anyone. Or connect him in any way with this murder."

Instinct warned Gilbert not to make this promise. If the man's evidence was of vital importance, there was a good chance he might be needed to present it in court. But Gilbert would not be able to weigh the importance of that evidence until he had heard it. It could be nothing. It was probably nothing. But perhaps it would lead to something really important.

"I promise," Gilbert said.

It was a short walk to the Church of Saint Mary the Virgin. The church was an oblong box of stone lying with one long end along the High Street. The simplicity of the design, lacking such fashionable things like a high tower (instead it had a squat one at the west end), round naves and vestibules, large stained glass windows, or fancy carvings about the doors, indicated that it had probably been built before the coming of William of Normandy. There were hundreds of churches like it all over England.

A small number of young men clad in black cleric's robes occupied benches outside the church. Only a handful had their hair tonsured, indicating that they had taken at least minor orders; mere students who had not done so kept their hair but were allowed the clerical robe as a sign they were affiliated with, and protected by, the church.

He studied the students with something approaching envy. They had to belong to the universities springing up in Oxford, which had grown out of schools originally established by the local churches. These original schools often taught only basic literacy or the rudiments of Latin and Greek. But others devoted themselves to more complex mysteries like arithmetic, geometry, astronomy, music, grammar, logic, rhetoric and theology in order to prepare the students for clerical careers; many bishops came from the ranks of such students now. The demand for learning had grown so much that universities had been established here and elsewhere that were organized like a craft guild, with the teachers as masters and students as the apprentices. Most of these universities were informal, centering around a teacher or small group of teachers who held their lessons in churches or rented houses and halls. Lately, however, a formal corporation comprising a

A Curious Death

university had been formed in Oxford out of the chaotic mess of some of the scholarly guilds. Gilbert wished he had their chance to pursue learning. His own education at his priory had been haphazard. He would have liked to learn more, but he had never had the chance.

Gilbert was shocked to see that some of them were reading books — outside in the daylight, where those valuable manuscripts could be dropped or damaged by the weather. He could not imagine that kind of recklessness with a book.

"Rabble," sneered John as he led Gilbert and Wymar by them. "Students! Always causing trouble! And the law cannot touch them!"

"I thought the king had ordered them out of Oxford," Gilbert said.

"He has," John said. "Some have defied the order, however, and the town aldermen are doing nothing about it. Palms greased to look the other way!"

Eight students were inside the church seated on a circle of benches not far from the altar. One of their number stood in front of the group, a book in hand.

The man with the book read out: "*Quod sit deus tripartitus et contra?*" He then launched into a discussion about the passage in church Latin.

Gilbert stood transfixed. He knew what this was! It was from Peter Abelard's book *Sic et Non*. Gilbert had once copied it at the priory for sale to another religious house. He had been so affected by the book's contents that he spent more time reading than copying, to his master's displeasure that the project took so long. The question the teacher quoted was one that Gilbert had struggled with for a long time.

"Nonsense!" John growled as he pulled Gilbert around the seated crowd.

"What's he saying?" Wymar asked; a peasant boy, of course he had no Latin, and this was just priestly babbling.

"He said, question, is God a Trinity or not?" Gilbert said.

"That's a silly question," Wymar said. "Everybody knows God's in three parts. The priests say so, don't they?"

"Not everyone is convinced," Gilbert said.

"Sounds like stuff people ought not to be meddling in," Wymar said.

"A lot of rot," John said, concurring.

The altar was on a wooden platform. Gilbert's feet thumped on the steps loudly enough to cause several heads to swivel in his direction at the disturbance. Gilbert mouthed apologies as his feet met carpet at the top of the platform and he stepped up to the altar itself, a large table of deep brown wood not covered by any cloth.

Beyond the altar, stood a marble statue of the Virgin on a wooden pedestal. The artist had carved her as a pretty woman with a frail face and prominent cleft chin, and a painter had given her blonde hair, blue eyes, rosy cheeks and red lips. She smiled down at Gilbert. It was oddly comforting to look into that sweet smiling face. Dimples showed at the corners of her mouth. A hand rose between her breasts with one finger raised. Gilbert felt as though he was in the presence of an actual flesh-and-blood woman rather than mere stone.

"Put your hand on her," John said, gesturing to the Virgin.

"Ahem, certainly," Gilbert said. He rested a hand on the Virgin's feet. They were bare, the nails delicately carved. The solemnity of the moment was sobering to the point he almost felt in tears.

"Swear to Our Lady that you will not reveal the name I am about to disclose to anyone at any time, no matter how useful they might be in your inquiry into the death of Miles de Dinesley," John said.

"I so swear," Gilbert whispered.

"Repeat the words!" John ordered.

Gilbert repeated them as well as they could be remembered, his voice catching.

"Was that good enough?" Gilbert asked when he finished. John nodded.

"Who was it, then?" Gilbert asked.

A Curious Death

"The name is Richard le Glasiere," John said. "I can't promise he will tell you what he saw, but you can ask him."

Chapter 11

"So, this glasiere was sharing a bathtub with a married woman who wasn't his wife!" Wymar said this with gusto, his emotions having been bottled up since the revelation by the need to keep silent

"The world is full of iniquity," Gilbert sighed. "Your mother will be unhappy I have exposed you to the corruptions of Gomorrah, you such an innocent babe."

"I am not innocent!" Wymar protested.

"You are the picture of innocence."

"Since when are you an expert on innocence and iniquity? You don't know a whit about what goes on in a village."

"I'm an innkeeper. You have no idea what goes on in an inn."

"A lot, apparently, from your tone. Do you get involved yourself?"

Gilbert shot Wymar a hard glance but said nothing.

"You're never tempted?" Wymar asked with false innocence.

It was clear Wymar was pulling what Gilbert had of a beard. So, he refused to be provoked. "I am a man of iron self-control and bottomless probity. I doubt we can say the same about you."

"Neither Glasiere nor this woman will want to talk to us," Wymar said, moving on from the debate about innocence.

"Glasiere might be willing to, if he can keep the woman out of it," Gilbert said.

Their steps carried them along High Street and in moments they were abreast of the Buckerel's wine shop. The elder Buckerel was visible through the windows bent over parchments with a dark expression that suggested to Gilbert that he was reviewing accounts and did not like what he saw. What most attracted Gilbert's attention, though, was a passageway next to the shop. Like many buildings in the center of towns, the shop was built smack against those on either side, and there was a vault through the buildings (with chambers overhead) into a courtyard. In the yard, a strapping

A Curious Death

blond man with a bulging satchel hanging from a leather strap over one shoulder was cinching the girth on a horse.

Gilbert entered the gate passage and called, "No deliveries today, Master Adam?"

Gilbert wasn't sure the young man was Adam Buckerel, but he resembled the elder Buckerel, only with youthful blond hair and a less sour expression. He was younger than Gilbert expected, too — barely twenty.

"What do you want?" the young man asked belligerently, indicating that he was, in fact, Adam Buckerel.

"Just a few moments of your time," Gilbert said, taking Adam's question as permission to enter the yard.

Adam frowned suspiciously. "What for?"

"I've a couple of questions. It shouldn't take long."

"Is this about Dinesley?" he snapped.

"Why, yes. It is."

"I've nothing to say," Adam said.

He vaulted into the saddle and kicked the horse into a trot. The passage was wide enough to admit a wagon, and Gilbert was in the middle of it. Adam did not attempt to slow down or swerve to avoid Gilbert, whose only recourse to avoid being trampled was to throw himself to one side. He collided with a wall and fell over.

"Nothing to say, except I'm not sorry that bastard's dead!" Adam called over his shoulder as he turned up High Street.

Gilbert staggered into the street, brushing off dirt.

"I hope you do better with Glasiere than this one," Wymar said.

Gilbert ignored this criticism. He stepped up to the window and met the elder Buckerel's hostile stare.

"Will your boy be back soon?" Gilbert asked.

"None of your business."

"It's official now, you know. Dinesley was murdered. The coroner has been persuaded of his error. Adam was there that day. He will have to answer for that at some point."

Buckerel's mouth worked as if he was about to spit. "He's gone to London. He'll be away for weeks."

"Sent him away, have you? To avoid awkward questions? Running away is evidence of guilt."

"It's business," Buckerel grated. "I've friends in London. I hope Adam can persuade them to work around the embargo — get us some wine. Nothing's allowed out of London these days going upriver."

"That's why the accounts look bad, eh? Nothing to sell and lots of debt."

Buckerel slapped the countertop. His parchments jumped and one fluttered to the floor. He did not attempt to recover it. "My business affairs are no concern of yours."

"And a happy good day to you, too, sir," Gilbert said with a mock tug on a forelock that he hadn't had in years.

The way to Glasiere's shop, which inquiry indicated lay on a street to the east of the castle, led through the heart of town, where the two main streets crossed at Northgate and Fish Streets. This spot was also the town's main marketplace. It was not a formal market day — that was on Fridays and Saturdays — but a few vendors had booths set up even so: a man and women hawking wooden bowls and carved platters; a knife maker showing off his knives, scissors and spoons, many of his wares hanging from a string stretched across the front of his booth, tinkling in the slight breeze; a pen of goats for sale by a rustic from the country; chickens in wooden boxes; and a few other odds and ends.

Gilbert halted in front of the bowl/platter seller's stall and stared at the goods. They were something Harry, formerly a beggar and now an accomplished woodcarver, would take a professional interest in. But Gilbert's mind was not on bowls and platters. Wymar was right. If Glasiere wanted his presence at the bathhouse kept a secret for fear of complicating his marriage, exposing his lover and risking death at the hands of a jealous husband, he was not likely to tell Gilbert anything

A Curious Death

about it. In fact, if Gilbert were that man, he would deny being there at all. So, simply knocking on his door and asking a few questions was not likely to get Gilbert anywhere.

There was something Gilbert could do about this possibility, however.

He turned on his heel and marched down Fish Street toward South Gate, one hand on his sword, which flapped awkwardly against his leg. Useless things, really, swords, unless you need to kill someone or scare him off, which Gilbert had not found to be necessary. But since he was with the army, it was a fashion appliance he could not do without.

"You're going the wrong way," Wymar said.

"No, I'm not," Gilbert said.

"But Glasiere's is that way." Wymar pointed westward.

"I am aware of that fact," Gilbert said. "There is something I must do first, before I see him. So, the way is not wrong. It's just a detour."

That detour led through the gate and along the path at the foot of the town wall to the lane heading southward to the Black Friar's Priory. Wymar muttered to himself about delays and sore feet — he paused twice to remove pebbles from his shoe, and then ran to catch up since Gilbert did not stop to wait for him.

A party of nine black friars was crossing the bridge over the mill run, the wooden structure swaying a bit since they marched in step, hands up their sleeves and hoods hiding their faces so that only their noses and chins showed. Gilbert watched them with some relief for this meant that perhaps Stephen would not be identified in his costume after all.

The friars took up the full width of the road, and Gilbert and Wymar had to step to the verge, for there was no way the friars would give way for them. And when the friars were passed, Wymar started for the bridge, but dashed back when Gilbert turned down the path that ran along the mill race and halted at the first of the bathhouses. Wymar may be a country boy, unfamiliar with the temptations of the large towns, but he had been down Lower Broad Street in Ludlow where the

Wobbly Kettle stood by the River Teme enough to know a bathhouse when he saw one. He had never been inside, though, but had only marveled at what it had to offer from the street and what others had to say about it.

"What are we doing here? You need a bath before you question Glasiere?" Wymar asked.

"You can wait here, or you can come in and watch a master at work," Gilbert said, pulling the door open.

"A master at picking nits," Wymar said under his breath just loud enough for Gilbert to hear.

"Continue such comments and you'll find yourself dining from the privy the next time you're at the Broken Shield," Gilbert said.

"Come now, Master Gilbert, just having a bit of fun!" Wymar said as he followed Gilbert into the hall, eyes alert for naked women and other marvels.

Wymar was sadly disappointed about the naked women, for the hall held mostly soldiers from the army drinking and playing dice and cards. There were women — two harried serving girls rushing back and forth, and three women seated on a bench at the foot of the stairs. But they were all clothed.

Wymar nudged Gilbert and pointed at the women on the bench. "Are those whores?"

"They are," Gilbert said.

"Oh, boy," Wymar gushed.

"Don't expect them to as much as talk to you unless you show them your money," Gilbert said. "Did you bring any money?"

"I didn't know we'd be coming here."

"Don't lie to me. You don't have any."

"Er, well, no. You've got all the money. Sure you won't lend me some?"

"I have to account for every penny to Sir Stephen."

"You really don't think he'll mind, do you? It's in a good cause."

"What would that be?"

A Curious Death

Wymar muttered something behind a hand that sounded like, "Losing my virginity?"

But before either he or Gilbert could say more, Hilde, the red-haired woman, descended the stairs, followed by a soldier so drunk that he was in danger of falling on her.

"Back again, are you?" Hilde asked Gilbert.

The drunken soldier reached the ground beside her without mishap and bent to peck her cheek. She allowed this, patted him on the shoulder, and said, "Thanks, love. Do you need some help getting home?"

"Nah, Hilde, I can manage," the soldier said with a grin. But as he turned for the door, one foot got in the way of the other and he fell on his face. This provoked a storm of laughter. He rolled on his back, waved his arms in acknowledgement, and said, "I'm all right! No need to rush over!"

Hilde crossed her arms at the spectacle. Then she asked Gilbert, "Are you here for business or pleasure?"

"Business," Gilbert said, to Wymar's disappointment. "Is Midge about?"

"She's in the back. I'll fetch her. But don't be long. As you can see, we're very busy."

Presently, Hilde returned with the young woman whom he had last seen cradling the dead body of Miles de Dinesley. She was more presentable now than she had been. Her hair was properly braided and tied at the back of her head, and her gown, though still sacklike, was not sopping and muddy, even at the hem.

"I will only need a moment, child," Gilbert said, as she stood before him, her thin arms crossed, her eyes appraising. He had thought her very young, and so her face and body, lacking a woman's round lines, appeared to be, but her eyes were cool and belonged in an older woman's face. "You know why I'm here, I trust?"

"Hilde said you want to talk about Dinesley," Midge said. "But you're not with the coroner's office. I remember you. You were there that day. Two alcoves away."

"You have an excellent memory," Gilbert said. "Is there somewhere quieter that we can talk?" He could hardly hear what people were saying even up close with the uproar in the hall from a hundred conversations going on at the same time.

"As long as you don't take too long. The customers get angry if their requests aren't met promptly. And I'm the only girl serving back there now."

There was no need to go into detail about what that meant. The servants, both men and women, who fetched drinks, towels and advised the water bearers of the need for replenishment did not undertake sexual duties for bathers.

"Certainly. Lead on," Gilbert said.

Midge took Gilbert into the bath chamber and out a side door to the yard, where a pair of goats grazed among the weeds. Beyond the towering woodpile to the left block all views of the stream as if they were in a secluded chamber.

"I think I'm in love," Wymar whispered in Gilbert's ear as they reached the yard.

"With Midge?" Gilbert asked, astonished.

"No, with Hilde," Wymar grinned. "I have a special passion for redheads."

"Well, keep it to yourself," Gilbert said.

Midge heard this, and she laughed, her hands on her bony hips when Gilbert turned to address her.

"Well, first things first, now that I have you here," Gilbert said. "Did you see anyone enter Dinesley's alcove at any time?"

"I didn't." She put a finger to her mouth, however. "Although when I do think back on it, I thought I heard him talking to someone."

"Any idea who?"

"Not a clue. I didn't think anything about it at the time, nor since, until now. It wasn't unusual for him to have company."

"By company, I suppose you mean the feminine sort?"

"Not always. Sometimes there were men."

"He wasn't inclined in that way?" Gilbert asked delicately.

A Curious Death

"Not as far as I know. They talked business, about money, payments for things."

"Do you know what things?"

"For not interfering." She scuffed a toe on the ground and looked down at it.

"Not interfering in what?"

"I don't think I should say."

"Why not?" Gilbert asked carefully.

"I could get in trouble."

"With whom?"

"The people with power," Midge said.

"I don't understand."

"You ain't supposed to."

"You know, Midge, what you say might remain with me, but if I have to have you summoned to give testimony, all the world will know," Gilbert said. It was an empty threat, but perhaps Midge would not see this.

Midge chewed on her lip. "There's gangs in town. Three of them. They've divided up the town and control the whores, gambling and such in their neighborhoods. And people pay them to keep order — or at least that's how it's explained."

"I don't follow that last bit." Gilbert thought he knew what she was talking about, however. But he wanted her to say it in her own words.

Midge took a deep breath and let it out in a rush. "If folk don't pay, they might suffer a mishap, like a fire, or a street robbery or a beating."

"They pay to be protected from the gang itself, in other words," Gilbert said.

"That's it."

"What did Dinesley have to do with this?"

"The gangs can't operate without the town aldermen and the castle constable looking the other way," she said.

"And I suppose someone puts coins in their palms for that purpose," Gilbert said.

"You got that right."

"And I also suppose that there are those who resent this."

"Indeed. It's on top of all the tithes and taxes folk have to pay. It can be a real burden."

"But you still haven't answered my question about Dinesley," Gilbert said.

Midge looked impatient, as if Gilbert should have worked this out already. "He was the constable's collector. He took the castle's payments. Every Monday, when he came for a bath."

"I see," Gilbert said, alarmed by this information. It could broaden the range of potential killers, who were likely to be very dangerous. He didn't mind risking a sore bum or feet to solve a riddle of death, but his own life was something else.

"Who makes up these gangs?" he asked to fill the silence, while he considered this shocking development.

"Students, mainly. They can get away with stuff ordinary people can't."

"Of course," Gilbert said. "They're clerics." Since the main purpose of universities was to prepare men for careers in the church, all students were regarded as clerics themselves, subject only to the jurisdiction of church courts and could not be charged or tried in hundred, county and the king's courts. This often meant that a student might get off free from any crime he committed, even murder.

"Did you or anyone else find any money in Dinesley's alcove after his death?" Gilbert asked.

Midge shook her head.

The door to the alcove shed cracked and a peeved face peered out. Midge saw the face and said, "I have to get back to work."

"There's one more thing," Gilbert said. "Did Richard le Glasiere occupy the alcove next to Dinesley's?"

Midge frowned. "Why, yes, he did."

"There was a woman with him. Who was she?"

Midge smiled slightly. "You know about that, eh?"

"I know he was with a woman. I want her name."

Midge breathed deeply. "Grecia le Goule."

"Who is Mistress le Goule?"

A Curious Death

"Her husband's a saddle maker. His shop's by East Gate. Why are you interested in her? You'll get her in real trouble if her husband finds out."

"I doubt he will," Gilbert said. "At least, not from me, if all goes well. Oh, and I almost forgot. Who occupied the alcove on Dinesley's other side?"

Midge's brows knitted in thought. "Soldiers from the army."

"Do you know who they were?"

"We have so many in now that I can't remember them all."

Gilbert dug into his purse and deposited a halfpenny into Midge's palm. "For your time, and thank you."

Midge dipped a curtsy, and hurried into the bathhouse.

Glasiere's shop had no sign announcing who lived and worked there. But since Gilbert knew the general area where to look for the shop, he identified it easily. Across the street from the castle's east wall, it was freshly painted and had ornate carvings of gargoyles, serpents and cherubim around the door, and along the eaves. The most striking feature of the house, however, was the windows themselves, for each one was fitted with glass panes, fitted in lead and wooden frames like shutters, blue for the ground floor with painted yellow flower designs, green with orange designs for the first floor, solid yellow for the second floor, and red for the two small windows on the third. The windows were a good way to advertise as glasieres were highly skilled window makers whose customers were the rich.

Gilbert lingered in the street for a few moments — admiring all that stunning glasswork before entering the shop while Wymar stared at a pair of girls carrying baskets who noticed his attentions and giggled.

The interior was separated into three parts, one with a wide and long bench for assembling windowpanes from painted sections of glass, a second for painting them, and a third for joining the painted fragments into a pane using strips of lead or copper. In the pane portion of shop, four young men were bustling around a table fixing painted panes to leaded frames that, when completed, would be a colorful mosaic in some church or the house of a rich man. In the paint shop, an older man was alone with brushes and various pots of paint. From where Gilbert stood, he could see that the painter was outlining an arm holding the handle of a sword on a piece of irregularly shaped glass about the size of two palms. The painter consulted a board propped on the table nearby with the scheme drawn in white that was being recreated in painted glass. On one table to the side, fragments of colored glass had been set out against a hand-drawn scheme, held in place by nails.

The apprentice looked over his shoulder and called, "Master! Someone to see you!"

The older man paused his paintbrush and looked back. He set down the brush, wiped his hands on a rag, and stood up. He was a tall man in a green, fur-lined coat. His forehead was high, his cheeks prominent, his chin firm and manly. He wore a slight but charming smile that did not fade when he saw who the apprentice referred to, even though it was obvious Gilbert was not a potential customer or an agent from a potential customer. Gilbert wondered if that smile was stuck in place.

"How can I help you?" Glasiere asked, folding long fingered hands upon his belt buckle.

"I just have a few questions — about Miles de Dinesley," Gilbert said in a low voice, leaning heavily on the Dinesley name. "Is there a quiet place we can talk?"

Glasiere's eyes narrowed and the smile faded to a gentle frown, proving that it was not stuck in place after all. "Yes, there is," he said. "Will you follow me?"

He led them to a small chamber at the rear of the shop which had a table with hand-drawn designs for windowpanes chalked out on its white surface. There was only a single chair

A Curious Death

in the chamber, but Glasiere did not take it. He stood with his back to the door.

"What is this about?" Glasiere asked. "Who are you?"

"My name is Gilbert Wistwode. I am an associate of Sir Stephen Attebrook. We have been asked by the Earl of Arundel to look into the circumstances of Dinesley's murder."

"And did you think I had something to do with it?" Glasiere asked.

"No. But I know you were in one of the alcoves beside Dinesley's and that you have some knowledge that might be useful."

"What makes you think that?"

"John the Archer told me."

Glasiere pursed his lips. "Is that all John told you?" he said slowly.

"He told me you were there, but not with whom. But I also happen to know from the staff at the Castle Keep who the woman was."

Glasiere looked alarmed. "It could cause me and my friend trouble if anyone came to know we were at the Keep on Monday."

"I don't want to cause you or your friend any trouble, but I need to know what you saw and heard," Gilbert said.

"Hmm," Glasiere grunted. The charming smile was long gone now and those deceiving lips were stretched venomously. "Will it be necessary for me to appear as a witness?"

"Perhaps not. Depends on what you have to tell me — and if I believe you," Gilbert said. His heart pounded at his audacity in the implied threat; he couldn't recall ever having spoken to anyone like that before. It made him giddy. Did Stephen feel like this — anxious yet oddly exhilarated — when deceiving people?

Glasiere's eyes flicked about the room as he considered his answer. At last, he shrugged. "Ask away. I'll tell you what I know. I think you'll be disappointed."

"Perhaps, but this is how the work is done: leave no stone unturned." Gilbert coughed and asked, "What did you see?"

"It wasn't so much as what we — I — saw, it was what I heard," Glasiere said.

"Go on."

"I was in the tub, enjoying myself, when there was a disturbance in Dinesley's alcove."

"Disturbance? That covers a lot of ground."

"Voices raised in argument. I didn't think anything of it, really. It happens more often than you expect. People drink too much and fail to control their tempers."

"Could you see who it was? Sometimes there are gaps in the curtains."

"There was. It was only enough to see someone with Dinesley."

"Did you see his face?"

"Who, Dinesley? Of course."

"No. The man he was speaking to."

"No. His back was to me."

"But you heard what was said."

"Some of it. People are loud in the Keep. There was an uproar, as usual."

"Tell me what you heard."

"Just a fellow complaining, rather bitterly, too, about Dinesley's pending marriage."

"Any idea why this fellow was complaining?"

"No, just something about the fact that Ysabelle — I heard that name plainly — was supposed to be for him, and that Dinesley had stolen her. Dinesley laughed. He could be a sharp, scornful bastard, if you know what I mean."

"You knew Dinesley?" Gilbert asked.

"Yes. I attended a few parties where he was there."

"I would not expect you to travel in the same circles," Gilbert said.

"Normally, we don't — didn't. But these were rather special parties."

"I don't see."

A Curious Death

"They were upstairs at the Keep. Rather loose parties, if you get my meaning."

"Back to the alcove," Gilbert gulped, scrambling to change the subject. He had heard of such parties, of course, although he had never met anyone who had actually been to such a party. Now and then they were condemned in sermons as wicked and sinful, for wild, unspeakable things apparently happened at them. He glanced at Wymar, whose attention had been wandering but now swerved back to Glasiere. "How did that fellow respond to Dinesley's laugh?"

Glasiere hesitated. He licked his lips, reluctant to go on. Then he said, "'I will make you pay for this, brother.'"

"Brother?" Gilbert murmured, disbelieving what he had heard.

Glasiere nodded. "Brother," he reemphasized.

"Oh, dear."

Glasiere chuckled humorlessly. "It might pose a problem, accusing the new heir to the barony of Hockesford of murder. Don't expect me to help you in any way with that."

Chapter 12

Stephen crossed one of the many bridges over the River Nene about Northampton and stopped. The town's west gate lay before him a short distance away, with the castle looming to the immediate north. The first real test of his disguise was coming. The thought made him nervous.

His eye wandered to the river. This branch of the Nene was little more than a shallow stream that flowed just west of the walled town.

The sally port cut through the wall somewhere in that direction, out of sight on the priory grounds at the north end of town. It would be quicker to find it within the town if he had more than a general idea where it was. If he could locate the exit to the sally port from outside town, he would have a far better idea where to look.

The fact a footpath led north along the town wall forced his decision. Stephen left the road and walked the path.

It was pleasant along the river, which flowed sluggishly southward between high banks. The grass was thick and sheep and a few cows grazing in the meadows regarded him with suspicion as he passed them.

Shortly, he came to a water mill, where the miller was loading sacks of flour into a handcart that a woman had brought out through a narrow postern gate in the castle wall. Both the woman and the miller waved at Stephen as he went by. Neither of them seemed to think anything of his walking the path. Perhaps it was often used by people to get around this part of town.

North of the castle was a water meadow where the grass bordering the path again grew thick and tall. Here and there, other paths diverged toward the river, and at one spot he saw a pair of boys fishing from the bank.

As he went farther north, the path skirted a boggy place where a small spring seeped through the turf and trickled into the Nene. The meadow got wilder. Weeds and small trees grew here and against the town wall, and patches of creeping vines the town aldermen had not cleared away slithered up,

A Curious Death

some as far as the crenellations — signs of inattention. But then money for maintenance of town walls often was short because nobody liked to pay the tithe for upkeep in times of peace. Collections lapsed, and fortifications often fell into ruin.

Stephen reached the top of the town where the wall curved to the east without spotting what he had come for. Could it really be here? Had Gilbert's memory played tricks on him? Had the port been filled in?

He walked back south along the base of the wall this time, wading through weeds and brush.

There was one place with a heavy growth of vines and a small ash and alder tree which obscured the wall. Could it be here, concealed by this riot of nature?

Stephen probed through the vines with his dagger. At first, the point clinked on stone. Then, it thumped on something softer. He pulled a handful of vines away.

The gap revealed a portion of a wooden door studded with rusty nails whose heads were as big as Stephen's thumbnail.

This was it.

Stephen cut a strip from his linen undershirt and tied the white strip to the branch of one of the alders covering the sally port to mark the spot.

Now to see where this gate opened inside the priory.

The priory gates were closed when Stephen drew up to them. Two armed guards wearing the red badge of a town bailiff on their coats sat on stools outside it.

"What do you want?" one of the guards asked Stephen without rising from his stool.

"To get in?" Stephen replied.

"Ya can't do that," the other guard said. "No one's allowed in or out."

"There's plague!" the first guard hissed in the sort of fake scary voice adults used on children. "The monks have it and so do some of the guests."

"The town's put the place under the interdict," the second guard said more normally. "You know what that means?"

"I've some idea. What kind of plague?" Stephen asked. "There are a lot of different kinds. Is it the pox?" The pox was a dreadful disease and everyone was terrified of it.

"It isn't the pox. Don't know what you'd call it," the first guard said.

"Makes you have the runs — explosive runs. Vomiting, too," the second guard said.

"Three monks and a traveler have died of it already," the first guard said. "It's nothing to play about with. The aldermen don't want it to get into the town."

"Dozens are sick. That's why there's an interdict," the second guard said.

"I get it," Stephen said. "No going in or out."

"That's an interdict for you," the second guard said.

"Thanks for the warning," Stephen said.

He retreated from the gate, wondering what he was going to do now.

The priory grounds were enclosed by a stone wall about eight feet high; at least, here along a lane running away from the entrance and the town's north gate, there was a wall. Stephen followed it to where the lane and wall turned left, and then another two-hundred yards to a turn right. At this corner, the wall turned westward and stretched a further three-hundred yards to the town wall. There were no other gates. The only way in was over the wall.

By this time, the streets were in shadow that had a soft orange hue from high clouds glowing with the sunset. Even though it was nearly April, the nights were cold and on hard ones, close to freezing. There was a house for Dominican friars, as he was pretending to be, in town. But he was reluctant to seek shelter there for fear of giving himself away.

A Curious Death

He might be able to fool common people in casual encounters but not other friars of the order.

Stephen did not relish hunkering in an alley or an orchard even with his thick cloak. And yet, that seemed the only course, since staying at an inn, when there was a perfectly good Black Friars house in town, could raise questions he might not be able to answer convincingly and his masquerade would be found out.

Stephen entered the apple orchard that sat to the south of the priory wall. It was not his first choice as a place to hide because you could see right through it and if he settled down now, he could be seen by any passer-by who might report him to the town bailiffs as a trespasser.

He came out on the street on the opposite side of the orchard, intending to look for a bolt hole in the small lanes in the area. There were often nooks on such streets that could be used to hide at night, but along every lane, the houses were built one against the other with no spaces between them where an enterprising vagrant or spy could settle in for the night.

Near the castle's north gate, he was about to turn deeper into town, when a figure clad in a somber black cloak that billowed about knob-kneed legs hurried out of the gate. The figure seemed sunk in his thoughts as he rushed past, but then he stopped abruptly.

The fellow took several steps toward Stephen and bent forward with a squint as if that might make his vision better in the fading light.

"Attebrook?" the fellow asked with astonishment and disbelief. "Stephen Attebrook? Can it really be you?"

The shock of being recognized struck like a sword thrust to the gut.

"I, er, Tom?" Stephen croaked at last. "Tom Boneyre?"

"God's knuckles!" Boneyre cried. "It is you! What's happened to you, man?"

"Nothing's happened to me."

"Nothing's happened? How can you say that! You've become a man of the cloth! You're the last person I would have expected to take holy vows! I thought you were bent on going to the continent, to go soldiering," Boneyre said.

"Well, I did. But I had a change of heart," Stephen stammered. It was not unusual for soldiers to enter religious life, but that usually happened when they were old and facing death with a weight of sin to account for.

"I would not have expected that of you in a hundred years. Speaking of years, how long's it been? Ten?"

"Something like that," Stephen said, wishing Boneyre would go away. They had been law clerks and students together in London that many years ago. Boneyre looked like he had stuck with it and had built himself a profitable practice.

Boneyre grasped Stephen's arm. "Well, old man. There's only one thing to do. You must come home to supper!"

As much as Stephen wanted to jerk his arm away and run as fast as he could, he could not resist Boneyre's tug without creating a scene — the guards at the castle gate were watching. So, he allowed himself to be led down the street.

They passed a stone building just visible behind another orchard. Boneyre waved at it, and said, "You'll be staying there, I expect!"

Stephen pondered this statement for a moment. "Oh, you mean Black Friars House? That's it?"

"You were searching for it when we met, were you? Bad directions, eh? Happens all the time. Come on, we're almost there."

"Almost there" was a wide marketplace. Two streets led out of it to the north. Boneyre took the righthand one, and a few houses on, he stopped at a narrow timber house that jutted up four floors from the ground. Its narrowness, so common in townhouses, did not detract from its grandeur, accentuated by carved filigrees about the windows. A modest sign over the door announced in French that this was the office of Thomas Boneyre, attorney at law.

"Well, here we are!" he said with pride. "Home!"

A Curious Death

Supper at Boneyre's house proved to be less onerous than Stephen anticipated. Boneyre asked a few questions about Stephen's activities since he left his clerkship with Crown Justice Ademar de Valance, but it was clear that Boneyre didn't care what Stephen said. Boneyre was more interested in boasting about his own successes — his flourishing practice, his beautiful new wife (who actually was rather plain) and their successful marriage (she was the daughter of a wealthy grocer), their healthy new son (who lay in a cradle by the supper table), their grand house, his plans to purchase a country estate of a gentry family fallen into debt, and his many connections among the nobility. The only rough moment arrived when the baby began to cry.

"Ah, Henry's hungry," the wife murmured shyly. She had not spoken during the meal, uttering only a "pleased to meet you," at Boneyre's introduction when they first arrived. She was much younger than he was, younger even than Ida, who was seventeen.

Boneyre looked annoyed as his wife scooped up the baby and retreated with him to a chamber at the rear of the hall. "We had to dismiss our wet nurse," he said.

The cook, maid and valet at the far end of the table dropped their eyes to their trenchers.

Stephen took Boneyre's statement and the servants' reaction to mean that, in fact, Boneyre hadn't employed one. Wet nurses were expensive and only the rich used them. Perhaps Boneyre wasn't doing as well as he wanted Stephen to think.

"Are you handling any interesting cases?" Stephen asked, to direct everyone's attention away from the issue of the wet nurse.

Boneyre brightened. "Why, yes! I've a case coming up before the sheriff's court tomorrow. My client stabbed a man over a game of dice. No one saw him but the accuser, however, and I've lined up a formidable line of declarants! More than the accuser! And of better quality!"

In criminal cases, a finding of guilt or innocence could turn on the number and quality of people, that is, their social standing, who appeared to swear to the accused's honesty and good character.

A thought blossomed in Stephen's mind, one that had simmered below the threshold of conscious thought since he had passed the castle's gate. A thought that created a huge temptation, one so great that it was overcoming his fear of being recognized in the castle. It would be dangerous to enter the castle. But it might be worth it — to the king and Lord Edward.

"That is fascinating," Stephen said. "I would like to see it."

"Why, there's no reason you cannot!" Boneyre said, pleased with the idea of being able to show off as Stephen thought he would be. "Be at the castle gate at Terce!"

It was an hour after sundown by the time supper concluded, and the clanging of the town's church bells ringing the curfew echoed down the street. Boneyre walked Stephen to the front door.

"My man will walk you to your accommodations," Boneyre said. "Can't have the night watch arresting you! They are very keen and watchful these days, and the punishments are harsh for being caught out after curfew. Even your tonsure may not shield you. The war, you know. They say the king's spies are everywhere."

"I had no idea things were so serious," Stephen said.

"You'd think after our victory in the west country, the king would come to terms," Boneyre said. "But he's a stubborn man. All this mess could have been avoided if he was more given to compromise."

"Victory in the west?" Stephen asked, puzzled. He wasn't aware of any victory by the rebels in the west.

A Curious Death

"Yes, in Gloucester, where we humbled Lord Edward!"

Stephen had been in the west country, and Gloucester in particular, when Lord Edward had clashed with a rebel force harrying the lands of Baron Roger Mortimer, one of the king's principal supporters. He remembered things differently than the story Boneyre told. Lord Edward had marched across the River Severn to aid Mortimer. The rebels had hoped to bottle Lord Edward up west of the Severn by seizing the bridges at Gloucester and Worcester and march on Oxford, but by skillful maneuvering, Edward had avoided the trap, and recovered the town of Gloucester, which had fallen to the rebels.

But Stephen said, "Ah, I hadn't heard."

"News doesn't get up to Northumbria very fast, does it?" Boneyre said. He clapped Stephen on the shoulder. "I will see you in the morning."

Holding a lantern on the end of a pole, the manservant led the way down the broad street, through the deserted marketplace, to the first street on the right past the market. He turned down that street and stopped at a covered gate in a low stone wall.

"Here we are," he said.

"Not seeing me to the door, eh?" Stephen asked.

"I can if you want."

"I can find my way across the yard. And I don't think the night watch will jump me before I get there."

"You could probably outrun them if you had to. Most of them couldn't run fifty yards without falling faint."

Stephen dug out a halfpenny for the servant, who was surprised to get it, and pushed through the gate. Often, friaries had houses at their gates for porters, but there was none here, which was a relief, since the porter's absence relieved Stephen of having to answer awkward questions.

The lantern had already disappeared around the corner when he reached the door to the Black Friars House. In the dark, Stephen couldn't tell much about it other than it was large, long and high — and quiet. Evidently, the friars did not stay up late. At least, it was unlikely he would be seen.

He went around the house to the back garden and groped his way across it in the dark, for there was no moon, tripping only once over a pile of spare lumber from some building project. The fall knocked the wind out of him, but it was better than plunging into an unseen privy. That had been known to happen, sometimes with fatal effect.

He emerged on the street behind the friary through a small stand of cherry trees separating one line of houses from another that ran down to the market. He paused here, eyes and ears straining for any signs of the watch. Often a town's night watch patrolled with lanterns as the servant had carried, but when they were bent on really catching wrong doers, they went without lanterns like the footpads they hunted.

There were no houses in the direction of the town's western wall. The space there was devoted to gardens and orchards; the landholders of unoccupied land often rented ground to town citizens so they could grow their own produce.

Stephen crept through the orchard, low-hanging branches that avoided his upraised hands raking his face until he came out on the narrow lane running beneath the priory's southern wall.

He scanned left and right, listening for human activity in his vicinity. Seeing no one, hearing no one, he leaped for the top of the wall and pulled himself up and over, almost losing his satchel with its change of clothes when it slipped from his shoulder. His landing, however, was not as graceful as his scramble over the wall, for he landed with a plop and fell on his butt with a jar that left him stunned for several moments. But mishaps and injuries were to be expected; burglary was, after all, a risky business with discovery and arrest being only two of them.

Here, in the lower portion of the priory grounds, was another orchard and a vast herb garden. Stephen crept to its end without fearing discovery, until he halted at a more formal

A Curious Death

garden, or what appeared to be a garden; patches of land had been divided by wicker fences with lanes between the patches. In the darkness, Stephen could not tell what grew in these gardens — the waning crescent moon would not rise for hours yet.

Gilbert said the guest house was against the priory's west wall. Stephen could make out several structures that way despite the gloom, so he wound through the garden plots in that direction. The night was quiet except for a dog barking somewhere in the town.

The first structure was a shed with a furnace that still radiated heat and stank of hot iron: a blacksmith shop. Next to it was a low pigsty, identifiable some distance away by its signature stench. Then there was another shed over a large woodpile where the skittering of small feet could be heard: the resident rats and mice, perhaps, for out of the dark a small shape streaked across Stephen's path. It was too large and ran too gracefully for a rat; he guessed it was the local cat. There then was a gap and after twenty paces a large stone building loomed against the wall with three sets of double doors on the ground floor, the kind which were the hallmark of a substantial cellar.

Stephen listened for movement in the sleeping quarters above his head. He heard murmurs, groans, and a muffled voice crying, "Oh, God! Not again! Deliver me!" And there was the sound like fluid being poured. Stephen shuddered. He hoped the pestilence did not seep through floors, for that was all standing between him and this disease.

He tried each of the doors. The outer two were barred, but the middle one was not. It creaked open at Stephen's pull.

He slipped inside.

If Stephen had thought it was dark and hard to get around outside, it was nothing compared to the guesthouse's undercroft. The cracked doorway presented a thin greyish crack at his back that provided no illumination of the interior, which was as dark as the inside of a mine after the candle went out. It smelled musty with an under-fragrance of that peculiar odor of molding grain that had gotten wet.

And it smelled of dog.

A chain clanked and there was a menacing growl out of the dark. Fear paralyzed Stephen. It was one thing to face cold steel, but quite another to face the charge of a massive, snarling dog.

But the dog did not charge, although it continued to growl and the chain continued to clatter. The ultimate threat arrived as the door behind him creaked ever so faintly and there was the whisper of a foot scraping on dirt.

Stephen instinctively stepped to one side and an object whooshed through the space where his head had been.

His attacker was not a large dog, but a very short man-shape. Stephen swept an arm across that person's throat while stepping behind him to throw him backward with the backheel. The attacker landed with a thud and an "ooff!" The growls changed to frenzied barking, punctuated by the clashing of chain links.

Without thinking, Stephen pressed a knee into the fallen attacker's side and drew his dagger for the killing stroke.

Yet his hand froze in midair by what he saw in the dim starlight cast by the open doorway. The attacker was not a man, but a girl, short and skinny as a sapling.

"What are you doing here?" Stephen hissed.

"Nothing," the girl spat. "And get off my chest, you bastard!"

Stephen lightened the press of his knee but kept the hold in place. He didn't see the weapon she had tried to brain him with now, but he wasn't willing to take the chance that she didn't have another.

"Can't they do something to shut that cursed thing up?" a voice said above him, barely audible through the din of howling.

A more muffled voice answered that the beast must have been after a rat; the cellar was full of them. Yet any moment, Stephen expected someone to come down to shut the dog up.

The girl voiced his concerns when she muttered, "Don't matter now. I'm caught. Someone will be down to shut Bill up."

"Bill?" Stephen asked. "That's your dog?"

"Of course, it's my dog," the girl spat. "You know that unless you're dumb as a post."

"I'll give the post a run for its money, thank you. But I didn't know."

"How could you not? You're one of the stinking monks."

"Well, I am not a monk. Don't be jump to conclusions just because I wear a cleric's robe."

She wiggled. "Are you going to stand on my chest all night, or aren't you doing to arrest me."

"I've no intention of arresting you. Can you shut that dog up?"

"Let me up."

"Only if you promise not to brain me."

The girl nodded, and Stephen removed his knee. The girl crawled to the dog. At her touch and with a few whispers, the dog fell silent, except for some rattling of its chain.

He listened for movement above his head, but this silence seemed to satisfy those trying to sleep.

"Why did you try to brain me?" he asked the girl.

"You *are* dumber than a post."

"To get your dog, by any chance?" Stephen guessed.

"My purpose doesn't matter now."

"Why is your dog chained up?" Stephen asked.

"You don't know?"

"Why would I? I'm not from around here."

"He bit the prior," the girl said.

"He bit the prior, just like that?"

"The prior touched me," she said.

"So?"

"He pulled my hair, forced my head back, and tried to kiss me. My family are villeins of one of the priory's estates, so he thought he had license. Like we're property or something, and he can do what he likes with us. I struggled. Bill was protecting me."

"I see. So, the prior took your dog."

"He means to kill Bill, or so the porter told my dad," the girl said. "If it weren't for this plague, Bill would be dead now. The prior's fallen sick with it."

"And you came here to get him out?"

The girl didn't answer this question. Instead, she said, "You're a tricky friar, aren't you. Come to steal some relics? This is the wrong place. They're up at the church."

"I told you, I'm not a friar. And I'm not interested in relics. I am interested in doors. One door in particular."

"This sounds like some sort of bad riddle. I'm terrible at riddles. Why don't you just speak plainly."

Stephen grasped a handful of the girl's shirt — she wore a man's tunic and stockings instead of a woman's gown, her hair bound up in a knot at the back of her head — and lifted her to her feet. He glanced out the door and scanned the priory grounds for any sign of movement or the sounds of alarm.

"There is a door through the wall in this undercroft, an old sally port," Stephen said. "If you help me find it, I'll get you and your dog safe away from here."

"Why do you want to find this sally port? To loot the cellar while everyone's asleep?"

"Yes, exactly. That's it."

The girl chuckled lowly. "For some reason, I don't believe you, but that is an offer a girl cannot refuse."

They had to find the door by feel since there was no light to see. The girl started at one end of the undercroft while Stephen started at the other and they worked their ways toward each other over boxes, sacks and barrels stacked against the wall that interfered with progress. Occasionally some of these obstacles had to be moved to allow a searching hand to drift over cold stone.

A Curious Death

"I've found it," the girl said. "I think."

Stephen fumbled his way to the girl, navigating by her heavy breathing. He ran a hand along stone until his fingers encountered a heavy door, iron-hinged and studded with broad-headed iron nails. Stephen's fingers told him that the door was wide and tall enough to admit a single mounted man, if he stooped over the horse's neck. It opened inward and was bolted with two iron rods that were secured with a padlock.

"This is it," he said.

Chapter 13

"This Serlo strikes me as the vicious sort," Wymar said as he held out his bowl to Kate, who was tending the pot, for another helping of porridge.

Kate, the wife of one of the archers in their camp circle, hesitated in stirring the pot. Wymar gave her a charming smile, and the woman's rather stern expression softened. She ladled another gob into Wymar's bowl.

"That's the last you get, you greedy dog," she said not unkindly.

"Thank you, mistress," Wymar said, who could brim with charm when he wanted something.

"What do you know about the fellow? You've never met him," Gilbert said, stirring his porridge without enthusiasm. It was like most porridges, thick with barley and oats, but many of the grains were still hard so that it often felt like the mess was filled with pebbles.

"I asked around. Apparently, he set a dog on fire when he was younger. One of his brother's favorite hunters. Caused quite a row in the family, apparently." Wymar stuck a finger in his mouth and massaged his teeth as if dislodging something stuck there. "They'd have been all right with it if it had been a cat. Nobody's got any use for a cat. But a dog! There are limits, don't you think?"

"They? Who's they? Where did you hear that?" Gilbert asked.

Wymar waved, vaguely indicating an unspecified location in the camp. "I went round last evening while you were snoring away to where the Hockesford party is camped. They're near Arundel's men. They don't like young Serlo. Had nothing good to say about him. Arrogant little prick was the kindest thing I heard, I think."

"Amazing they would have said as much, given he's the heir now."

"They were drunk."

"And you remained sober enough to wring that out of them?" Gilbert asked.

A Curious Death

Wymar gave a lopsided grin. "They were drowning their sorrows and I gave them a sympathetic shoulder to cry on."

The cook cut in, interrupting this fascinating conversation, "Cut me some more wood for the fire before you go, will you, Wymar? When you've finished up."

"Of course, mistress," Wymar said through a mouthful of porridge that dribbled down his chin. He wiped the chin, licked the back of his hand, and nodded.

"That's a good lad," the cook smiled.

Gilbert scooped up the last of the porridge and tossed the dirty bowl in a nearby bucket.

At their tent, he strapped on his sword, glad for the first time that he had it, even if he was more likely to hurt himself than someone else.

"Hurry up with that. Do you think Serlo can be found with his men, or with his new wife?" he called to Wymar.

"If you were Serlo, where would you be?" Wymar asked with a leer.

Serlo was not with the lovely Ysabelle at their chamber in the king's hall or anywhere within the castle, but with the army, and it took Gilbert most of the morning to find him.

They finally came upon Serlo at an open field north of the king's house, where cavalry units were exercising. The men were armored and wearing big pot helmets that concealed their faces, so it was impossible to pick out Serlo among those changing from one formation to another at the shouted orders of the commander while engaging in mock charges and retreats. Finally, a bystander pointed him out to Gilbert.

"Course you can't see their faces," the bystander, an elderly archer, said. "That's the point of them helmets — so you don't eat one of my arrows. Look at their shields! The Hockesford arms! The sword with three pears."

"Pears," Gilbert said. "Not very warlike."

The archer chuckled. "I'll not argue with that. Who knows why families choose the arms they do. Maybe their ancestor had a fondness for pears."

"Or pear wine?"

"Ha! Foul stuff! Fit only to pickle corpses."

"Hmm," Gilbert said. "You may be on to something. It would certainly help with the smell."

The old archer slapped a thigh and laughed. "So it would!"

The exercises finished and the horsemen walked their beasts to the edges of the field, where their squires and grooms waited to help them dismount and to collect their gear.

Gilbert caught up with Serlo as he handed his shield and lance to a young man who must be his squire. Serlo removed his helmet and regarded Gilbert in an unfriendly way.

"Wistwode, aren't you?" Serlo said dismissively as he dismounted and handed the reins to the already burdened squire, who missed his grip on them.

"You useless bastard!" Serlo screamed at him.

The squire, who was older and looked big enough to break Serlo in half, took the dressing down with a carefully straight face. "Your pardon, my lord."

"I inherited the lout from my brother," Serlo said to Gilbert as he strode toward the spot where several ale barrels had been set up. "I shall have to replace him, I suppose." He took a cup but did not see that Gilbert was served.

"So, what are you doing here?" Serlo asked.

"I have undertaken to continue the inquiry into Sir Miles' death," Gilbert said.

Serlo looked startled. "You have? I thought you just followed Attebrook around, like a puppy."

"I am a little more than a puppy," Gilbert said.

"So, do you have something to report?"

"After a fashion. I have taken a statement from a witness who claims you were in the Castle Keep and spoke to Sir Miles in his tub shortly before he died."

Serlo's mouth opened, shut and opened again.

"You had an argument," Gilbert said. "What was it about?"

"It was nothing. A dispute about a loan."

"The name of your wife came up. There was mention of a claim she had been promised to you."

Serlo's nostrils flared. He breathed heavily and leaned forward with balled fists. If he had been a bigger man, Gilbert would have worried about being attacked. But Serlo did not seem the type. He was a bookish man. He had ridden well in the exercises, but his handling of his lance was awkward. He was not the sort to engage in a direct attack. At least, Gilbert hoped so, keeping an eye on Serlo's hands in case he went for his dagger.

"Ysabelle and I have known each other since we were children," Serlo said at last. "Mother said she would speak to her father for me and arrange a marriage."

"I thought you were destined for the priesthood," Gilbert said.

"That was my father's idea. Not mine."

"And you thought that marrying Ysabelle would save you from that fate?"

Serlo tapped his thigh with his whip but didn't reply.

"But that did not work out," Gilbert said.

Serlo sneered. "My brother had my father intercede! Miles told Father it was the best way to join our family to Ysabelle's. She is an only child and when that wretch of a father of hers dies, her lands will be ours. We'll be one of the richest families in the North! Miles persuaded Father that he was the better match as the heir so this could come about."

"Whereas only you would have taken possession of your wife's lands when she inherited," Gilbert said.

Serlo's mouth worked, but he did not reply.

"Money, a woman. Reason enough to kill him," Gilbert said with false mildness, for every nerve in his body was tingling with trepidation that he could say such a thing out loud. It was the sort of rash thing Stephen would say.

Serlo stood tense and shaking, his face pale. "And yet I did not!"

"So you say," Gilbert said.

"I was not alone. I have a witness to the whole thing. He will tell you everything."

A Curious Death

Chapter 14

Finding Serlo's companion, one Godfrey de Maunsfield, meant retracing his steps to Saint Mary's Church.

Out of curiosity and in hopes of finding another lecture going on, Gilbert stuck his head into the church, but the only live things he spotted were sparrows flying among the high rafters and a pair of women on their knees before a figure of a saint to the right of the altar. It was quiet except for the low murmur of the women's voices and the fluttering of wings.

He pulled his head out of the church and looked around for the tavern Serlo had named, The Crow. Three taverns were in view from where Gilbert stood, but he didn't see an establishment with a sign that indicated it was The Crow.

Two streets ran north from High Street on either side of the church. Gilbert looked down the western street and saw nothing that looked like it might be The Crow. He found it, however, on the eastern street, which terminated at Smith Gate — a large sign of a crow with a tankard clutched by one foot.

He and Wymar went inside.

It was dim, except for a low hearth fire that filled the air with choking smoke from what must have been wet wood. A few rush lights glimmered in the fog to provide what little illumination there was.

There were few men about, for it was still midday. They appeared to be soldiers bent over their cups and a few black-robed students. Several looked in Gilbert's direction until he shut the door, plunging the hall back into dimness. Then they turned away. A dice game was going on in a corner which didn't pause at his appearance.

But then one of the players rose and approached Gilbert, rattling the dice in his cupped hands. He was a tall man, broad shouldered and slim waisted. His wrists were thick, his forearms muscled. He had a square face, brows that went straight across, deep-set eyes and domed head with hair cut in the clerical style, yet he wore a burgundy coat with green and yellow stockings beneath his black student's robe. He smiled without humor at Gilbert, who felt threatened by his confident advance and wanted to flee. But Gilbert stood his ground and resisted the urge to put a hand on his sword. He felt Wymar stir beside him. Wymar must feel threatened, too.

"Let's see. Fat little lump of a man with no hair. You must be Wistwode," the player said. He dropped the dice from one palm to another. "I've been expecting you."

"Expecting me?" Gilbert said, nonplused.

"Serlo warned me you'd be coming."

"Ah," Gilbert replied, sensing what must have happened. As soon as Gilbert turned his back on Serlo at the practice field, Serlo must have ordered a man to rush ahead to warn Godfrey de Maunsfield to expect them — to ensure they got their stories straight, perhaps? "You're Maunsfield, then."

"Right," Maunsfield said.

"You should know what I'm after," Gilbert said.

"You want to know about our visit to Dinesley."

"Miles de Dinesley, yes."

Maunsfield's tone dripped with hatred, which caught Gilbert by surprise. He hadn't expected Maunsfield to harbor any animus toward Dinesley, or even to know him.

"Let's have a seat," Maunsfield continued, gesturing to a vacant bench and table. He waved at the man at the bar and held up three fingers. "You're paying, of course," Maunsfield said to Gilbert.

"You didn't like Dinesley, I take it," Gilbert said, as they sat down.

"For such a silly looking little man, you're quite smart," Maunsfield said sarcastically.

"I do my best. How did you know him?"

Maunsfield stared into the dimness. His lips worked. He said, "We had dealings."

"What kind of dealings?"

Maunsfield's mouth twitched. "We are both wrestlers. A year ago, the day after Palm Sunday, at the market, we had a match."

"Don't tell me. You lost."

A Curious Death

Maunsfield rubbed his left elbow. He nodded. It seemed to take a great amount of effort to perform the nod, but Gilbert could understand that. It hurt to admit defeat. Most people couldn't do it. They made up excuses instead.

"Bastard broke my arm, even though I'd yielded. He was a vicious swine. He liked hurting people. I thought I could take him, thought I'd teach him a lesson. Didn't work out, though." He flexed the arm. "Took me almost a whole year to get full use of it back."

"What were you and Serlo doing at the Castle Keep last Monday?"

Maunsfield let out a deep breath. "I owed Dinesley money. Went to deliver it. Serlo had nothing to do, so he came along."

"You owed Dinesley money? Or were you delivering it for someone else?"

Maunsfield's eyes narrowed. "You best not ask more about that, if you don't want to end up hurt, or worse. Let's just say, I owed him a debt. A lost bet, eh?"

"All right. What happened when you got there?"

Maunsfield shrugged. "Not much. We exchanged a few words and left."

"What words?"

"Weren't me who did the talking."

"Serlo, then."

Maunsfield's fingers tapped the table. "It was about my sister."

That caught Gilbert aback and it took a moment to get his thoughts back on course. "Your sister? Ysabelle de Baresworth?"

"Do I have to draw you a picture? We share the same mother, different fathers."

"Of course. What did Serlo say about Lady Ysabelle?"

"If was an old grievance. Serlo had entreated his mother to arrange a marriage between them, but Serlo's father interceded. Poor love-struck bastard. He's been filled with disappointment ever since. Idiot let it show Monday. Miles loved it when he caused people pain. He'd bullied Serlo since they were children, and now this."

"What did Serlo do?"

"Poor bastard cried."

"Did he say anything about getting even?"

"He might have done. I don't remember."

"Then what happened?" Gilbert asked.

"We left, is all."

"Dinesley was alive when you left?"

"Laughing so hard I thought he would shake all the water out of his tub."

Gilbert drained his ale cup and stood up. "Well, that's that, isn't it?" He paused for a moment. "How much money did you deliver to Dinesley?"

Maunsfield let another moment pass before answering. "What's that got to do with anything?"

"I'm not sure. But as far as I know, no money was found in Dinesley's alcove. That must have implications. I'm sure that the constable is not happy about it."

Maunsfield's eyes narrowed as he contemplated how far Gilbert's knowledge extended. But rather than deny what he had been up to, he said, "The constable is not happy. He didn't believe us when we said we paid."

"So, he's demanded you pay again."

"That he has."

"I assume from your reaction that this was a substantial sum."

Maunsfield snorted. "More than a little man like you sees in a year."

"Life is full of difficulties. I'm sure you'll find a way out of this jam." Gilbert meant the retort as a lame way to have the last word. But as soon as he uttered it, his vision swam with a bolt of realization. He knew he should probably not say anything about it. But his curiosity got hold of his tongue, and he blurted, "You'll pay a call on Joce Buckerel again, won't you?"

"Why would I do that?" Maunsfield growled.

A Curious Death

"Because there's money to be made there."

"What makes you think so?" Maunsfield's voice held a mixture of animosity and caution.

"Because you know a secret the Buckerels don't want made public."

"That's nonsense."

"You learned the secret from Serlo. And you saw a way to profit from it."

"What secret is that?"

"I don't need to say what it is. We both know."

Maunsfield laughed. There was no humor in it, though. "What if Buckerel owes me money? It's none of your concern."

He drained his cup, scooped up his dice and stalked out of the tavern.

Gilbert and Wymar remained at their table. They had paid for a pitcher of ale to lubricate the interrogation of Maunsfield, and it was only half finished. Gilbert did not believe in the waste of food or ale, a firm resolve which overpowered his impulse to run; no telling whether Maunsfield would return with some of his gang to rough him up or worse. On reflection, though, Maunsfield probably would do nothing. He thought himself above the law because of his clerical status as a university student. And he was probably right.

"That's another dead end," Wymar said, refilling his cup. "Even if they're the guilty parties."

Gilbert sighed. "Perhaps. It is curious that their stories are so consistent. Not word for word, but in the important parts."

"Are you saying that they agreed on what to say?"

"They could have. Maunsfield strikes me as the sly type, more so than Serlo. He might be clever enough to have coached Serlo. But if they are lying, we have no way yet to prove it short of torture."

"From what you and my lord have told me, the earl might enjoy a bit of that."

"I'm not giving FitzAllan the chance. If we're going to solve this, we'll do it without breaking any fingers or lopping off any ears."

"Have you given up on the Buckerels, too?" Wymar asked.

"I don't know. They have reason to want Dinesley dead. And Adam apparently is the sort to act rashly."

"And he was there that afternoon," Wymar said.

"Yes. But no one saw him among the baths. And how would he have known which tub Dinesley occupied? He'd have had to ask one of the staff. I'm sure that would have been remembered, and no one said anything about it."

"He could have peeked through the curtains until he found Dinesley, couldn't he?"

"If that was Adam's method, he'd have looked in our alcove, and I had my eyes on the passage. I'd have seen him."

Gilbert tapped a finger on the table as another thought occurred to him. "You know, it could have been robbery."

"What do you mean?"

"You heard Maunsfield — the gangs are paying the constable for the right to extort money from the townspeople. There was a lot of money in that alcove, and it's disappeared."

"Maunsfield and Serlo killed Dinesley for money?"

"I doubt it. But maybe someone else could have."

"Yet no one heard or saw anything untoward," Wymar said.

"There is that," Gilbert said. It had seemed like a good idea, but, like the others, it ran into a small problem called lack of evidence.

"Time to give up, I suppose," Wymar said glumly.

"Maybe not," Gilbert said. He remembered something that had slipped his mind. He delved into his pouch and fumbled about for the button Stephen had given him. His fingers found it and he held it up to the light. "There is this."

"A button? Why's that important?"

A Curious Death

"Stephen found it in Dinesley's alcove. Our killer might have lost it."

"Phew. Anybody could have lost it. Buttons fall off coats all the time."

"They do," Gilbert said. "But it's all we have to go on at the moment."

Chapter 15

Stephen's first thought was to clear the stacks of boxes, sacks and barrels away from the sally port and to send the girl and her dog through it to safety. But there was so much stuff piled up before the door that it would have taken him the rest of the night to move it and then put it back. So, he turned his attention to freeing the dog from his chain. This was something he approached with reluctance since he had not made friends with the dog, and Bill didn't seem interested in being friends with Stephen, as Bill growled when he sensed Stephen scrambling closer. But the girl crawled to the dog and quieted him so Stephen could get to work.

The chain was secured with a padlock. Ordinarily, such a lock would be a decisive impediment, but Stephen had come prepared. He fished out a skeleton key on a thong about his neck from beneath his friar's robes. Ida had acquired its twin in London in order to help him escape from one of the city's many gaols. He hadn't needed much persuading to realize the usefulness of such a universal lock-breaking tool and had a smith make him a key of his own — just in case he might need it to further his burgeoning career as a burglar. So far in this happy career, he had learned to break into houses by climbing through upper story windows on ropes secured to the roof, smashing through the plaster and wattle set between the timbers of many buildings, and by the use of magic keys. What might come next, he wondered. He had once escaped from a lockup by burrowing under one of the walls. Perhaps he might someday find a reason to reverse the process to get in rather than out.

A few moments of twisting and turning the key in the lock and the thing popped open with a soft clunk.

Stephen gathered up the chain and its lock, and he went out to the yard with the girl leading the dog by its collar.

"That'll make them scratch their heads about how he got away," Stephen said.

"Scratch enough to bleed, I hope," the girl said.

Then they went to the southern wall of the priory.

A Curious Death

Stephen fashioned a harness about Bill with the chain and pulled himself to the top of the wall. He hauled Bill up while the girl supported the dog from below, and between them they managed to lift Bill, who was as big and heavy as his growl had indicated, to the wall. Bill was not happy with this treatment, but he made no sound other than a low growl that caused Stephen's insides to vibrate. When Bill had reached the top, he squatted unsteadily before Stephen and they were face to face. For a moment, Stephen feared that Bill would latch onto his face — he had seen dogs attack this way and it never turned out well for the recipient. But Bill just sniffed Stephen's nose and looked at the girl. Stephen leaned down and pulled her up, then let her down on the other side. They repeated the procedure for Bill and Stephen dropped beside them.

"You know you can't go back to your village," Stephen said. "If Bill turns up there, the prior will just seize him again. And he will assume you freed Bill and there will be consequences."

"I suppose so," the girl said. She looked into the dark distance, obviously considering her prospects, which were bleaker than she had thought them to be. She probably hadn't given much consideration to what she would do when she freed Bill.

"Any idea what you'll do now?" Stephen asked.

"I thought about running away," she said.

"It helps to have somewhere to go," Stephen said. "There is something you can do."

"What?" the girl asked.

"I know a place you can go and be free."

"Where is that?" she asked in a tone that said she didn't believe such a place existed.

"I have a manor in the west. You can live there."

"You? Have a manor?" she asked skeptically. She pointed at his head. "With a shaved head like that?"

"I know it's hard to believe. Take advantage while you can."

Stephen told her how to get to Kislingbury and find shelter at the Picots' manor.

"Wait there until I return," he said.

"You're not coming?"

"I have some other business here first. But when I get back, we'll start the journey. What's your name, by the way?"

"Begilda. What's yours?"

"Stephen."

"Stephen what? If you're gentry you've a last name, too."

"That's enough for now. If I don't show up in two days, make for Oxford. Ask after a man named Gilbert Wistwode at the army camp. Tell him I sent you and to take you back to Ludlow."

"Ludlow," Begilda repeated.

"My manor's near there. My wife will take you in."

"You're sure about that?"

Stephen nodded. "When morning comes, I would go out the south gate, if I were you. It's furthest from the priory. We'll shelter in that orchard there until sunrise," he said, pointing to the orchard on the other side of the lane. He didn't like having to hide there, but it would have to do. "Then you get on as fast as you can."

A Curious Death

Chapter 16

On Friday morning, Gilbert went to see Joce Buckerel at his shop on High Street.

One of Buckerel's clerks told him the master was in the cellar taking inventory, so Gilbert went back outside and down the stone-paved incline. He heard voices on the way and when he reached the bottom, he saw Buckerel and another clerk in the light of a candle set upon a barrel top.

Buckerel and the clerk fell silent as Gilbert reached the bottom.

"God's bunions! You again. What is it now?" Buckerel said with irritation.

"We need to talk," Gilbert said. "It's best if we speak alone."

Buckerel chewed his lower lip. Then he said, "James, go back up to the shop."

He crossed his arms when James' footsteps on the incline ceased and the clerk's shadow followed him into the street. "Go ahead. Spit it out. I am a busy man. I haven't time to waste on your speculations."

"I want you to summon Anne so I can question her. And I want to see your wardrobes," Gilbert said.

"You impertinent little piece of shite!" Buckerel burst out. His hands formed fists which he held rigidly at his sides, his posture tense and trembling as if he only managed to restrain the urge to strike Gilbert with the greatest of effort. "How dare you —"

"I know who your blackmailer is," Gilbert cut Buckerel off. "If you cooperate with me, I will give you his name."

Buckerel panted heavily, the noise reverberating in the confines of the stone cellar. "How do you know this?"

"I discovered who it was during my speculations, as you called them. He confessed to me." Well, as good as confessed, Gilbert thought, crossing invisible fingers.

"This hardly seems a good bargain, if you think my children guilty of murder!"

"If you refuse, it will be a confession. Surely you see that."

It seemed to take a very long time for a clerk to run to the Leke house and return with Anne Buckerel.

Gilbert waited in the street with Wymar while the elder Buckerel retreated into his shop.

The first indication that Anne had arrived came from Wymar, who had been watching women passing on the street and whose head swiveled about and came forward as if he was a hunting dog which had just spotted the game.

Gilbert followed the boy's gaze and saw the clerk sent to fetch Anne. Behind him was a girl of dazzling beauty. She had delicate and serene features, and thick brown hair falling about her shoulders visible through a silk veil.

Her father must have been watching for her from a shop window, because he hurried out as she came up, perhaps worried that Gilbert would speak to her before he could intercede.

"You needed to see me, father?" Anne asked.

Buckerel nodded. "This irritating little man has a few questions for you."

"For you both," Gilbert said.

Anne looked Gilbert over with confident, self-possessed eyes. "This must be the fellow who called for me a few days ago, when I was feeling unwell."

"Not your ladies time, was it?" Gilbert said. "But something quite different."

"He knows," Buckerel said.

"Ah," Anne said calmly.

"The wardrobes first, then the questions," Gilbert said.

He strode into the house without waiting for Buckerel's answer.

The wardrobes were, of course, in the first floor bedchambers. Even though a wealthy family like the Buckerels had more clothes than the ordinary person, it did not take long to search through the chests. Some of Adam's garments were festooned with buttons, as was the current fashion, but none of them were silver. Nor did any of them match the button hiding in Gilbert's pouch. It was the same for his father's and Anne's clothes.

Down in the hall with the servants sent away, Gilbert extracted the button and laid it on the table.

"What's that?" the elder Buckerel sniffed.

"Have you seen its like before?" Gilbert asked.

Buckerel prodded the button. "No. Should I have?"

"And you, mistress," Gilbert asked Anne. "Have you ever seen one like it?"

"No," Anne said in her musical voice, eyes holding Gilbert's with a confidence that seemed intimidating in one so young.

"Were either of you at the Castle Keep Monday afternoon?" Gilbert asked.

Both said no.

"Adam was," Gilbert said.

"Of course, he was," the elder Buckerel said. "It was business. Nothing more."

"Did he know that Dinesley was there as well?"

"Why would he?"

"It was Dinesley's habit to refresh himself every Monday at the Keep — and to collect money from the student gangs plaguing the town."

"I did not know that," Buckerel said. "About Dinesley, I mean. I knew about the payments. Everyone knows the gangs are paying tribute to the town and to the castle."

"And you, Anne? Did you know?" Gilbert asked.

"I do not pay attention to such things," she said. "They are none of my business."

"Where were you Monday afternoon?" Gilbert persisted.

"I was at my mistress's house, as she told you."

"Ill. But not with your woman's time."

"Well, it is a sickness only women are prone to," Anne said, eyes level.

"An illness that involves vomiting?"

"You are familiar with it!" Anne said with a small laugh.

"My wife has had children and was bothered by it early on." Gilbert looked at Anne's lap. "Isn't it about time that you found another situation? Until …?"

Ann sighed. "I suppose it is. I have selected Godstowe Abbey as my lying in place. Perhaps you know if it. Rosamund Clifford is buried there. I rather like the symbolism."

"That is fitting under the circumstances," Gilbert said. Rosamund Clifford had been the mistress of King Henry the second of that name and had given him, according to rumor, at least two children. Godstowe was a Benedictine nunnery, and should do nicely for the delivery of her child in secret.

"What about your promise?" Buckerel said. "We've done what you demanded."

"You have," Gilbert said. "The man who is troubling you is named Godfrey de Maunsfield. He is a student at Balliol College."

"What makes you think he is, in fact, the one?"

"He is a close associate of Serlo de Dinesley. I have no doubt that Dinesley told Maunsfield of your trouble. It's the only way he could have learned of it. And he admitted to me that he intended to extract more money from you. You see, he carried the students' payment to Dinesley last Monday, and no cache of money was found in Dinesley's alcove. The constable has demanded that the money must be immediately replaced. So, you can expect a visit from Maunsfield any day."

Back on the street, Wymar paused and glanced at the Buckerel house. "The fact you didn't find a coat with matching buttons doesn't mean they didn't do it. Does it?"

"No," Gilbert said. "But it makes it less likely, I think."

"Do you think that Maunsfield is alone in this blackmail? Couldn't Serlo de Dinesley be involved, too?"

A Curious Death

"That's a possibility," Gilbert said. "But we have no direct proof of that. And anyway, there's nothing we or the Buckerels could do about it even if we did."

Wymar snorted. "If Serlo's involved, whatever happens to Maunsfield won't stop the extortion."

"That could be, that could be. But I hope we have found a way to put a stop to the extortion."

"Do you have some clever plan for dealing with Serlo?" Wymar asked as they neared the castle's main gate. "Like you did with the Buckerels?"

Gilbert shook his head. "I've nothing in mind so devastating and persuasive."

"He isn't going to answer questions about that button of yours. And if he is willing, I'll wager he won't tell the truth."

"That is a problem," Gilbert said as they came up to one of the gate wardens, who was leaning against the wall of the passage, looking bored. "But I have an answer for that." I hope, he said to himself.

"State your business," the warden said without leaving his crucial position holding up the wall.

"An inquiry for the earl of Arundel," Gilbert said.

"Oh, yes. You've been here before."

"Say, I was hoping to have a word with Serlo de Dinesley. He is the earl's kinsman, you know. I understand he and his new wife have taken chambers in the castle."

"They're occupying the deputy constable's chambers for the time being. Until the army marches and we get a new deputy."

"And those chambers would be where?"

"In the hall, of course."

"That was masterful," Wymar said as they started across the bailey.

"Watch and learn, young worm," Gilbert said. "You are in the presence of greatness."

"A great appetite, maybe."

"Keep it up and I will tell Sir Stephen of your disrespect. He will have you flogged."

"Will he, now?" Wymar said, but with some hesitation. He did not know Stephen well enough to discount the threat as a bluff.

Once in the hall, questions to a few servants led them to a stairway to some upper chambers at one end, which led to a dark passage illuminated by a single slit of a window at the far end.

Gilbert counted the doors until he reached the second from the end. He knocked on it, heart in his mouth, hoping that the right person answered.

The door opened.

It was the wrong person, a prim woman of about thirty with the look of a lady's maid.

"Is Lord Serlo here?" Gilbert asked, trying to keep his voice low and not high with the tension he felt.

"He is not," the lady's maid said. She stood there not volunteering anything else.

"And Lady Ysabelle?" Gilbert asked.

"She is not here, either. What ever would you want with her?"

"Not her, actually. Nor Lord Serlo. I was hoping to speak to Lord Serlo's body servant."

"What do you want with Hugo?" the lady's maid demanded.

Gilbert extended a hand. The button lay upon his palm. "I believe Lord Serlo may have lost this. At the jousting ground."

The maid bent over Gilbert's palm for a closer look. She straightened up and called over her shoulder. "Hugo! There's someone to see you!"

Shortly, a man in his twenties with a long moustache and long slender hands came to the door.

"What is it?" Hugo asked.

Gilbert held out the button. "I think your master lost this at the jousting grounds."

A Curious Death

Hugo picked up the button and turned it around in his long fingers.

"Have you been with Lord Serlo long?" Gilbert asked, as if making polite conversation.

"Five years next month," Hugo said, frowning as he returned the button.

"Ah, this must be a great change for his lordship from his student lodgings."

"It is, quite."

"About the button? Is it his lordship's?"

"He has nothing like it. I am afraid you are mistaken."

"Oh, I see. My apologies for disturbing you."

"I thought we were going to wrap things up here," Wymar said as they recrossed the bailey to the main gate.

"It is a matter of baby steps," Gilbert said. "Tedious baby steps, pursuing some possibilities while eliminating others, until we reach our goal."

"I had no idea this would be so boring. I'm going back to camp."

"Go ahead. You've been a dead weight, anyway."

But when Gilbert arrived at the guild hall, Wymar was still with him. And indeed, Wymar found a seat on a bench under the porch to wait while Gilbert went inside.

He sought out the town clerk and asked for a list of the town's goldsmiths, since these craftsmen worked all sorts of precious metals including silver, and tailors. The clerk received this request with a raised eyebrow and a great helping of I-have-better-things-to-do-than-dealing-with-this-rot.

"What do you want this for?" the clerk demanded, placing his palms on the parchments which were as thick as fallen leaves on his writing table. "I am quite busy, as you can see."

He waved Gilbert away and took up a quill.

But Gilbert stood his ground.

"Your pardon, sir," he said. He removed the silver button from his pouch and held it out. "I'm trying to find out who made this. It is part of a murder inquiry."

"Murder inquiry? What murder inquiry? Wait! Is this about Miles de Dinesley?"

"It is."

The clerk appraised Gilbert with an expression that suggested he did not approve of the man who stood before him. "You're not what I expected of Stephen Attebrook. I thought he was a much younger man and . . . more fit. A fighting knight of some prowess, or so I heard."

"I'm not Sir Stephen. I am his clerk."

"Indeed. And why has he sent you rather than come himself? Am I too lowly to bother with?"

"It's not that. Sir Stephen has been called away momentarily on the king's business."

"So you say," the clerk said. "Murder . . . humph! If anyone deserved it, Dinesley did."

"I have gathered that he was not very popular in some quarters."

"He was an arrogant arse." The clerk sighed. "Still, murder is a nasty thing. Very well, I'll give you what you need." He rattled off the names of four men Gilbert took to be the goldsmiths and where their shops could be found.

"And what about tailors? How many are there?"

"Tailors?" the clerk mused. "Forty-one, I think."

"Forty-one!" Gilbert exclaimed. "I think I'd better write this down. And where they can be found."

"You are a troublesome little man," the clerk said. He found a blank sheet of parchment freshly scraped clean of the letters that had formerly occupied it, which Gilbert had to pay for, and shoved a quill pen and inkpot cross the desk. "You know your letters, I hope. Because I'm not going to waste my time copying out your list. Are you ready?"

Gilbert dipped the nib into the inkpot, poised the quill over the parchment and nodded.

A Curious Death

The nearest goldsmith's shop was three doors down from the guildhall. It consisted of a vast room on the ground floor divided into three sections by partitions. Each compartment had its own furnace with leather bellows protruding from the sides. At the rear, beneath large windows, through which a great stone house and courtyard could be seen, were tables strewn with assorted tools — chisels, hammers, pincers, rasps and such. Two workmen tapped away, one shaping a bowl on a small anvil, the other fashioning a cup. The proprietor — distinguished by his green wool coat lined with a fox fur collar — bent over a wax carving, shaping it with a curved knife.

Along the walls were shelves displaying recently completed goblets, belt buckles, assortments of rings, chalices, and candle sticks.

The proprietor, whose name of Albertus Garbutt was painted in yellow over the door, noticed Gilbert's interest. "Are you in need of something, sir?"

"Yes, I was hoping you could help me," Gilbert said, approaching the open window. He set the button on the turned-down shutter which acted as a counter over which business could be conducted without having to enter the shop. "I am trying to find out who made this. Or if anyone has asked for a replacement."

"Hmmph!" Garbutt grunted. He picked up the button and turned it over. "No maker's mark," he murmured. He retreated into the shop and returned with a white linen cloth and a stone. He wiped the button with the cloth, which came away with black streaks upon it. Garbutt nodded as if that meant something. He sniffed the button before putting it back on the counter and placing the stone beside it.

"What's that about?" Gilbert asked, mystified.

"Just a few tests," Garbutt said. "All silver tarnishes, as this item has done. If it was adulterated with another metal, you can often tell by the smell. And that's a lodestone. Silver, like gold, doesn't react to the stone like other metals do. Often a silver patina is applied to an iron core and the thing passed off as pure. So, as far as I can tell as we stand here, this button is pure silver, alright. But who made it?" He shrugged. "I can't say. It's expensive even so."

"Is it really?"

"The metal's expensive. Making the die takes time and some degree of skill."

"But you and your guild members could do it."

"Oh, certainly. Any competent journeyman could do it."

"And no one's come to you for a replacement?"

"Not yet."

Visiting the other three goldsmiths took the rest of the day, with suitable detours and delays for meat pies and stews to alleviate Gilbert's hunger for real food rather than the contemptible porridge that passed for army rations. The answer he received was the same — none of them had seen this button before and had no idea who made it.

A Curious Death

Chapter 17

In the twilight before Friday's sunrise, Stephen rose and tried to make himself presentable, free of twigs and leaves in what hair he had left and cloak, so neither Tom Boneyre nor the wardens at the castle gates would suspect he had slept rough. Begilda helped clean him up.

She stood back to examine him as if admiring a bit of craftwork. Daylight revealed that she was a small girl, boyish in figure, thin, with gangly arms and legs, freckled cheeks, and dull brown hair. Her eyes were overlarge for her face. But they were determined eyes and the set of a thin-lipped mouth suggested determination. Stephen supposed she was not even fourteen.

"I guess I should be going now," Begilda said, looking to the east, where the rising sun cast an orange glow on the underside of a cloud at the horizon. "The gates should be open by the time I get there. Kislingbury, you said."

"You know where it is?" Stephen said.

"I'll find it. It's somewhere west of here, I think."

He nodded. "About an hour's walk."

"Right. Come on, Bill."

Stephen watched her disappear through the orchard, his thoughts drifting to a letter. Had it not been for this letter, he would be on his way out of town with Begilda.

The letter had arrived at Stephen's Ludlow townhouse shortly before he and Gilbert departed for Oxford.

Ida had come back from the burned ruins of their manor of Priors Halton to see him off to the war. They and the other members of the household — Harry the legless woodworker, his wife Joan, Harry's young son Johnnie, and Stephen's toddler son Christopher — were at the dinner table when the knock sounded at the front door. Joan, the housekeeper, rose from the table and answered the knock, returning with a bemused expression and the letter.

"He didn't even wait to be paid. He just went off without even a good day," Joan told Stephen in astonishment. Deliverers of letters usually were paid by the recipient rather than the sender.

Stephen lay the letter on the table between him and Ida without tearing the seal, which was a plain yellow daub without any impression of a seal to identify the sender, and reading it, even though the manner of its delivery indicated that it was a very important letter

Now and then, Ida threw a glance at the letter, an indication of her curiosity about it and what trouble it might portend. But she made no attempt to reach for it, although she had not shied away from reading Stephen's letters in the recent past.

But, at last, when dinner was finished and Joan and Harry's son John cleaned off the table while Harry swung himself on his massive arms toward his shop at the front of the house, Ida prodded the letter with a finger.

"Well, aren't you going to read it?" she asked.

"I might just let my dinner settle first," Stephen said. He could tell she was burning with curiosity about the letter's contents. So was he. But he was enjoying watching her fidget. He had lately begun to notice how attractive she was. At seventeen, nearly eighteen, she was astonishingly lovely, blue eyes the color of the summer sky, hair the color of ripening wheat, a rosebud of a mouth, a graceful neck. She was his step-niece and he wasn't supposed to have impure thoughts about her; society looked upon their union, though not as real as the gossipmongers thought, as incestuous and brimming with scandal.

"No, you won't. You're as eager to find out what's in it as I am," Ida said, her mouth turning up at the ends.

"All right, then," Stephen said. "Have at it. I hope it's not bad news."

"If it is, you will sit still and take it like a man," Ida said, taking up the letter. She broke the seal with a slender forefinger and unrolled the parchment.

A Curious Death

She frowned. "It's written in English!" Those who were literate tended to write in French or Latin, even if their first language was English, which was true of most people. Almost no one but low merchants corresponded in English.

Ida read: "'To S from M, greetings.'" She regarded Stephen with narrowed eyes. "I hazard a guess that you are S, but who is M?"

"It's a poor attempt at code," Stephen hedged, oddly discomforted. He had heard about coded letters but had no idea how it was done.

"Code, is it? Hmm. Does this have anything to do with spying?"

"Uh, umm, sort of."

"Sort of, then yes. How did you get caught up in such a sordid business?"

"I stumbled into it, like you might into a privy."

Ida's nose wrinkled as if at a bad smell.

"Go on, aren't you going to tell me what she has to say?" Stephen said.

"She? M is a woman?"

"Yes."

"Led astray by a woman. Pathetic. What's her name?"

Stephen hesitated. "Margaret."

"Maaarrgaret. Well, then." Ida raised the parchment sheet as though she was a town crier reading some pronouncement in the town market. "'I have received new information. O is being held by one of F's household knights. His name is Walerand de Greystok. They are at N, as I told you. I hope you will still find them there and will be able to do what has to be done.'"

The sheet sank to Ida's lap and she fixed him with a hard stare. "What does all this mean?"

"O is a boy named Oliver, Margaret's son." Stephen told her. He almost didn't tell her the story behind the letter. But she could be annoyingly persistent and would, no doubt, wheedle the story out of him. So, he went on, Margaret was Margaret de Thottenham, a widow who was a spy for the rebels. Last month, when they met by accident in Leominster, Margaret asked him to find and return to the boy to her so she would no longer have to do the bidding of Nigel FitzSimmons, the rebel spymaster.

"Northampton, isn't that a rebel stronghold?" Ida asked after a moment to digest the story.

"Yes."

Ida snorted, not believing that Stephen had told the whole truth. "You would risk your life for an enemy?"

"Margaret saved me from a sticky end several times. I owe her a favor. She's called it in." He didn't tell Ida that they had been lovers, and this, as well as her help, accounted for his sense of duty. While his marriage to Ida was a sham, he had the feeling that she might not like to hear all there was to their relationship.

Ida rose and spun the parchment sheet at Stephen. "When will you be leaving for Northampton, then?"

"I'm not sure I'll be leaving for Northampton at any time."

"Oh, of course, you will, you mush-headed fool."

Ida marched from the table to the stairs and climbed to their bedchamber. Stephen did not watch her go, nor did he turn his head when the door slammed. That night, he slept in a corner of the hall.

Boneyre said to meet at the castle's main gate at Terce, which was about two hours after sunrise, the time when most officials had finished breakfast and were ready to conduct business. There was no fixed way to determine when Terce or any other hour arrived — they were approximations subject to a great deal of individual interpretation. So, Stephen went early to the gate.

He stood to one side of the road leading through the castle's main gate, a two-fold fortification, with an outer bastion consisting of an earthen embankment palisaded on top, a wooded bridge over a huge ditch and a formal stone

A Curious Death

gate house of two hulking towers flanking the narrow gate itself, as a crowd streamed over the bridge and into the bailey beyond the gate. The guards paid no special attention, as they would have on any other occasion. Normally, you couldn't just walk into most castles when you felt like it. You had to have a reason for being there. But a sheriff's court, which heard all sorts of cases ranging from murder, assault and rape, to land disputes and, if the parties consented or the king permitted, will contests, debts and fraud. This meant the court was always well attended by litigants from town and countryside, as well as by people who just liked to watch the proceedings; they were a form of entertainment that served to lighten what otherwise were drab work-a-day lives. It was odd, though, that the rebel commanders allowed the sheriff to hold his court in the castle. Stephen would have thought the rebels would require the sheriff to find another venue, such as the town's guildhall. But perhaps they were making some sort of political point, such as how much support the rebels had from this sheriff and how much they trusted him.

A light rain started falling as Stephen stood in the street before the gate's bastion. He was glad for the rain since it gave him an excuse to pull up his hood. Hoods were excellent for concealing a man's face and making it hard for others to identify him. He was less worried about that than he had been the first time he passed the castle. The more he'd thought about it, the more likely it seemed the Ludlow men loyal to Montfort and the barons had gone to London, where Montfort himself was raising a second rebel army. But it didn't hurt to be careful.

Stephen hadn't been on station for half an hour when Boneyre came hurrying up, his knobby knees visible as he churned along, followed by a gaunt man who had the look of a clerk.

"Damn this rain," Boneyre complained as he drew up. "Careful there!" he turned to the clerk. "Get nothing wet!"

"Yessir," the clerk intoned on a deep voice while checking the flaps on his bulging satchels, which probably held a copy of Glanvill's tome and assorted parchment writs.

"Let's not waste the day here," Boneyre said. He hurried into the gate with Stephen and the clerk on his heels.

When Stephen reached the bailey, he understood why the rebels might allow the sheriff to hold court here. This part of the castle was circular in plan, the outer walls at least twenty feet high. Another, lower wall cut this circle in half, creating two baileys. In this one, the outer bailey, there were timber buildings built against the walls housing a long timber barn capped with a thatched roof, a stable and paddock, a blacksmith's furnace and forge, other workplaces for carpenters and masons and other craftsmen necessary for the upkeep of the castle without whom it would rapidly fall to ruin, a wood pile and others whose function Stephen could not identify. In addition, there was a large timber building that had the look of a chamber block. Next to it was a long low structure that could only be a hall where those who lived in this bailey took their meals because next to it was a round kitchen with two chimneys belching smoke, the cooks visible through open windows hurrying about their task of making dinner. Behind the kitchen, the rounded form of the apse of a small chapel poked out.

Beyond the bisecting wall, the enormous great tower reared toward the low sky, flanked by the tile rooves of the great hall, what looked like a housing block and a chapel or church. That part of the castle could only be reached from the bailey where Stephen stood by a small gateway. It was guarded by two men leaning against the wall on either side of the gate, as guardsmen will do when not under the eyes of a superior officer. Stephen knew the castle had another bailey to the south of this one and it, too, could only be reached through a small gate, also guarded. So, the riffraff who had come for the court could not wander at leisure among the army that was camped in the lower bailey.

A Curious Death

While he had halted to make this visible inspection, Boneyre and the clerk had almost disappeared in the crowd surrounding a large tent erected in the middle of the bailey, the place where the court would be held. Stephen spotted the clerk's head above those around him and made after them. Boneyre seemed heedless that he'd left Stephen behind, but Stephen put that up to nerves rather than rudeness. Boneyre was concentrating on what he would have to do and say when the sheriff called his case, and had no room in his thoughts for anything else.

Stephen ambled about the edges of the crowd, keeping his eye on the gate to the lower bailey. He had no idea how to get through it, and he hoped that some opportunity would present itself.

Before long, he had passed around to the other side of the court tent, where the kitchen was. The kitchen emitted delicious, yeasty smells of baking bread, which meant there was a bakery here, too. He paused at the window, savoring the scent of fresh bread, and of roasting haunches on spits at the fireplaces, dripping rendered fat into iron pans. He hadn't eaten for some time.

One of the cooks caught Stephen staring at the food. "Hungry, brother?" the cook smiled as she set down a tray of buns. She poured honey over the buns and offered Stephen one of them.

"Thanks," he said gratefully. A hot honeyed bun was the nearest thing to paradise on this sorry earth.

He licked his fingers and the cook handed him another. Then she turned to other work so that was the last of the free buns.

Beyond the low hall and chamber block, he came to the massive barn. It was over two-hundred feet long and was curved to fit against the castle walls, forming a sort of amphitheater like a ruined Roman one Stephen had seen once in Spain. It had three doors along its length. The middle doors were open and four men repairing a wagon wheel blocked the entrance, an impediment which provoked loud protests from a gang of men who had just drawn up in another wagon to fetch supplies for the lower bailey.

So they are feeding the army from this barn? Very curious. He wondered how set they were for provisions. A well-stocked barn could mean the army might hold out in the castle for considerable time if Lord Edward and the king put them under siege, the usual way of taking castles; storming them was dangerous and expensive in the lives of men that the royalist forces could ill afford to lose.

He lingered in the doorway and exchanged a few pleasantries with the men repairing the wagon, while the gang from the lower bailey hurried around with sacks and barrels which they loaded onto their wagon with the help of a ramp of two boards.

Stephen could not see far into the barn because it was dark despite an array of narrow windows just below the roof. But he could tell that it bulged with supplies: enough to feed an army for weeks, perhaps even months.

Disquieted by this finding, Stephen tarried until the loaded wagon began its journey around the crowd to the gate to the lower bailey. He followed the wagon, which the guards saw coming and had the gate open to receive it.

"What can I do for you, brother?" one of the guards asked as he started to pull the gate shut.

Stephen had thought furiously about what to say to such a question as he approached the gate, and was well prepared for once. "I've been asked to deliver a letter to Walerand de Greystok."

The guard looked Stephen over, found nothing to arouse any suspicion, and let him through the gate.

The gate led to a wooden bridge spanning a deep ditch. The lower bailey beyond the ditch was a spectacle to behold. The bailey itself was impressive enough, a stone-walled enclosure twice the size of the other part of the castle. It was packed to the brim with tents of many colors, blue, yellow, green, red, purple, and every combination. All were arrayed in circles about cooking fires so the colors seemed to whorl about within the confines of the castle's whitewashed walls. You could almost see the whorls spinning. A horse paddock holding perhaps two-hundred head, filled almost a third of the enclosure.

Surveying the whole, Stephen reckoned there must be about four or five hundred men in the lower bailey. This was the force — sufficient to hold the town itself let alone the castle — that Lord Edward's army would have to defeat; taking the town while leaving the castle to hold out was a useless victory. Stephen imagined that Edward must have a plan, but he could not think of what it might be.

Stephen crossed the bridge to the lower bailey.

Finding Greystok required the usual tedious inquiry of asking people if they knew him and where he could be found. Most of the people Stephen spoke to didn't know Greystok, but at last, a man-at-arms pointed at a gap between two tents where a red and green one could be seen.

"That's his tent, brother," the man-at-arms said. "Although you won't find him there. He's at the paddock, working a young horse."

"How will I know Greystok?" Stephen asked.

"Middling tall, red hair, short beard. Hard to miss."

Stephen thanked his informant who turned away to sniff at the contents of a cook pot hanging from a hook and chain over a campfire and to pinch the bottom of the woman tending it. She slapped his face, but in a playful way.

Stephen fixed the red-and-green tent in his mind, along with its location, which was near a small sally port that opened into the street near the town's west gate, then turned toward the paddock.

When he reached the edge of the thicket of tents, Stephen saw a red-haired man in the company of four men-at-arms leaning against the paddock fence observing a young black-haired boy lunging a stallion. Now and then the men shouted some instruction cast as a good-natured insult at the boy, who received these verbal attacks with a smile and a nod without changing how he handled the stallion, as if he didn't take them seriously. If this was Margaret's boy, he was large for seven, and gave every hint he would grow into a large, muscular man — in sharp contrast to his small, frail mother. Many boys that age had cherubic faces, and this lad was no exception, although it also gave hints of a lean hardness to come. His cheeks were ruddy and his eyes were a flashing blue — exactly as Margaret had described him. One of the watching men added the name Oliver to an insult, removing all doubt.

That man caught Stephen's attention and his body experienced an abrupt chill. Even if Stephen hadn't been so focused on Greystok and the boy, he would not have missed this fellow. The man stood out from any crowd, big, blackbearded, clad all in black coat and hose. His name was Gervase Haddon, and he knew Stephen. They had met in the Broken Shield Inn an age ago when Haddon had delivered Nigel FitzSimmons' answer to Stephen's challenge to a duel. When Stephen and FitzSimmons had fought with sharp steel in the Ludford village churchyard, Haddon had been one of the supporters who had arrived with FitzSimmons to witness the fight.

Stephen's first impulse was to dash back to the concealment of the tents. But that would have drawn attention to himself, and Haddon seemed not to have spotted him. Stephen forced himself to turn and walk unhurriedly away.

When he had put tents between himself and Haddon, Stephen took several deep breaths to calm a pounding heart and forced himself to think.

Now that Stephen had confirmed Oliver was here, what next? He couldn't bundle the boy under an arm and run for it. But if Edward's army came soon and the castle fell, especially if it fell without bloodshed, there would be a chance.

But the castle wasn't going to fall. A hundred men were sufficient to defend it against storming. With five hundred it was impossible. And starving them into surrender was impossible, since it was stocked well enough to hold out for months. Moreover, Simon de Montfort would not sit idly by if

A Curious Death

Edward invested Northampton. Montfort would march immediately to the castle's relief. There might be a major battle, and battles were risky. There never was any certainty of winning one, which is why commanders preferred to avoid them. Edward might feel the same, and march away. Or he might lose — a real possibility if the army encamped at the castle sallied, to join up with the relief army. Edward and the king would be outnumbered then.

There wasn't anything Stephen could accomplish here, and he wandered back to the bridge to the upper bailey, turning these thoughts over in his mind. He paused at the bridge, casting one last look behind him ... and stopped. Something below him and before his eyes suddenly registered. There was no barn or other storage place for provisions for the army. This meant that the only stores were in the great timber barn in the outer bailey behind him, where the sheriff's court was taking place.

The glimmer of an idea began to form in his mind. The audacity of it, the danger involved, and the slight likelihood of success made his mouth run dry and his limbs tremble.

He slid his hands into his sleeves, as friars and other clerics often did, and returned to the outer bailey, eyes on the ground, mind a whirl.

He was making his way through the crowds about the tent toward the little chapel behind the kitchen when Boneyre called his name.

There was no avoiding Boneyre, so Stephen halted and turned around.

"You saw it, eh?" Boneyre cried. His homely face was flushed and split by a huge grin.

Stephen almost said, "Saw what?" but then he remembered. "Ah, your case. Of course. Wouldn't have missed it for anything."

"Got my man off!"

"A brilliant piece of work," Stephen murmured. "Your gift should be substantial." Lawyers trained at the inns of court in London, as Boneyre had been, did not accept payment for their services. When representing private parties, it was customary to receive gifts.

"It shall," Boneyre said. "Sir Hugh is a wealthy man. Will you be staying?" He waved toward the great tent. "Brings back old memories, eh? Hard to tear yourself away."

Stephen nodded. He could care less what happened in that tent.

"Well, I must be off," Boneyre said. "I've other work to do. Enjoy yourself. It was good to see you." He clapped Stephen on the shoulder as if they had been old friends instead of casual acquaintances, spun about and hurried away.

Stephen loitered among the crowd at the sheriff's court after all. It was the best place to avoid notice and questions about why he was here. When the court concluded and the crowd broke up in late afternoon, with most of the spectators and participants streaming toward the main gate, he turned toward the little chapel behind the kitchen. The place smelled of two tallow votive candles guttering by the door, dust and wet wool. He had to share the chapel for a while with a couple of elderly women, who were the source of the wet wool aroma and who prayed at the altar for the soul of a son who had died recently. Their presence forced Stephen to assume a posture of prayer himself, instead of what he wanted to do, which was lie down behind the altar and get some sleep. Sleeping in orchards could be uncomfortable and he had been up several times during the night. He wasn't much for prayer either, though, and spent the time examining the painted frescos on the white-plaster walls: Joseph and his colored coat, Mary holding the infant Jesus, Jesus preaching on a mound to a multitude with a fish in his hand, visions of the crucifixion, ranks of figures that had to be saints.

At last, the women fell silent, stood up and tottered toward the door, awkward with the stiffness of kneeling for a long time. Stephen rose as well when they were gone, working out his own stiffness as the supper bell rang distantly.

A Curious Death

Prudence warred with temptation. He was starving since he hadn't eaten all day apart from those two honeyed buns. It was risky to slip into the servants' hall for supper, but he considered whether to chance it. With the army here and many noblemen and their households, no doubt much of the overflow of the underlings would eat with the castle servants. One stray friar was not likely to be questioned.

Yet he paused with his hand on the door latch as he had second thoughts. On reflection, it seemed too much of a chance to take. His supper would have to wait.

Stephen licked his fingers and pinched out the two votive candles. He retreated to the altar, where he sat down cross-legged. If anyone entered, he would assume a praying posture. The sight of a cleric making a vigil would not arouse any suspicions. He should be safe here until it was time to act.

Night fell. It was cold, damp and dark in the little chapel. There would be no moon tonight; it would appear as a sliver in the dawn, a waning crescent. It would be a good night for those up to no good to be about their sinister business.

As it became too dark to see, Stephen began pacing up and down along one wall, a hand on the plastered stone to gauge his way: five steps one way and five steps back. He was nervous about what was coming and he was glad no one could see him.

Every so often, he stuck a head out of the door to listen. There was some merriment going on at first in the servants' hall, marked by a clamor of voices that had hardly slackened when supper concluded. Meanwhile, faint music could be heard from the inner bailey: the high-born being entertained by a band of players. Gradually, however, the clamor at the servants' hall slackened over time until it was gone.

Stephen went out to peer through a crack of a shutter into the hall. The hearth fires had burned low and only a few people could be seen as silhouettes moving about, spreading pallets and opening blankets: servants without a room of their own, only a place on the hall's floor.

He went back to the chapel, changed into his rustic's clothes and stuffed the friar's robe into his satchel.

He waited another eternity, which was really a bit less than an hour from the march of the stars overhead. There was a disturbance in a henhouse — a fox Stephen would have guessed if this had been the country. Perhaps it was a wandering rat.

He waited a few more minutes until the hubbub subsided, then plucked four votive candles from a clay pot beside the rack and slid into the night.

Stephen slipped to the hall, and hugged its side until he came to the round kitchen. He tried the door, but it was barred. Normally, castle kitchens weren't shut up tight, even though there was food in the storeroom that could be stolen. This was so because castles were like little villages and there wasn't much likelihood of theft. It was different now, he supposed, with all the strangers within the walls, for a barred door meant that someone was inside. He had been counting on getting in. Beside each of the three fireplaces, he had seen a small metal pail. Such pails were used to carry embers in the morning to other hearths and fireplaces where the fires had gone out so they could be restarted. He had planned on stealing one of those pails and a shovelful of embers. Now that might not be possible.

Stephen retreated to the hall to rethink his plan.

The prudent thing was to give up and flee to the church. But he didn't. He forced himself to his feet and crept along the hall to the barn. The first door he tried was barred. The middle and largest one was secured with a padlock bigger than his fist. Stephen took out his skeleton key and went to work, but after almost a quarter hour of fiddling, the lock would not yield. Some locks were immune to magic keys after all.

Almost as an afterthought, he tried the last door. It was neither barred nor locked. The fragrant, delicious smell of dried hay greeted him when he opened the door, and he realized why this part of the barn was not locked — it held the hay stores for the castle. Horses had to eat just like men, but men were not likely to steal hay as they were sacks of grain, barrels of dried or salted meat, or tuns of wine.

Dry hay, said a voice in his head. There was a way after all.

Stephen felt his way inside, dropping to hands and knees to crawl along around stacks of hay until he came to a far corner. He listened for the sounds of habitation: barns often were trysting places or abodes of those not welcome in the hall. But he heard no sounds of men, no snorts, no coughs, no snores, no rustling while someone turned over in his sleep. The place felt almost church-like in its silence; it certainly smelled better.

Locating a supporting timber by feel, he stacked a pile of hay at its base. He took up one of the candles and cut it down to a nub as long as his thumb. Then he fumbled into his belt pouch for a small leather purse. This was not a purse containing money. Instead, he extracted one of his three remaining cotton balls. He had acquired them several years ago while returning from a raid into Granada. He and his friend Rodrigo had been passing a field containing these odd plants. They had gone brown except for white balls hanging from the branches. When Stephen asked Rodrigo what those strange plants were, Rodrigo said, "That's cotton."

"Doesn't look good to eat," Stephen said.

Rodrigo laughed. "The Moors don't eat it. They make fabric from it."

"What?" Stephen asked skeptically.

"From those little balls. It turns out like linen. Don't ask me how it's done. It has other uses, though," Rodrigo said, sliding from his horse.

He walked a few steps into the field and plucked handfuls of those little balls from some of the plants.

When he got back to the road, Rodrigo handed over some of the little balls while putting the remainder in his pouch. He said, "You keep them. They are useful for starting fires, too."

"How does that work?" Stephen asked.

"I'll show you when we get back."

The how turned out to be simple, and Stephen applied Rodrigo's lesson. He got out his flint and struck sparks from it with the pommel of his dagger. Some of the sparks fell onto the cotton ball, which caught fire.

He could have shoved the flaming ball into the hay, but that would have resulted in an immediate conflagration that could give him away — nothing burned faster than dried hay. He needed time to flee, which was the purpose of the candle.

He lighted the wick and blew out the cotton ball. In a short while, the wick would burn down and flop onto the hay, thus starting the fire. Many a house fire had been ignited in this way. By that time, however, he should be away. He set the candle down and smoothed hay around it.

Then he made for the door as fast as he could go in the dark.

A Curious Death

Chapter 18

Half an hour passed without any sign of a disturbance. Stephen marked the time at the door of the chapel, looking with one eye through a crack into the yard. There wasn't much to see from this vantage point — the kitchen and the side of the hall, which masked the storehouse. His heart had not stopped galloping since he returned and struggled into his friar's habit.

He was beginning to think that he'd failed, that perhaps someone had been in the hay room after all and, spotting the candle, had put it out.

Then he saw an orange glow beyond the hall. He held his breath, feeling dizzy with fear and anticipation.

He should stay in the chapel, out of sight, but the glow drew him into the yard. When he came around the kitchen, though, he gasped at the sight. Flames were licking skyward from the thatched roof, small yet, tickling the low clouds, but now visible to all.

At the same time, voices of watchmen at the gate began crying, "Fire! Fire!"

A bell clanged.

It seemed only the time it takes to draw a single breath before a frenzied crowd had poured into this part of the upper bailey, shouting, screaming, crying, bellowing orders, rushing about.

And in that same time, the fire had grown so that half the thatched roof of the barn was ablaze. The firelight was so bright that it seemed as though a small sun had landed on the roof. The heat was intense. Stephen felt toasted, and he was at least fifty yards away.

People ran for the barn's doors and, after a struggle with the lock on the main door, forced it open and rushed inside. Lines of men formed to pull out what they could of the supplies before the roof collapsed because everyone knew that the building could not be saved. Not enough water from the single well could be drawn to make any difference, and there weren't enough buckets anyway.

What buckets could be found were needed to put out fires on adjoining buildings, ignited by sparks flung off by the roaring thatch.

This effort seemed to be successful until the supporting timbers in the hay room gave way. Flames and sparks burst upward as if from the mouth of a volcano. Sparks rained on the hall and the chapel, setting little fires all over the roofs that quickly grew in size and united, writhing like orange and yellow demons, mocking those who watched to do anything.

With the collapse of the hay room's roof, the fire shot through the rest of the barn, driving out those trying to save what they could. Large patches of flaming thatch plunged into the inferno, revealing structural timbers as thick as trees taken freshly from the forest that were ablaze themselves. Although a sizeable pile of stores lay in the middle of the yard, it had to be a small portion of what the fire was destroying before Stephen's relieved eyes. His plan had worked. There should not be enough for the rebel army to withstand a long siege of the castle.

Now, he just had to get out.

Stephen edged through the crowd to the main gate. Some instinct caused him to pause before approaching the gate and to observe first before making a move. And he was glad for this precaution. Several people asked the five gate wardens to pass through and were refused. This seemed odd behavior in the face of this conflagration, odd not to let people out, but odd also not to let people in to help fight the fires. Whatever the reason, he couldn't get out this way.

Across the bailey, however, he saw that the gate to the lower bailey was open and men were streaming up from below, joining the crowd in doing what it could to battle the flames.

It would have to be this way, if at all.

Stephen slipped around to that gate and stood by hoping neither of the two men guarding it would notice him in the

A Curious Death

comings and goings. But he was in luck, for their attention was more on the flaming buildings and the chaos than on who went in and out. The random friar was not something people paid much attention to anyway, like an undistinguished bit of furniture, seen but not registered in the mind or memory. Stephen waited until a party of four soldiers pushed against the tide of incoming men to get down to the lower bailey. He joined in at the end and got through without the guards making any noise about it.

The bridge over the ditch separating the upper baileys from the lower one was so choked with soldiers that Stephen didn't bother with it. He slid down the slope to the bottom of the ditch and clambered up the other side.

With some difficulty in the dark, he located the sally port near Greystok's tent. It was closed and barred, but not guarded. It was too risky to push up the bar and escape, though. There were many people nearby watching the fires in the upper baileys, and they were sure to notice. He would have to wait.

So, Stephen found a spot by a campfire, curled up using his satchel as a pillow and laid down. His stomach gnawed with hunger and it was a long time before sleep found him.

Stephen woke up to the smell of frying bacon and the stench of burnt timber. The wind had shifted during the night and carried smoke over the lower bailey, and the colorful tents and those sleeping outside were covered with a fine coating of soot. He wiped his face on the skirt of his robe and hoped for the best.

He visited the privy and when he returned, the sally port was open and people were going in and out, although there were a pair of officers overseeing traffic who barred a few of those from leaving, common soldiers who probably would use their temporary freedom to cause trouble in the town.

Stephen got in line to go out, the procedure being that the officers let a dozen or so men out, then held the departing line back while a roughly equal number of those on the outside seeking admittance were allowed in.

The line shuffled in such a way that Stephen found himself at the head of the next group to go through.

The line waited until the officer barring their way with a baton dropped it and waved them forward as those who had entered filed past into the lower bailey.

The man at the end of that line, however, stopped dead as Stephen went by him. He stared hard at Stephen, recognition dawning in his feral green eyes.

It was Gervase Haddon.

Once on the street, Stephen walked fast toward the west gate, trying not to run and not daring to look behind him. Haddon may have known him, but he had not called out an alarm yet and Stephen didn't want to draw attention to himself in case he did.

When he reached the gate, he chanced a look back. Haddon and two other black-clad men had just emerged through the sally port, held back until those behind Stephen could get through — thank God for officious officers who followed the rules no matter what.

Haddon pointed in his direction and he and the two men with him ran toward the gate. They each carried a sword.

"Stop him!" Haddon cried. "Stop that man!"

The gate warden, the sole guard within the gate, looked around to see who Haddon meant. There were several possibilities within the gate besides Stephen, a tinker loaded down with a bulging pack from which pots, jugs and spoons dangled and clashed together as he walked; a carter leading his cart; a young man with books under one arm, perhaps a student.

The guard decided Haddon must mean the student — students were always guilty of something, getting drunk, gambling, quarreling, getting in fights — so he grabbed the

A Curious Death

young man, who struggled against the arrest. The two fell down in a flurry of robes and white ankles.

Stephen ducked around the cart and broke into a stumpy lope for the bridge over the west branch of the River Nene.

In his younger days, Stephen had been quick on his feet, such that he often was the first person picked when sides were chosen for football. But since his injury, he couldn't run nearly as fast. In fact, Ida had beaten him in a footrace away from Priors Halton the night their manor had been raided by rebel supporters and burned.

Houses stretched for almost two-hundred yards on the south side of the road to the bridge, which led to a forested, uninhabited island, before crossing another branch of the Nene.

Somehow, Stephen reached the bridge before his pursuers or anyone coming out of a house to intercept him. He pounded across, hearing their feet thump on the bridge boards.

There was nothing Stephen could do. He couldn't outrun them or outfight them — they were three men with swords and he had only a satchel and a dagger.

Yet surrender surely would lead to a terrible fate. If he was captured, he would be questioned under torture about why he was skulking about Northampton Castle garbed and tonsured as a friar. And, since everyone talked eventually under torture, he would confess that Edward sent him there to reconnoiter the town's defenses, which would lead to questions about Edward's intentions and the disclosure he intended to attack here and not in the south. If Stephen was killed, though, the secret would not come out and the pain leading to his death would be transitory, even a mere nothing — when he had lost his foot, he had felt only a thump, a knock, a jar, easily endurable. He hadn't realized part of his foot was missing until after he knocked the Moor who had taken it off the wall of Rodrigo's castle. It seemed the only way.

Things were unfolding so swiftly that, once his decision was made, there was no time for second thoughts or regret. Mind filled with the emptiness that came upon him in a fight, Stephen skidded to a stop at a spot where the road across the island took a slight turn so he was out of view of the town gate, pulled his dagger, and turned to face his pursuers.

They were strung out in a line, as often happens, since few men all run at the same speed, so some will forge ahead, others will lag behind. The first one, taken by surprise, tried to slow and raise his sword, but Stephen was too quick: he drove his dagger into the man's heart, feeling the blade jar painfully on bone, then slip into the man, whose feet carried him by Stephen. The dagger stuck and would not come out, and Stephen lost his grip on it.

Haddon was the next man. He slowed and drew his sword.

"Fancy seeing you here," Haddon sneered. "What possible business can you have in Northampton, I wonder."

He set the point of the sword at Stephen's neck as if he expected this to bring about Stephen's surrender, instead of seeking revenge for his dying man. This was a mistake.

For surrender was not in Stephen's mind. He swept the blade aside with his satchel, and pounded Haddon on the throat with a backhanded blow. The hammer's blow struck Haddon's windpipe, which collapsed with a crunch. Haddon's face went white. His hands flew to his throat as his mouth worked like a fish's and he uttered choking noises.

Stephen paid no more attention to Haddon, for he was dying and no longer a threat. He recovered Haddon's sword just as the last man rushed up. This man glanced from his companion with the dagger protruding from his chest, to Haddon, on his knees, his face blue now, lips purple, spittle flying from his mouth, but no breath passing his lips.

The black-coated pursuer wasted not a heartbeat — he cut down at Stephen's head, but as Stephen moved to parry with his satchel as if it was a shield, his adversary deftly cut around to the other side.

A Curious Death

Stephen brought his sword across his body to the outside guard and the blades tinged at the impact, which was so strong it jarred Stephen's arm.

Even so, Stephen answered with a thrust to the face which the other man set aside and returned an upward cut to Stephen's belly that would have laid him open if he hadn't anticipated it and pivoted aside.

A pause occurred, and quiet, punctuated by their heavy breathing.

It was obvious that Haddon's companion was a good swordsman, yet just as Stephen had taken his measure by this exchange, so he had taken Stephen's, and realized that overcoming Stephen would not be the easy task he had supposed it to be. Sword dueling without armor was one of the most dangerous things a man could do. You could give a man his death blow yet, before he died, he could cut or thrust back and end the victor's life. Skill often gave way to chance.

The companion seemed to think that the danger was too great after all, and it probably was, since Stephen had his satchel shield while the companion had nothing of the kind. A fight with a bare sword against a man armed with sword and shield was a losing proposition. He stepped back. Then he ran toward the bridge.

Stephen suddenly realized that if the man got away, he would alert riders who could come out and eventually run him down. He couldn't let that man escape.

He gripped his sword at the cross and threw it like a spear. The silver blade arched through space and lanced into the companion's back. He collapsed on his side, gripping the part of the sword that had passed through his body, a look of surprise and disbelief on his face before he died.

Stephen pulled the bodies into the wood so they would not be found immediately and hurried toward Kislingbury.

Chapter 19

As Gilbert emerged from Robert Tauk's tailor shop on Fish Street, he stepped on a pebble. Stepping on pebbles was a common hazard of everyday life, often distracting and uncomfortable, but this pebble felt as though he had trod on a nail.

He muttered a few selected curses as he hung onto Wymar's arm with one hand and explored the state of his sole with the other. A few swipes of his fingers and his fears were confirmed. The sole at his big toe was parchment thin and there was a small hole at his big toe.

He set down the foot, contemplating what to do about this. He had only the one pair of shoes and a dwindling supply of money. Yet if he didn't do something about this, the hole would grow to consume the shoe, exposing Gilbert's tender foot to the elements.

By a bit of good fortune, there was a cobbler's shop a short distance up Fish Street. Gilbert made his way there, favoring the damaged shoe.

The cobbler was alone in his shop, where he was cutting leather.

"Need help?" the cobbler asked, observing Gilbert's hobbling gate.

"I've got a hole in my shoe," Gilbert said. "Can you mend it?"

"Why not just buy a new set?"

Gilbert suppressed a sigh. Cobblers always tried to sell you a new pair of shoes rather than mending the damaged ones; there was more money in it for them. "I'm short on coin."

"Let me see."

Gilbert handed over the shoe. The cobbler inspected the sole. "I can slap on another sole, if you like. Next Tuesday all right?"

"What! Next Tuesday? You mean, you'll have it done by Tuesday?" The prospect of going about with only one shoe for four days appalled Gilbert. His foot would be cut to

A Curious Death

ribbons on the cruel stones and ruts of the town's streets. His examination of the tailors would be significantly delayed — he couldn't count on Wymar to visit every one of them and ask the right questions if he did. Soon the army would march, and he had to march with it if he was to take custody of Oliver de Thottenham on Stephen's behalf and escort the boy to Ludlow — the only reason why he had come along. The slim chance of finding Dinesley's killer that remained would be gone.

"That's what I said."

"Are you sure you can't get it done today? These are all I have."

"Cost you extra."

"How much extra?"

The cobbler said, "Three pence altogether."

Gilbert winced. A full pair of shoes usually cost about four pence. It was more than he was willing to pay. But he supposed that if he had to, he must.

He reached for his purse, but Wymar stayed his land.

"How much for that patch of leather?" he asked, the shoemaker, pointing to a scrap on the end of the table.

"That?" the shoemaker said. "A half penny."

"Can you afford that?" Wymar asked Gilbert.

"I suppose," Gilbert grumbled. Even spending a half penny hurt at this moment.

"Give the man a half penny," Wymar said. He stretched across the counter and despite the distance was able to reach the fragment of leather.

The shoemaker, busy taking Gilbert's money, did not object.

"Come on," Wymar said when the exchange was concluded.

"Why? Where are we going?" Gilbert said. "And what did we want with a scrap of hide?"

"I'm going to fix your shoe with it," Wymar said. "But I left my best knife at camp."

"What do you know about fixing shoes?" Gilbert asked, feeling a bit indignant.

"I've had to repair a shoe more than once. It's not that hard. We just cut another sole and put that *inside* the boot — no sewing required! It'll last long enough for us to get back to Ludlow, where you can have a proper repair done."

"Well, then," Gilbert said, stepping out but wary of the hole in the shoe and the damage the road might do to his foot between here and camp. "Let's see just what you can do."

Gilbert was limping toward High Street past the shop of Arthur Dingle, tailor, when he heard a vaguely familiar voice coming from within the shop.

He would have gone on, thinking nothing of it since he had already interrogated Dingle about the button, if Wymar hadn't stopped to gawk through the open window.

"What is it?" Gilbert asked irritably.

"Only my heart's desire," Wymar sighed.

Wymar had so many heart's desires that Gilbert still would have walked on. But at that moment, the curtain parted at the rear of the shop to reveal a woman in her shift standing on a small pedestal with Dingle and his wife, who was his chief assistant, draping a rich rust-colored fabric embroidered with unicorns upon the woman's outstretched arms and arranging the falls of fabric about her waist and legs. The tailor and his wife were conducting a fitting for a new — and very expensive — gown.

The woman was Hilde from the Castle Keep.

"What are you looking at?" a man's voice said sharply at Gilbert's elbow.

It was the Keep's barman, Richard.

"I, er, ah, nothing," Gilbert said, realizing that he shouldn't have been staring at the partly clad Hilde.

"Hello in there!" Richard called through the window. "Mind the curtain!"

The tailor's wife snapped the curtain shut.

A Curious Death

"I daresay," Gilbert managed to say through his surprise at finding the barman here and his embarrassment. "That will be a very nice gown when it's finished." — As if he was admiring the fabric and not the woman.

"Yeesss. I've just come into an inheritance," Richard said. "It is but a pittance but enough for us to get married and move to Wallingford. We hope to open a tavern there."

"A wedding gift, then?" Gilbert said, nodding toward Hilde and her new gown.

"I thought it fitting for her to have a wedding dress," Richard said. "Don't you?"

Richard entered the shop without waiting for an answer.

Chapter 20

Stephen reached Kislingbury an hour later. He was relieved to see that Begilda and Bill had found the Picot's manor and were waiting in the stable.

It was still early, so he changed out of the friar's habit into his archer's simple clothes, and they set off south without a good-bye or a thank you to Lady Picot, who probably was glad to see them go.

Late that afternoon, they picked up the Roman road south of Towcester, where the going was easier. Roman roads had a habit of running straight from one place to another, and he remembered from the journey northward that this one led through Bicester and on to Oxford. It was relatively well marked, too, unlike many English roads, which sometimes dwindled to footpaths and even played out.

However, the sun had nearly set when he and Begilda finally gained the road, and the horse, having come twenty miles from Kislingbury carrying the both of them, had grown tired. Stephen hopped off and walked the last mile with Begilda's hound trotting at his heels until they reached a small village, where the road took a sharp turn to the right at the end of the village's main street. He'd had fantasies of reaching Oxford in a single day, although the distance was forty miles, but it was not to be and he turned his mind to finding them a place to sleep and forage for the horse.

They stayed the night in a barn for a farthing (the dog was free) and at first light continued to Oxford. It was only another twenty miles, but early in the morning the mare threw a shoe. Stephen held up her foreleg and surveyed the damage: the shoe hung by a single nail. He pulled off the shoe and put it in his satchel. It was still a good shoe, after all, and not to be wasted.

"I know you were getting used to the luxury of riding, but we'll have to walk," he told Begilda.

She shrugged philosophically and ruffled her Bill's neck. "Doesn't matter. Never liked being on a horse that much,

A Curious Death

anyway. Do you know how many people are killed by falls from horses?"

"Too many," Stephen said. "It's a knight's occupational hazard."

So, they didn't reach Oxford until almost sundown.

The road from Northampton came into the town from the north and went right by the king's house and the army's campground.

Stephen veered into the camp and found his tent and their campfire. No one was minding the fire, or at least no one was raking out coals for cooking since it seemed that supper had concluded.

Gilbert, who was seated on a stump soaking in the fire's heat on this cool evening, waved at Stephen when he came up. "Ah, the prodigal returns."

"You didn't save anything," Stephen said with some displeasure, although to be fair, Gilbert had no reason to anticipate his return and take appropriate steps.

"He ate my portion, too," Wymar said.

"Did not," Gilbert said. "You made yours vanish before I had a chance to lunge for it." He called to one of the women bent over a pair of buckets, washing the supper platters and kettles, "Kate! Have we anything left for a visitor?"

Kate straightened up and wiped her hands on her apron. A put-out expression flickered over her face but disappeared when she saw the visitor was Stephen. "I have a bit left, sir," she said and strode toward her tent.

"And something for the dog, too!" Stephen called after her.

"Dog? What dog?" Gilbert said. He caught sight of Bill and then Begilda standing at the edge of the tent circle.

Stephen beckoned to them. "Find a seat for yourself, Begilda."

Wymar eyed Begilda with polite interest. Even though Begilda was not yet a woman and was travel worn, dirty and wearing a poor woman's discarded gown that was patched and frayed, she was nevertheless pleasant to look at. Wymar leaped to his feet and waved to the log on which he had been sitting. "Please!"

Begilda could spot admiration and interest when she saw it. She curtseyed and accepted Wymar's offer.

"I'm Wymar," Wymar said.

"Are you, then," Begilda said.

Kate emerged from the tent with a half loaf of bread, a quarter round of cheese, and a clay pot of butter. Bill the dog looked on with interest as these were handed out, and Stephen spread butter on his half of the half loaf with his spoon. Bill thought that perhaps a bit of the cheese was meant for him, but Stephen was unwilling to share. Kate returned to the tent and came back with strips of dried beef, which Bill found more appetizing than the cheese, for all of it was gone in a flash of frantic chewing.

"Do you have any more of that?" Stephen said. "I wouldn't mind a bit."

"Sorry, sir," Kate said. "All out, I'm afraid."

"Who is this?" Gilbert asked the question that was on everyone's mind, for they were not alone here in the circle of tents.

"A friend," Stephen said after swallowing a mouthful of bread. Even though it was a bit stale and hard, it was the most delicious thing he had eaten in days, not to mention the only thing besides a pair of honeyed buns that he had eaten since his supper at Tom Boneyre's house. "She helped me out."

"And when did you get into the habit of picking up young girls?" Gilbert asked.

"She has nowhere to go," Stephen said. "I promised to take her back to Priors Halton if she helped me."

"Ah," Gilbert said as if that made all things clear, although it didn't unmuddy the waters at all. "Say, did you find what you were looking for?"

Stephen nodded. "I did. On both counts."

A Curious Death

After that not very satisfying supper, Stephen walked over to the king's house.

Despite the fact it was after sundown, the hall was lighted by two fires and wax candles placed all about. A band of musicians played on the walkway above the entrance, while three jugglers and band of mummers wearing fantastic costumes consisting of masks, deer antlers and long feathers performed between the two hearth fires. As his finale, one of the jugglers tossed one of three batons he had been juggling across the fire, and leaped to catch it, to the shouts of approval from the spectators.

Stephen looked around for Lord Edward without much hope of spotting him, and wove through the crowd toward the stairway to the chambers on the first floor. But as he reached the foot of the stairs, he spotted Lord Edward in earnest conversation with several other magnates, including Roger Mortimer and Percival FitzAllan, earl of Arundel.

FitzAllan noticed Stephen first, and snapped, "Take your hat off in his grace's presence!"

Stephen was wearing his wool cap to hide his cleric's haircut and he did not raise a hand to remove it.

"You impudent wretch!" FitzAllan shouted at Stephen's obvious refusal. He reached for Stephen's head, but Lord Edward grasped his hand.

"It's all right," Edward said. "There's a reason for this."

"A reason, your grace?" FitzAllan sputtered.

"Yes," Edward said. "Gentlemen, if you will excuse me, I must have words with Attebrook."

They went outside into the dark. A light rain had begun to fall, and Edward put up his hood. He leaned close and said softly, "Have you anything to tell me?"

"In fact, I have," Stephen said, and he recounted in brief what had happened at Northampton.

Edward slammed a fist into a palm when Stephen finished. He grinned. "I have them now!" He grasped Stephen's arm. "Come! We must see the king straightway!"

Edward did not wait, but walked as fast as his long legs could carry him, which was a trot for ordinary men. Stephen caught up with him easily, since he wasn't much shorter, and they turned together down Saint Giles Street toward North Gate.

The gates were closed for the night, of course. Edward stood there as if expecting Stephen to do something, and it was a moment before Stephen realized he was supposed to knock. He drew his dagger and hammered the pommel against the iron-stubbed gate panel and cried, "Open the gate for his lordship, Lord Edward!"

After a few moments there were grumbling noises on the other side, and a small panel opened. It was too dark to see any face behind it, but whoever was there said, "Lord Edward? Is it really Lord Edward? Is this some kind of joke?"

"It is no joke," Edward said as the man behind the portal held up a lantern so that he could see those in the street seeking entry to the town.

"It's really him!" the voice said to someone inside the town.

"Then open the damned gate, you idiot!" another voice replied. "You can't leave his lordship waiting."

The sound of fumbling and clanking followed as bolts were thrown aside and bars lifted, and a door within a door only wide enough to admit a single man on foot swung open.

Edward motioned for Stephen to go through first. He stepped through to find that six or eight men — it was a bit too dark to get a full count of them — were waiting with spears and shields, probably the entire complement of the gate guard.

"Your lordship!" apologized the man who had spoken to them. "We didn't realize …"

"No matter," Edward said, and hurried away down Northgate Street.

A Curious Death

They had to go through the same ritual at the castle gate because it, like the town gates, was shut for the night and ordinarily allowed no one to pass, except on urgent business — or by payment of a small amount of money to the guards' ale fund.

The king was, like Edward had been, in the hall surrounded by magnates. He said something that had his brother Duke Richard, doubled over in laughter and slapping his thigh, while the others about them both laughed but in a more restrained way.

The king paused in the middle of another witty comment as Edward marched up. Henry lifted a wine cup to his son. "What the devil brings you here this time of night? Out of wine at my house?" Like all the nobility, he spoke French. His came out of his mouth in an accent that Stephen placed as being north of the Loire River.

"I've had my fill of wine tonight, father," Edward said. "Can I have a moment?"

"A moment, but not for drinking?" Henry asked with a smile, and Stephen noticed that his handsome face was flushed about his graying brown beard and the ears that poked out of his flowing brown-gray hair were cherry red.

The king was drunk.

"Can't it wait until morning?" Henry asked.

No doubt the best thing to do was come back in the morning, but Edward was in a fit of enthusiasm. "If I may impose, your grace."

"All right, all right."

Henry stood up and noticed Stephen for the first time. His eyes wandered to Stephen's knit hat, which was still on his head, where it was not supposed to be in the royal presence. The king, even though he was a stickler for dignity, said nothing about the hat. A servant, seeing the insult of the hat, stepped forward to remove it, but Edward raised a hand to stay him.

"Attebrook's had a rather unfortunate and embarrassing haircut — at my request," Edward said. "It's best if no one sees it, my lord."

Henry looked puzzled. "Oh, ah — I see." He handed his cup to a servant. "Have this filled. I'll be right back."

The king led them to a corner of the hall where his presence scared off a couple of squires and two girls who were becoming too familiar with each other.

Henry stroked his beard. "You've found out something, I take it."

Edward surprised Stephen by letting him tell his story rather than repeating what he had heard. Henry listened, his dog-like gentle eyes thoughtful and more clear than they had been when he stood up.

When Stephen was done, Edward launched into an explanation of his plan, which Henry heard out.

Henry said nothing when Edward finished. A silence settled on the corner, although it seemed more of a thoughtful, rather than an awkward, one to Stephen.

"What do you think?" Edward asked.

"Have you discussed this with any of the others?" Henry asked.

"Not yet," Edward said. "You know our need to keep this secret."

Henry chuckled. "It seems to be working. I have heard from friends in London that Montfort intends to move on Rochester. He plans to draw us south, then summon the men at Northampton to fall on our backs when we confront him. If he had an inkling what madness you're cooking, he'd be on the road already." Rochester Castle and the town were held for the king by John de Warrene, earl of Surrey. "Speed in this thing is of the essence. If we are to do it."

"You've changed your mind?" Edward asked cautiously.

A Curious Death

Henry tapped his chin. His ears were still red and his face flushed. Was he making a decision he would reverse later, when he had time to regret it?

"No," Henry said emphatically. "We'll do it."

He turned his eyes again on Stephen. "You know the place, Attebrook. You will command the force to open the sally port." He said to Edward, "See he has the pick of the men to make it happen. I do not want this plan to fail."

Chapter 21

Gilbert awoke Monday morning to an empty tent, the smell of burning porridge and a leaden feeling of despondency about what he had to do today. He had slept in yesterday, as it had been Sunday, and no one likes to be bothered by inquiries on a Sabbath day. But today, it was back to fishing for tailors.

He stuck his head out of the tent and shouted at Kate by the fire, "Take a care, will you? The porridge is boiling!"

Kate removed her hands from a tub where she was washing shirts and wiped them on her gown. "You're an expert on porridge now?"

"I know I don't like mine burnt!" Gilbert said.

"You give it a stir," said Kate, returning to her laundry. "I'm otherwise occupied."

Gilbert wrapped his blanket around his shoulders and scampered on bare feet to the fire, where he moved the pot, which sat above the coals on spindly iron legs, to the edge of the fire. He stirred it with the wooden spoon set nearby for that purpose. It was like stirring sludge, which was how it had appeared every morning. You could plaster the side of a house with it, Gilbert reflected gloomily. But that's all there was to eat in the army when you weren't a rich knight, apart from dry and often moldy cheese. He found a bowl and ladled himself a portion, avoiding blackened fragments that arose from the bottom of the pot. At least the grains had cooked down and were soft this time so he didn't break a tooth. He sat on a log by the fire to eat.

"Where is everyone?" Gilbert asked Kate. For the tents here and nearby were deserted except for a few women and children. Even that new girl Stephen and brought back from Northampton, Begilda, and her dog were gone.

"Gone off for exercises," Kate said. "Called first thing this morning. Went off without breakfast. Don't you eat all of it! They'll be back soon!"

"Sir Stephen and Wymar, too?" Gilbert asked, setting down the spoon he had used to draw out a bit more porridge.

"And that girl, too," Kate said.

A Curious Death

Gilbert thought about tracking Stephen down. He hadn't had a chance to tell him the progress, if it could be called that, he had made in the search for Dinesley's killer. Stephen hadn't returned to the tent until late, when Gilbert was already asleep, and had gone straight to bed.

But a search for Stephen could take most of the morning, and Gilbert still had much to do, none of it enjoyable. The tailors were spread all over town and not located on a single street as was the custom in many towns, and he had spoken to only a third of them at best. He looked forward to several more days of dreary trudging around, asking the same questions of impatient men who didn't want to be interrupted for the Dinesley business. The days were never long enough for the difficult business of keeping one's head above water, and diligent men didn't like sacrificing precious time on distractions and frivolities.

He patted his poor, abused stomach, tossed his dirty bowl into a bucket and went to find his shoes.

The first sign that something was amiss came at dinner time. Gilbert took a table at a tavern called the Purple Pheasant and ordered half a roasted quail, a bowl of stewed beans, bread and butter. But when the meal came, he could not smell it, for his nose had begun to fill with fluid and snot ran from his nose, which he hastened to catch with a handkerchief.

The servant who brought his trencher look horrified as Gilbert blew into the handkerchief, almost threw down the trencher and fled to the rear of the tavern.

Gilbert wondered what had got into the man, wiped his face and chin of snot, and attempted to tuck into his dinner.

Except the quail, which should have been delicious, for it was tender and dripping with juice, tasted like old leather. Gilbert chewed slowly, both disappointed and alarmed. The inability to enjoy his food was appalling; dinner was the highlight of his day.

Yet, it was a sin to waste food, so he couldn't push it aside. He forced himself to choke down every bit, paid his bill, and returned to his search of the tailors.

As the afternoon dragged on, without any progress, Gilbert found himself becoming so tired that he often failed to watch where he placed his feet. This caused him to stagger occasionally, potholes and gullies being so common that making one's way along often involved a bit of a dance to avoid them, and that drew hostile looks from people nearby, who shied back, some making the horned sign of the devil. At first, Gilbert was unaware of this, but as the church of Saint Michael at the Northgate came into view ahead, a barrage of dirt clods flung by a pack of wild children shouting, "Be gone, you poxied lout!" struck in a flurry. He stopped to wonder what they were shouting about.

It was true he felt unusually tired, but then he had been walking most of the day. It was true his voice sounded a bit hoarse, but he had been questioning unhelpful tailors most of the day. And it was true his nose was running like a stream. But ... Hmm. He felt his cheeks. His hands were cold, but his face was hot. How to explain that? It was probably nothing. Hands were usually the coldest part of one's body, anyway.

The last straw, however, was his reception by the servant of the tailor whose shop was in the shadow of the church. The servant took one look at Gilbert, felt his forehead, snapped, "Be gone, you foul host of pestilence!" and slammed the door.

"Host of pestilence, am I?" Gilbert said to himself.

Well, he was feeling a little out of sorts.

While he urgently needed to continue his canvas of the tailors, what he really needed was some rest. Just one night's good solid sleep. That would do it.

His feet led the way to Northgate, which was just round the corner. It wasn't far from there to his tent and his pallet. If it were only a feather mattress rather than stuffed with straw. Now, that would be nice!

A Curious Death

Chapter 22

The sounds of a dry, hacking cough finally forced Stephen out of bed about half an hour before sunrise. The coughing had been going on for some time, but he had tried to ignore it. He had got in late last night — planning for his part in the attack on Northampton was more time-consuming and complex than he had imagined it would be. He needed a clear head, for there was still a lot to do, and for that he needed sleep. The racket was impossible to ignore now, though.

In the twilight, he saw the silhouettes of Wymar and Begilda, who had also sat up at the tortured sounds coming from Gilbert's pallet.

"Woke you, too, did it?" Stephen said to them.

"It sounds bad," Wymar said.

Stephen crept on hands and knees to Gilbert's side. He put a hand on Gilbert's forehead.

"I'm sorry I woke you," Gilbert croaked, then burst into more coughing that racked his rotund body. Between coughs, he wheezed like a smith's bellows.

"You've a fever," Stephen said.

"No! No! I'll be all right!"

"No, you won't. You're not to get out of bed for anything other than to pee, understand?"

"Not even for breakfast?"

"Not even for that. Begilda will watch over you. Won't you?" Stephen asked, turning his head toward the girl.

"Of course, sir," she said.

"She'll bring you breakfast, and dinner and supper," Stephen said.

"None of that awful porridge! Please!" Gilbert moaned. "It'll kill me!"

"Right. No porridge."

Stephen pulled on his boots and wrapped his cloak about his shoulders against the morning chill — he had slept fully dressed, which was the usual practice when traveling. He dug into his purse and poured out a palmful of coin. He gave Begilda the money.

"For his sustenance, and yours. Look after him while we're gone. If he needs a physician, there should be enough there to cover the fee," Stephen said.

"Yessir," Begilda said. "Can I feed Bill out of it, too?"

Stephen nodded.

He picked up his sword.

But Gilbert threw off his blanket and tried to sit up. "I'll be all right. Really! I've got work to do! There's Oliver!"

"Never mind Oliver," Stephen said. "Wymar can bring him back. Then you can take him to Ludlow when you've recovered." This was why Gilbert had come along, to fetch Oliver back to Ludlow if Stephen managed to free him from Nigel FitzSimmons' grip.

"But what about Dinesley! I could continue that work!"

"I don't see how you can," Stephen said. He shrugged. "Anyway, from what you've said, there doesn't seem to be much likelihood you'll find his killer at this point."

Stephen pushed Gilbert back down and spread his blanket over him. "Rest now."

"I'm sorry!" Gilbert croaked.

"You've nothing to apologize for," Stephen said.

"Yes, there is!" Gilbert said. But he did not say what that might be. He closed his eyes, looking miserable.

"Well," Stephen said lamely. "Take care of yourself. Begilda will look after you."

Gilbert did not open his eyes. But he nodded that he had heard.

"Right, then," Stephen said. "Don't die on me while we're gone."

Receiving no reply to that cheery exhortation, he rose and left the tent.

Northampton was waiting.

A Curious Death

Chapter 23

The full impact of how mad this scheme was did not hit Stephen until he crossed the wooden bridge over the River Nene and approached Northampton's South Gate. He had been so busy with preparations over the last few days that there had been no room in his mind for anxiety, fear or doubt. But now that he was about to take the final step, he had plenty of all three, and the realization swept his breath away. The king's opening gambit in the war that was about to begin in earnest hinged on what he did within the next day. For the king needed a quick victory. Without it, his cause might fail upon Northampton's walls, for storming the town was the only choice should the sally port not open. So many good men might die in the attempt that the king would be undermanned for the rest of the struggle.

These thoughts made Stephen light-headed with anxiety and he stumbled and might have toppled over if Simon Feran had not grasped his arm.

"Are you alright?" Feran asked. He was a tall man by English standards, which meant he was a few inches shorter than Stephen, but broader with strong forearms from wielding swords and lances. He, like the six others of the party, were clad in the black habits of Dominican friars. They had their hoods up, since they had revolted at the suggestion that they shave their heads as Stephen had done to make the disguise really convincing. Worse, the men didn't look like clerics. Monks and friars often had a bookishness about them, with narrow often starved faces and slender hands. These men were blunt and hard, the faces of knights used to fighting and risking their lives.

"It's nothing," Stephen muttered.

There was no turning back now.

A one-horse cart laden with sacks of grain and a half dozen barrels had stopped in the gate passage while the gate guards counted the sacks and barrels to assess the toll charged for entry into the town. As Stephen reached the rear of the cart, he dropped his hood to give the guards at the gate a look at his tonsure.

The three guards on duty hardly glanced at the friars as they squeezed around the cart, since religious men were of no interest, which eased Stephen's anxiety more than a little.

The driver of the cart, however, locked eyes with Stephen for a moment. Just when Stephen thought with some alarm that the driver would nod to him, the driver's eyes slid away. The guards did not seem to notice this.

Stephen led the way down the main road from the gate to a large church on the righthand side with a marketplace to its north. It was afternoon now, so he figured the church would be deserted. A small group were praying in the nave, however. The men and women glanced with some curiosity as the false friars filed by them to the transepts, where Stephen noted there was a doorway leading to the outside at the north one.

"This should work," Stephen said.

The men dropped their satchels and stripped off their clerical robes. All wore peasants' brown coats and dull stockings beneath the robes, which went into the satchels. They left the church by the doorway leading out to the market without being seen by those praying or anyone else.

It was then but a short walk to the Marehold marketplace near Boneyre's house. Stephen remembered seeing an inn just up from the market which had an inner courtyard where they could conduct some necessary business later away from the street. The proximity to Boneyre's house raised the possibility that Stephen might run into the lawyer, but it had to do, since it also wasn't far from the south wall of Saint Andrews Priory, which reduced a more worrisome chance of running into the night watch later.

The innkeeper, a hard-eyed man, nodded when Stephen asked for a chamber for them all.

"I've no rooms, but you're free to sleep in the hall," the innkeeper said.

Stephen had hoped for a chamber, since one would keep them out of sight until it was time to ask.

A Curious Death

"What about the loft in the stable?" he said. "We're used to sleeping in barns. And the straw will be more comfortable than hard ground."

"Suit yourself. Where are you boys from, anyway?" The innkeeper's question could be just casual conversation, but there was a hint of suspicion in it that alarmed Stephen.

"All over. Take your pick," Stephen said. "I'm from the west country, myself. I can't speak for the rest of them."

"And where would you happen to be going? Seems to me brawny boys like you could make a good bit of coin if you signed up at the castle," the innkeeper said.

"We're sailors, if you must know, and not much given to fighting on land," Stephen said. "Our ship burned at London and we're looking for another one. A factor found us an engagement, and we're to meet the boat at King's Lynn." This was a small port on the River Ouse three days' walk away.

"And you believed him? Sounds like a wild goose chase to me."

Stephen shrugged. "We know where his family lives, if there's trouble."

The innkeeper slapped his thigh. "All right, then."

"What's for supper, anyway?" Stephen asked.

"Boiled beef and peas mixed with turnips," the innkeeper said, and turned away to another pair of customers who had just come through the door.

"That was the worst lie I ever heard in my life," Feran said as they sat down at a table. "My dead aunt could have done better."

"It was the best I could do," Stephen said.

"I hope it doesn't get us arrested."

The loft was large and filled with fresh hay, and when the group climbed the ladder, they heard no scurrying feet of rodents that liked to inhabit lofts, which was a good thing, because at night rats were known to scamper across sleeping bodies and even to nibble on ears and fingers.

The men spread their blankets on the hay, including Stephen, who then sat down by the ladder, where the light from the open door was the best.

"I suppose we should get this over with," Stephen said, removing his knit cap.

"I never fancied myself a barber," Feran said, "but in this case, I'm happy to do the honors."

"Hack away," Stephen said. "It's not much different than shearing sheep. Have you done that, at least?"

"You'll be so pretty when I'm done," Feran said, opening and closing a pair of scissors.

"Just watch the ears," Stephen said. "I'd hate to lose one."

It was dark by the time Feran had applied a razor to Stephen's head so that he was as bald as Gilbert, except all over.

"Not even any blood spilled," Feran said. "I charge extra for that."

"You are an artist," Stephen said. "I'll square up tomorrow."

Feran put the razor back in Stephen's satchel with the scissors and lay down on his blanket.

"Once I slept in a field where I had to pick cow shite out of my hair in the morning," Feran said. "This is much better."

"I'll take the first watch," Stephen said, removing the hourglass from his satchel. The men stared at the hourglass, which had been loaned by Lord Edward, for it was a rare thing and none of them had seen one before they had been recruited for this mission. Stephen upended the hourglass and they watched the sand fall from the upper bulb to the lower one before one-by-one falling asleep.

Feran woke Stephen and moved off to rouse the others. Stephen put the hourglass back in his satchel and went out to the yard. It was a clear night filled with bright stars so that they would be able to see where they were going.

A Curious Death

The other men filed out to join him. They descended the ladder and went out to the yard, where the one-horse cart, still filled with its sacks and barrels, sat by the door.

The cart driver was asleep on a layer of grain sacks, but woke silently when one of the men shook his foot.

The cart driver lifted the lid on one of the barrels and flung down an old linen curtain. He reached into the barrel and started removing canvas sacks that clinked faintly and were very heavy, for they were filled with mail and the men's helmets. While the men sorted out who belonged to which sack, the cart driver went to work emptying a second barrel, this one filled with swords. After these had been handed out, he opened a third barrel, much larger than the others, and passed out shields.

"We'll change in the stable," Stephen said, glancing around the interior of the courtyard. Like many such courtyards, there were porches on the various floors linked by stairways to allow guests to reach their rooms. He saw no one, but wasn't willing to take the chance that someone might be awake.

It was too dark inside to see well, but the men had so much practice donning mail that they could do it by feel, and it took very little time before they were armored and had belted on their swords, helmets tucked under an arm and shields hanging on their backs. One knight had a heavy axe more suitable for chopping wood than hacking heads and limbs, while Stephen removed a hacksaw from his canvas bag.

One of the men wandered into a back corner to relieve himself. From that dark spot suddenly came a yelp of indignation, some thumps and thrashing about, and two young voices begging for mercy. The knight reappeared at the door with a skinny young man and a slender woman, her hair down, mussed and with random bits of straw in it, by their collars.

"I caught these two lurking about," the knight said. He gave his captives a shake.

"We weren't lurking!" the young man protested. "We were asleep until you peed on me!" He seemed defiant until he got a look at the men. Then he gulped and became frightened. "Who are you?"

"We should kill them both," Feran said. "They'll tell first thing."

"No," Stephen said. "Tie and gag them, and put them well in the back. By the time they're found in the morning, it will be too late to make a difference."

Stephen paused at the end of the passage connecting the inn's courtyard with the street. He listened, heard nothing, and stuck his head around the corner. A pair of dark figures was hurrying toward him from the Marehold marketplace. He pulled back and waited, hoping they would pass by without seeing him. But when the figures came abreast of the passage, one spotted the knights and took off running with the other one close behind.

"That's a pair who're up to no good," Feran said.

"All the better for us," Stephen answered. "They're not likely to sound an alarm, are they."

The priory was only a short distance from the inn, which they covered in a slow jog. At the base of the wall, they gathered their breath and then one after another, the men boosted each other up until only Stephen remained. Feran reached a hand down from the top of the wall and pulled Stephen up far enough for him to lay across the top on his stomach. Then Stephen swung his legs over and dropped to the ground with more noise than he would have liked.

All was quiet with the priory grounds, however. So, after a moment of tense listening, he led the men through the extensive herb garden, the jingling of mail in his ears and the scent of rosemary in his nostrils.

Ahead to the left, Stephen could plainly see the A-shaped roof of the guest house projecting above the town wall, since the sky had begun to lighten. It would be sunrise in less than an hour. A rooster crowed to the right where there was a rustling of many wings as the priory chickens began to awaken. They passed by a pigpen where two sows came to the fence to see who was out and about at this unusual hour, perhaps expecting an early breakfast.

Once at the guest house, Stephen tried the center door, expecting it to yield as it had the first time. But it stuck fast, and in the twilight's dimness, he realized it had been padlocked. The result of Bill's escape, perhaps?

Stephen had his choice of his skeleton key or the hacksaw to deal with this obstacle. Because the hacksaw was likely to make noise and take longer, he lifted the thong around his neck over his head for the key. After some fumbling, the lock gave way and Stephen tossed it aside.

He opened the door. While outside it had grown light enough to see a man's features, it was dark as the inside of a sack in the cellar.

"William, Richard, you're on the door," Stephen said to the two knights who were to guard the entrance.

He entered the cellar, followed by the others. He fumbled across the cellar, feeling for obstacles in the general direction of the sally port. He stumbled and fell only once, before encountering the large stack of barrels and sacks that he and Begilda had found blocking the port. He edged around the stack and ran his hands over the jagged stone of the wall for a short way, then met the heavy oak panel studded with thick iron nails.

"This is it," Stephen said with relief. "Get that shite out of the way."

"Quickly, now," Feran said. "And try not to make any noise."

By the time the men had cleared enough space at the wall so Stephen could fit through the gap enough to work on the door, the twilight had brightened as sunrise drew near. Stephen felt for the iron bolts and the padlock that secured them. Once he had his hands on the lock, he deployed his skeleton key again. But the key did not move within the lock no matter how much Stephen struggled with it. The lock remained frozen.

"What's the matter?" Feran asked.

"I think the lock's rusted solid," Stephen said.

"Better hurry," Feran said. "People are moving about upstairs."

It was true. There were knocks and bangs on the floorboards above and the clamor of voices. The door to the first floor opened and the thumps of footsteps could be heard on the stairway as several people came out of the house, descended to the yard and headed off toward a privy.

"Sard it, they would have to take this moment for a piss," said William at the doorway. "Don't friars believe in chamber pots?"

"If you were a friar, would you want to spend your mornings emptying chamber pots?" Richard said.

"That's what servants are for," William replied. "I'm sure they've got enough of them."

"Hey, you!" a voice outside shouted. "Who are you? What are you doing?"

"My lord!" Richard called into the cellar. "We've been found out!"

At the moment, alarm bells began to ring in the town.

"I think the king has arrived," Feran said.

And the sally port was still not open.

A Curious Death

Chapter 24

King Henry stopped in the middle of the bridge over the River Nene. He removed his helmet, threw back his mail coif, and pulled off his arming cap. He stuffed the arming cap into the helmet, which he tucked under one arm.

Ahead lay Northampton's southern gate. At this distance, at the edge of a long bowshot, dark round balls that were the heads of the town garrison could be seen in the crenellations on the wall, along with sparkles of sunlight off burnished helmets, armor and spearhead. Henry examined those men — more appearing at every moment as alarm bells clanged urgently — with dismay. Northampton would be a tough nut if he had to storm it. With luck, he would not. But now that the die was cast, he would have no choice. His prestige demanded an attack. A retreat would be seen as weakness, and he could not afford that. People obeyed kings only when they appeared strong. Weak kings were deposed and usually killed.

A third of Henry's army was drawn up in three long lines stretching across the road running to the south gate. In the front were archers, five hundred of them. In the second line were the infantry and dismounted sergeants with assault ladders set out in the grass by each formation, another five hundred. And behind the infantry were the mounted knights and sergeants, two-hundred-fifty, give or take. They looked impressive from Henry's vantage point, and he hoped those on the town's halls would be deceived in thinking it was his entire force.

His advisers had told him this was not a good place to attack the town. The river stood at the army's back and there was only one bridge across it. If the garrison decided to sally and Henry's men broke, they would be trapped against the river and slaughtered.

Henry nudged his horse forward and rode through the lines toward South Gate. His advisers had pleaded with him not to put himself in danger by riding close to the walls, but he had decided to take the chance anyway. He rode helmetless so that the men on the walls could have no doubt who he was.

Even though he had a golden crown signifying his identity welded to the top of his barrel helmet — the gold in fact was polished bronze — the impact of his appearance unhelmeted would be greater.

He halted about forty yards from South Gate, which consisted of two square towers flanking the gate passage.

He heard the murmur of astonished voices at the top of the wall. The most common thing was "It's the king!" Henry could not help smiling because despite the fact these men were his enemies they still regarded him with the reverence he was due as king. Thinking of this helped to allay the undercurrent of anxiety he felt at the possibility that some unseen man up there was training a crossbow at him. His uncle Richard had been killed by a crossbowman as he rode close to a besieged town, and Henry did not relish repeating that experience.

"Where is Lord Simon?" Henry called out, meaning not the elder Simon, his brother-in-law, but the elder Simon's son, who was in charge of the forces here. "Still in bed, I suppose!"

"He is on his way, your grace!" a voice answered.

"It is rude to keep me waiting," Henry said.

"Our apologies, your grace!"

"And see that's he's properly dressed! I won't talk to a man still in his nightshirt!"

Presently, there was a stirring on the wall. A familiar face appeared in one of the crenellations, uncoifed and unhelmeted as Henry was.

"What kept you, Simon?" Henry said. "Sarding your mistress?"

Simon cleared his throat. "I am surprised to see you here, your grace."

"That was the idea," Henry said. "Surprise."

"Where is my cousin Edward?" Young Simon asked, gazing at the army.

"Where he belongs," Henry said, gesturing to the throng behind him. There was a man with the mounted knights who was wearing Edward's surcoat and whose squire was carrying

A Curious Death

Edward's flag. It was part of the deception. To conclude the gesture, Henry swiveled back and pointed at Young Simon. "Soon he will be where you stand."

"Boldly stated, your grace," Young Simon said.

Henry shrugged.

He said, "If you surrender the town and castle, I will allow you and your men to march out with your arms and horses, with the proviso that all take an oath not to bear arms against me again."

"A pardon?" Simon asked.

"Rebellion against your sovereign lord is treason, so you've a guilty conscience, eh? Well, if you want to think of it as a pardon, you have my leave."

Henry hoped for a flat-out rejection, but instead, Simon hesitated.

"I must consult the barons," Simon said.

"If you must. You have half an hour. Then the game begins."

Chapter 25

The alarm bells fell silent.

"Hurry up, for God's sake!" Feran hissed over Stephen's shoulder.

"I'm working as fast as I can," Stephen gritted. The hacksaw was not making much headway against the lock, primarily because of the way the lock was positioned against the rod and the door: he couldn't make a full stroke with the saw, only small ones. "What's going on out there?"

"The men who called ran off toward the church," William said from the doorway.

"To the chapter house, you mean," Stephen said. "They've gone to warn the prior. William, Richard, Henry. Michael — get to the priory gate house." He didn't have to say more. He had told them earlier that seizing the priory gate was as essential to their success as opening the sally port. Opening the port only gave Lord Edward access to the priory grounds. The army would be trapped inside unless Stephen's men held the priory gate.

He resumed struggling with the saw and lock. After a dozen draws, he felt the notch he had created. It was only a quarter of the way through, if that much. At this rate it could take an hour.

He heard voices, not from behind him or in the priory yard, but outside, through the door. Someone pounded on the sally door and called out, "My lord! Are you there?"

It was Wymar.

"I'm here, but I'm having a bit of trouble with the lock," Stephen said.

"You must hurry!" Wymar called. "Lord Edward is here and the attack on the wall will start at any moment!"

No sooner had Wymar said this, Stephen heard the distant clamor of hundreds of voices shouting at one.

"Any moment, he says," Feran said. "It's already started!" He raised the heavy axe. "Get out of the way! You're getting nowhere!"

A Curious Death

Stephen darted back as Feran swung the axe at the lock. The head ricocheted of the iron padlock and nearly hit Feran's leg.

"Stop that!" Stephen said. "There's another way!"

He bent to examine the hinges. They were as he thought. The part attached to the wall stuck up like an L or a thumb while the part attached to the door was an O ring that fit over the thumb.

"Give me the axe." Stephen turned to a pallet that had been cleared of sacks but not moved. He chopped a board loose, which he gave to Feran.

"Put one end under the door and lift up," he said.

Feran looked confused by this order but hurried to comply. The hinges creaked and held, indicating that they were as rusted as the lock. But Stephen had an idea — he struck upward against the top hinge with the blunt side of the axe. At first the axe rebounded without effect. Stephen put all he had into the second blow while Feran, getting the point, pulled up on the board with all his might.

He pounded twice on the lower hinge to loosen it and then aimed the next blow at the upper hinge again. That blow dislodged the O ring from the thumb, and both men threw themselves backward to avoid being crushed by the door, which toppled inward at them and landed with a bone-crushing thud.

Wymar stood silhouetted in the doorway, looking dumbfounded.

"Nice to see you, too, Wymar," Stephen panted as he lay upon his back, grateful that the door had missed him.

He scrambled to his feet and beckoned Wymar to enter. "Let's get this thing out of the way."

Stephen and Wymar wrenched the door free of the last hinge, and with Feran's help, lugged the door out of the way.

Now it was Stephen's turn to stand in the doorway. Thirty yards away, across the Nene, Lord Edward sat upon his horse surrounded by household knights, with the rest of the army behind him.

Stephen stepped outside and waved. "It's all clear!"

At Stephen's wave, Edward crossed the stream and trotted to the doorway, followed en masse by the army in a flowing river of men and horses. Edward raised a hand at Stephen as he passed and bent down to enter the sally port. One by one, the men of the army followed.

Battles are confusion and chaos for those in them. If you are in the front rank, you cannot see further than the man in front of you and, perhaps, those on either side of him, and you are frantically busy defending against blows with your shield, taking terrific thumps on the head if you aren't quick enough, being jostled by the men beside and behind you, sometimes being struck on the backswing by your friends' weapons as they raised swords and axes to smite the enemy. For those in the rear, you can only know what's happening a man or two in front of you, for broad shoulders and shields block your vision, and all you know is that a seething mass lies before you, which might part from time to time as a wounded man stumbles back or is passed along to the rear, where he falls to the ground, perhaps to be stepped on by those pressing against the men in front of them.

So, all Stephen could see when he emerged from the priory was a crowd of men a hundred yards down Saint Andrews Street. The spears in the rear ranks stood upright and swayed back and forth, while glints of rising and falling swords and axes could be seen over their heads accompanied by the clatter and clunk in a mad cacophony when the weapons landed on their targets.

Over the uproar, he heard men shouting on the next street over, Broad Street, so fighting extended there as well.

He lifted his helmet when he reached the rear of the crowd on Saint Andrews Street, and asked the first man he came to, "What's going on?"

"Your guess is as good as mine," said the soldier, armed with a spear, a simple pot helm and a padded jacket.

A Curious Death

"They say that the enemy sallied out to meet us when they realized we'd breached the wall," said the soldier next to him.

"Done a good job, too," said the soldier who'd first spoken. "We haven't moved in a while."

Stephen considered this. "You men," he shouted to those nearby. "Follow me!"

About fifty heard him, one of them a knight who seemed to be their commander. "What are you up to?" the knight asked.

"I know a way to get behind that lot," Stephen said, gesturing at the scrum.

The knight nodded and gestured to his men. "After us!"

Stephen went to the nearest house on the right. He didn't want to do what had to come next, but there wasn't a choice. So, he kicked in the door and pressed through the shop to the hall and the back garden. "Make sure they all follow," he said to the knight. "There's no time for looting."

"Right," the knight said and turned back to check on the men, pushing them toward the rear of the house.

Stephen leaped a wicker fence, crossed another back garden, and invaded the house across the way in the same manner, pressing through to the street beyond, a lane that ran along the priory's wall. Then it was off at a jog to the south.

He reached one cross street just below the end of the priory grounds that ran into Saint Andrews. He stuck his head around the corner and saw men running up Saint Andrews toward the fight — more soldiers from the castle.

So far, no one from the garrison thought to block this lane as well, but it was only a matter of time before the idea occurred to one of the enemy's commanders.

Since the way seemed clear, Stephen led the little band down the lane to the next cross street, which he recalled emptied into the Marehold marketplace. He turned down that lane, glancing behind to make sure the men were still with him.

At the Marehold, Stephen said, "This is it. Half of you face up toward the priory, the rest toward the castle! That way we'll catch them in the rear, but they won't catch us!"

He clapped on his helmet and stepped into the Marehold.

His sudden appearance startled some stragglers from the garrison who looked at Stephen in bewilderment, perhaps thinking at first that he was one of them since he had come from a place where no enemy was expected.

But he cut down one spearman and pushed another over with his shield, which sent the stragglers running, removing all doubt that he and his companions were not friends.

Stephen paused here to order the men, pushing a few about unceremoniously since they couldn't seem to understand simple orders. When he had his two lines, he ordered one to charge the enemy in the rear on Saint Andrews Street while the other line faced toward the castle in the south and covered their backs.

Stephen's spearmen crashed into the enemy with leveled spears as if they were jousting on foot, killing and wounding many in the rearmost rank who were caught unawares before jabbing and pushing against the next one.

Cries of mercy began to go up from the enemy as men threw down their weapons and fell to their knees.

A gust of satisfaction swept through Stephen at the success of his wild plan, but a shout behind him dispelled it.

"They're coming!" the knight who led this contingent shouted. "Get ready to receive cavalry!"

Cavalry? Stephen thought with alarm. *A cavalry charge?* Here, in the center of town? A cavalry charge by armored knights was a formidable and frightening thing. Few men on foot had the courage to receive one, and he doubted that this rabble, for that's what they were, armed farmers owing feudal service to the knight, could manage it.

He spun around to see the charge. There were indeed five mounted knights on the street with infantry pelting behind them, their horses pounding toward his frail formation. A few

A Curious Death

spears stuck out from his rear line, but not enough to deter a determined charge.

His own sword felt like a thing made of butter in his hand — swords were not the best weapon for the dismounted man against an armored rider unless he was willing to kill the horse. But someone had dropped a spear nearby and Stephen, transferring his sword to his left hand, picked up the spear just as the first of the enemy knights struck the shield wall.

The leading enemy knight, who was a few strides ahead of his companions, drove his spear through the forehead of one of the infantry while his horse literally knocked into the air the three men behind him and bowled over those on either side.

The enemy knight dipped his lance point toward the ground to disengage it from the dead man's head and, spotting Stephen, turned toward him. Stephen only had time to bring up his shield to deflect the lance, but instead of thrusting at either man or horse, he set the spear point on the ground between the horse's forelegs. The spear pole tripped the horse and it went down hard, turning a somersault, the crashing hindquarters narrowly missing the knight who had pitched over the horse's head.

The knight lay dead or stunned, so Stephen turned back to the line to face the next threat.

But there was none. Another rider had penetrated the line, but he was being dragged from his horse while the other three pulled back from the charge, and the line of infantry closed against the enemy.

Stephen stalked to the fallen knight who was sitting up now, holding his head. Stephen removed the man's helmet and put his sword on the fellow's neck. He was several years younger than Stephen with a friendly handsome face — and the Montforts' insignia on his shield and surcoat.

"Do you yield?" Stephen asked.

The young man looked up at Stephen with disgust, although that softened a bit when he realized he was surrendering to a knight and not some peasant. "I suppose I must."

"Wise choice. Excellent ride, by the way."

Stephen helped the knight to his feet. "Who are you?"

"I am Simon de Montfort," he said. "I'm not *that* Simon. I'm the earl's son."

"Stephen Attebrook, at your service."

"You're handy with a spear, I see."

"I've had some practice."

Chapter 26

Word of Young Simon's capture spread quickly among the defenders. Those trapped between Stephen and the royalist contingent surrendered, while those between Stephen and the Marehold melted away, first in two and threes, and then en masse. The royalists pursued the enemy down Saint Andrews Street, but by the time they reached the marketplace, the enemy defending Broad Street had heard about Young Simon's capture and also were fleeing. Stephen's group would have laid into those rebels and cut down as many as they could if Lord Edward had not ridden up and shouted that his men must to let them go.

"We shall not shed the blood of Englishmen if it can be helped!" Edward bellowed. "Follow them to the castle!"

While not enthusiastically received when they were winning, the men obeyed the order and slowed to a walk. There was no need now for a pelting pursuit.

As Edward watched the men obey his command, he caught sight of Stephen standing in the middle of Saint Andrews Street with his captive. A smile broke out on Edward's face, and he trotted up to Stephen and Young Simon.

"What have you got there, Sir Stephen?" Edward asked. "That's a very big trout!"

"Just something I picked up," Stephen said.

"Well, Simon," Edward said, "are you ready to mend your ways?"

"I do what I am obliged to do for my father," Simon said darkly.

"You've always been stubborn," Edward said. He turned to two household knights behind him. "Bring Montfort along. He will fetch a great ransom. Come, Attebrook. There's still work to do."

Edward trotted off toward the castle to the south. Stephen, lacking a horse, followed as quickly as his aching bad foot allowed; it often troubled him when that he wasn't occupied with facing imminent death.

There was a great crowd outside the castle's main gate. In the narrow streets, it seemed as if the whole army gathered here.

Edward worked his horse through the throng. The two household knights in charge of Young Simon followed Edward so that those on the castle walls could get a good look at the younger Montfort. The crowd was noisy and jubilant, as if this was a horse race or football game. Edward held up a hand for quiet and the tumult gradually subsided.

Edward turned his attention to the enemy upon the walls above his head, in particular to a tall, thin man in his forties with a receding hairline and a pinched face.

"Hello, Peter!" Edward called, and Stephen realized who that pinched-faced man was, Peter de Montfort, a cousin of the more famous elder Earl Simon de Montfort.

"I see you, my lord," Peter said.

"You've misplaced Young Simon," Edward said.

"An unfortunate turn of events," Peter said.

"Defeat is an unfortunate turn of events. And you are defeated, whether you want to admit it or not. I understand your barn caught fire a few days ago," Edward said. "All your supplies, gone — poof! Literally, up in smoke."

"We're fine for supplies," Peter said, clearly startled that Edward was so well informed.

"Let's not play games," Edward said. "It doesn't become a man in your position. You've enough left for, what? A day or two, if that? Then you'll have to eat what horses you have, and even then what will the men eat? It's starvation for them, eh? Can you keep order among them when they're going hungry?"

"Earl Simon will be along soon."

"He won't get here for at least a week. It will take two days for your messengers to reach London, maybe even three. Then it will take a day for him to get organized, and then another three to march here." Edward rubbed his strong chin.

A Curious Death

"And if it looks like Simon's on the way, I'll simply storm the walls. Your men can't be counted on to fight. They already know it's hopeless."

As Peter listened to Edward, another figure spoke into his ear. Stephen went cold. That figure was an old acquaintance, Nigel FitzSimmons. If anyone was Stephen's blood enemy, it was FitzSimmons, who had tried to have Stephen killed more than once. FitzSimmons and Peter de Montfort engaged in a heated exchange that, because it was whispered, could not be heard by the men below. But FitzSimmons was angered by it and not satisfied with what Peter had to say. He sneered and disappeared behind a merlon.

"I must speak to the barons," Peter called down to Edward. "I will give you their decision in the morning."

Stephen stood in the street, staring at the top of the castle's wall as the royalist officers led their contingents off on siege tasks assigned to them by the army's leadership. Since he had no leader other than Lord Edward and he had been given no orders, he thought hard about what he had just seen, trying to make sense of it. What had occurred between Peter de Montfort and Nigel FitzSimmons had been important, but he wasn't sure what it was. His tired brain failed to provide an answer.

Wymar found him in the street at last. "My lord," he said, striving for Stephen's attention.

"Ah, Wymar, it's good to see you avoided getting killed," Stephen said, still gazing at the wall.

Wymar looked put out. "They wouldn't let me get involved in the fighting."

"They?"

"After I lost track of you, I fell in with a bunch of fellows. But they put me at the back. Nothing happens in the back."

"It's safer there," Stephen murmured.

"I can fight!"

"No, you can't. Not yet. In time, perhaps." Stephen dragged his eyes from the wall, where sentinels kept watch but the leading men had disappeared. "Have you seen Feran and the others?"

"I passed them in that wide place, like a market."

"Where were they headed?"

"Back toward the priory. Where I left their horses."

"Hmm. Let's go find them."

"What are we doing?"

"I wish I could say."

Stephen hobbled back toward the priory, his left foot aching at every step, as it often did.

"Run ahead and see if you can catch Feran and the others," he said to Wymar. "Ask them to wait for me."

"Yessir," Wymar walked faster and put some distance in a few strides between him and Stephen.

"I said run!" Stephen said.

Wymar broke into a trot.

"Do you remember how to get there?" Stephen called to Wymar's back.

"I know the way!"

Feran and the others in the group that seized the sally port were waiting with their horses inside the priory gate.

Stephen limped up and put a hand on the neck of Feran's horse.

"What happened to you?" Feran asked. "Wounded?"

"You mean my foot?"

"Your foot, your leg."

"An old injury. Just aggravated it."

"What do you want? We were about to ride to the camp for a bite to eat." None of the group had eaten anything since their meal at the inn.

Stephen told him quickly what he wanted. "I can't force you, but it would be a great favor if you helped."

A Curious Death

Feran stroked his chin. "What do you say, boys? Let Sir Stephen tackle those rascals on his own?"

"I don't suppose it matters if it doesn't take long," one of the others said.

"Right, then," Feran said. To Stephen he added, "What are you waiting for? Someone to fetch your horse?"

On the west side of the River Nene, there was a line of trees that Lord Edward had used to mask the movement of the portion of the royal army that had entered the town. Stephen, Feran and the other knights waited within that line of trees, hopefully invisible to anyone on the west wall of the castle. Not far away, the wheel of the castle mill creaked in the languid current.

"I'm getting hungry," Feran said.

"You're always hungry," one of the other knights said.

"Someone could ride down to the camp and fetch a bite," Feran said.

"Not a bad idea," another knight said.

"Especially if Attebrook's thinking about asking us to spend the night here," Feran said. "If I was them, I wouldn't try it until after dark."

"You may be right about that," Stephen murmured, although he had a feeling FitzSimmons would move before dark. He would gamble that the royalists had not discovered the little mill gate in the walls of the upper bailey and thought to post a watch upon it. That's what Stephen would do in FitzSimmons' place — get out as soon as possible and trust to your horses' speed to get away safely. But he was asking a lot of these men based only upon a feeling.

They had been here an hour and seen no movement. Worried that he had been too late, Stephen sent Wymar to the mill, and Wymar reported that he found no sign that any mounted men had crossed the stream anywhere nearby.

One hour dragged into a second and then a third. The men grew impatient, some pacing back and forth, others seated and muttering.

Then Feran, at the edge of the trees, said, "Something's happening."

Stephen peered around an elm. The little mill gate had opened and a helmetless armored man was leading a saddled horse through it. He peered about and called back to the gate, and mounted as another man came out. One after another, four more armored men passed through the portal and mounted their horses. Stephen's lips curled, for one of these men was Nigel FitzSimmons. The surge of hatred he felt for FitzSimmons caught him by surprise and made him dizzy, so that he almost failed to register that the last figure through the portal was a child. Even a hundred yards away, Stephen could see it was Oliver de Thottenham.

The horsemen walked their animals through the river and clambered up the far bank.

"Time to go," Stephen said, and the men ran for their horses.

They clapped helmets on their heads as they crashed through the tree line, galloping to intercept the enemy.

Alerted to the fact they had been discovered, FitzSimmons' men spurred their horses, but it was quickly clear that they could not avoid a collision with Stephen's companions.

"On them!" FitzSimmons shouted. "Right! Right!"

FitzSimmons' men knew their business and swung right with the grace of a flock of birds, assuming a V-shaped formation with four at the front and FitzSimmons, Oliver and another man behind. The three in the vanguard leveled lances and bore onward so quickly that the gap between the antagonists closed in only two or three heartbeats.

Stephen ached to get at FitzSimmons and strike him down for all the pain and fear that man had caused him, but he had to break through the vanguard first. He went at the leading man who, helmetless, leveled his point at Stephen's

A Curious Death

vulnerable throat. At the last moment, Stephen shifted his sword to the left side in what the Italians and Spaniards called the guard of the woman, point upright and hilt on his left breast — one of the best positions for countering a lance thrust.

And it was a good thing, for his enemy suddenly dropped the lance point to spear Stephen's horse — but he beat the shaft aside and swept the sword around into a middle cut that caught the lancer in the face.

This all happened faster than it takes to blink, and Stephen shot by the enemy without seeing him fall.

FitzSimmons was before him now; no one was between him and Stephen.

Stephen drove spurs into his horse, who responded with a terrific leap that, had he not been prepared for it, could have bucked him out of the saddle. He leveled his sword and drove forward, death in his mind.

He had a glimpse of FitzSimmons' startled expression, as if he had not expected any of his men to fail.

Then another of FitzSimmons' men came from behind the master spy and charged Stephen, sword held high to deliver a powerful blow.

Stephen could not reach FitzSimmons without dealing with this threat. He only had time to drop his sword to his right thigh to offer his head as a target as the FitzSimmons man delivered a vicious downward cut at Stephen's neck. But Stephen was prepared. He thrust out his blade, intercepting the cut and stabbing the rider in the face. The momentum of the two charging horses added such force to the blow that it went clear through the man's head and the blade stuck there, torn from Stephen's hand as the men separated.

Stephen wheeled his horse in an impossibly tight circle and reached his dying adversary as FitzSimmons charged toward him. Stephen leaned over and jerked his sword free as FitzSimmons struck two-handed with an axe. Stephen knocked aside the blow, and in an instant the two men were circling each other, striking, evading, retreating and charging in the intricate and deadly dance of single combat.

How long this dance went on it was impossible to say. It seemed like an eternity, yet was likely no more than moments.

Before it was tragically cut short.

Something hard and pointy struck Stephen a tremendous blow in the back — a lance point that broke links on his mail shirt and penetrated the thick padded jacket beneath it. He could feel, as if in slow motion, the point enter his skin and muscle and sticking on a rib. The force of the blow unbalanced him. He struggled to keep his seat and not to fall.

But this gave FitzSimmons his chance. Rising in his stirrups, he struck Stephen a terrific blow on the helmet.

Stephen felt the helmet give way and split.

It was the last thing he felt before all went black.

Nigel FitzSimmons was seldom frightened, but these last few moments had been an exception. When the royalist knight had burst through the vanguard, killing his lead man, took down Roger de Herland with a marvelously skillful thrust to the face, and then engaged him in a single combat that had been going against him, he had felt the wings of death upon his soul. It had frightened him badly.

He had time to catch his breath and his composure, because the battle had reached a stalemate. Three of the enemy were down, wounded and knocked about, but not dead, and all the attackers who could move had drawn off. FitzSimmons wondered why the enemy did not continue their attack because he was now outnumbered.

But when FitzSimmons looked down at the man he had fought, he began to understand why.

The split helmet had come off in the man's head and he lay face up on the grass.

It was his old enemy, Stephen Attebrook. He must be the leader of this warband. When the leader fell, often a band would lose heart. So it must be now, thank God.

A Curious Death

And it looked as though FitzSimmons had just killed him, for he had a wound on the head where the axe had penetrated the helmet, coif and arming cap. There was blood on his face.

It was a man FitzSimmons hated with all the passion of his body and soul.

"God's blood!" exclaimed the companion who had saved him, Walerand de Greystok. "I know that man!"

"What? How?" FitzSimmons asked.

"I saw him! In the castle! Just a few days ago!"

"In Northampton castle?" FitzSimmons was so overcome with shock, surprise and disbelief that his voice rose to a screech.

"At the southern gate! I was coming in. Gervase Haddon was with me and saw him too — and pursued him with two of our men! None returned!"

FitzSimmons had heard the story from Greystok. Haddon had run off, shouting over his shoulder that he had found a spy. FitzSimmons had been alarmed that Haddon disappeared and the search mounted afterward had not found a body. Now what happened was as clear as still water.

"They're dead then, after all," FitzSimmons growled, anger rising. He had suffered so many insults at the hands of the man who lay in the grass at his horse's feet, and retribution for every one of them had eluded him until now. A warm feeling of satisfaction, made sweet by its long denial, spread through him.

"Give me your lance," FitzSimmons said.

FitzSimmons pushed aside some of the mail protecting Attebrook's left thigh with the point and thrust the lance into the flesh. Attebrook didn't twitch. Good. Dead after all.

FitzSimmons smiled. He had his vengeance on this troublesome man at last.

A splash of color in the trees to the south caught FitzSimmons' eye — more horsemen approaching at a gallop. It could only be royalist cavalry who had heard the commotion.

"We must fly," FitzSimmons said.

"But, sir," Greystok said. "What about —" He waved at the FitzSimmons' men who had been unhorsed but were still alive, and at Oliver de Thottenham, who was being led away from the field by a squire.

"We'll have to leave them," FitzSimmons said. "Unless you want to end up paying a ransom."

Greystok shook his head. He was well off, but ransoms could break even the richest families.

They rode fast for the trees to the west.

Chapter 27

Saturday afternoon, the fifth of April, a terrible sensation roused Gilbert from a fitful, feverish sleep. It was an odd thing, like nothing he had ever experienced before — a terrific fluttering of the heart as if a frantic bird was imprisoned in his chest.

"What's the matter?" Begilda stuck her head in the tent. "Master Gilbert! Are you alright?"

Gilbert sat up, hands over his wounded heart. The fluttering was subsiding, and he felt the heart beating normally, although it seemed a tad fast.

"I think so," he said. He rubbed his face. "I had a dream. A terrible dream."

"What about, sir?" Begilda asked cautiously. Dreams were often significant, especially bad ones.

"I saw Stephen. Lying on the grass."

"Oh!" Dreams about people could be especially important.

"There was something dark on his face. Like blood." Gilbert shook his head. "I don't know. It was hard to tell." The memory of dreams often faded quickly, and this one was no exception, leaving only a sense of disturbance and disquiet behind. "It's probably nothing."

"But, sir!" Begilda said, alarmed at this disclosure. "The lord!"

Gilbert blew his nose on a rag and lay back. His nose was as plugged as an ale barrel and he had to breathe through his mouth, which was as dry as a parched stream and sore in spots. "It's just a dream. I've been having some strange ones."

"Just the fever then?" Begilda asked, although she could not keep her concern from her voice.

Gilbert patted her hand. "Probably nothing."

He closed his eyes, and the breath rattled in his dry throat.

Begilda returned to her place on a stool outside the tent and picked up the sock she had been darning. The sock sat on her lap for a long time before she went back to work.

Gilbert's fever broke during the night, and by sunrise, he felt much better. He ate some of that foul porridge by a fire that only Begilda attended since everyone in their tent circle — like almost everyone else in camp — had gone to Northampton with the army. As much as he complained about the porridge, he was glad for it because he had had only weak broth since he fell sick. Broth goes right through a man, like wine, prompting him to rise to pee during the night, a torture when he is sick, while porridge sticks to the ribs despite its defects. What he wouldn't give for a mince pie, though.

A mince pie and a bath. He had sweated profusely during his confinement, and he smelled foul, even to himself. You knew it was bad when your own odor offended you.

Tramping about Oxford had given Gilbert a good sense of what could be found in the town, but he was aware of only one place where he could get a mince pie and a bath at the same time.

He stumbled back to the tent for his purse, which he could not locate.

Begilda rose by his pallet, his folded blanket on one forearm. "What are you doing now? I've just straightened things up. You're making a mess."

"Looking for my purse."

Begilda fished in her pouch and came out with said purse.

"What are you doing with it?" Gilbert asked suspiciously.

"I needed money for your medicine and food for the both of us. Where else was I to get it?"

"Oh, yes. Is there any left?" he asked with some alarm, fearing the loss of the mince pie.

"Some. Enough to get us through, I suppose, until Wymar gets back."

"Let me see it, then." Gilbert held out his hand, visions of mince pie causing his mouth to water. He inspected the contents of the purse, and while their funds were significantly depleted, there was enough for mince pie, a bath, and for food and shelter on their return journey to Ludlow.

"You've been frugal, I see," Gilbert allowed grudgingly.

"You've got something on your mind," Begilda said. "What is it?"

"How would you like a mince pie and a bath? When was the last time you had one?"

"The mince pie or the bath?"

"Both."

"I can't remember."

"Then let's go."

Having an intention was different than having the ability to carry it out, however. Gilbert got no more than a dozen paces when he got dizzy and collapsed. Begilda helped him back to the tent, with Bill's yapping encouragement, where Gilbert remained until the afternoon, and the three of them made it to the Castle Keep on the second attempt.

Despite the army's departure, the bathhouse hall was almost full when they arrived. They found seats at one end of an occupied table, had two mince pies each (they were small) and scraps for Bill, and having paid up for that tied Bill's leash to a table leg, and went to the doorway leading to the tub room, where they ran into Hilde. Gilbert requested two tubs.

"We've none unoccupied at the moment," the redhaired Hilde informed him. "But I'll ask if anyone wants to share." It was not uncommon for strangers to share a tub, even men with women when none were available for single occupancy. But people could refuse, which might mean a long wait.

"I'm surprised to find you here," Gilbert said.

"Why?" Hilde asked with narrowed eyes.

"I ran into your betrothed, Richard, few days ago. He said you were leaving town, for Wallingford, I think he said."

Hilde smiled, an expression that only affected her mouth. "We are. But not yet."

"Ah, your wedding dress — it takes time to be made."

"Dresses do, sometimes."

"Well, best wishes to you. We've come for a bath. Are there any tubs with only women in them?" Gilbert asked. "My servant here, as you can see, is a young girl of tender age. It wouldn't be right if you put her in with men."

"There are two," Hilde said. "I'll see. Back in a moment."

She returned shortly and beckoned them to follow. She stopped at the second alcove on the left. "Your servant can use this one." She pointed to the fourth on the right, the same one Dinesley had used on the day he died. "The fellow in that one says it's all right."

As Hilde went back to the hall, Gilbert paused at the opening in the curtains of the death alcove. That it was still being used was a bit unsettling, but then people died in houses that were not abandoned afterward. But in those houses, a priest had usually performed an exorcism to dispel any lingering spirit who might cause trouble. Gilbert doubted that had happened here.

Gilbert shivered, pushed the curtain aside and entered.

The tub had only one occupant. He was a man slightly older than Gilbert but with gray hair and a thick beard that was sopping with bath water. He had a bulbous nose in the middle of a carewarn face.

The man said something that sounded vaguely like English. But the whole of it made no sense to Gilbert.

"I beg your pardon?" Gilbert said.

When the fellow spoke again, his words, though garbled and tortured, seemed to say, "I said, get in here and close the curtain. You're letting in the wind."

"Sorry."

"You're not from around here," the bather said.

"No, I'm from the March."

"Ah, the West Country. I thought so. You can hardly talk English."

"And you?" Gilbert began to undress.

"Northumbria. Born and raised on the Holy Island itself. I'm Hugh Nelonde."

A Curious Death

"Gilbert Wistwode," Gilbert said, easing into the tub while trying not to slosh out any water, as you paid by the bucket. He sank down with satisfaction, for the water was warm and soothing, and there wasn't much dirt scum on top. "You're a long way from home, then."

"Ah, me work brought me here," Nelonde said.

"What business are you in?"

"I'm not in business!" Nelonde said, offended. "I'm a soldier!"

"Oh," Gilbert said. "I'm sorry. Why aren't you with the army in Northampton, then?"

"Northampton? That's where the king's gone? How do you know?"

"I've a friend who's with the army. He told me."

"Well, I'll be. No, I'm at the castle."

"Part of the permanent garrison, I take it."

"You take it right," Nelonde said with pride.

"Did you know Miles de Dinesley?"

"Course I did. He was the deputy constable."

"Did you know that he died in this alcove, in this very tub?" Gilbert said. He wasn't sure about the tub, but he enjoyed the shock value of the claim.

Nelonde shot to his feet, sending a wave that smacked Gilbert in the face and washed over the sides. "You're having me on."

"No. I was here at the time. Just a bit down that way."

Nelonde settled back down. It had to be cold standing up and all wet. "You think it's alright?"

"You know what they do with houses when someone dies. I expect they did the same here."

"I hope so. I wouldn't want that bastard haunting me. He could be damned unpleasant when he had a mind to."

"Dinesley?"

"Who else did you think? My old man?" Nelonde said.

"I'm just surprised you'd speak of him that way."

"I can now that he's dead. Even though you're not supposed to speak ill of the dead." Nelonde scowled. "The bastard once had me pull a full night's watch. Just because I didn't clean his mail to his satisfaction."

It took a moment for Gilbert appreciate the importance of this. But then he remembered from conversations with Stephen about how castles were run. The watch stood for an hour, sometimes two, but not for a full night, since they had duties in the daytime to fulfill. To be forced to remain on watch a whole night meant a difficult following day.

Nelonde went on, "He could be a bastard to those who didn't give him what he wanted."

"How so?"

"It was mostly women. He fancied them. He had the charm, and he seemed to like employing it. But if the woman refused?" He threw up his hands.

"What do you mean?" Gilbert threw up his hands in the same way Nelonde had done.

"He forced her."

"As in rape."

Nelonde nodded.

"How to you know this? Privy gossip? Rumor?"

Nelonde drummed his fingers on the edge of the tub. "I heard about one from someone who was there."

Gilbert was shocked at this, but he said nothing. Sometimes it was better to do that than ask a question.

Nelonde said, "It was one of Dinesley's retainers. He told me. We were out drinking in the town, and he had a little too much. And the thing bothered him. He wasn't right with it. It was a weight on his soul. He had to unburden himself."

"I see," Gilbert said. There was a long silence. Nelonde did not seem eager to fill it, so Gilbert asked, "What happened?"

"You know Elias de Fanecurt?"

"He's one of the town's coroners, isn't he?"

"Right. He had a wife. Pretty young thing. Don't know how an old gnome like Fanecurt ended up with a woman like that. Money, probably. It's always the money with that crowd. Anyway, Dinesley took a shine to her. Saw her in the market, followed her home. Fanecurt has a townhouse, you know. Went over when Fanecurt was out of town on coroner business. Spent a lot of time with her. But apparently she rejected him." He took a deep breath. "Because a couple of months ago, Dinesley and several of his boys rode out to the Fanecurt manor when she as there alone and ... and he raped her. The servants found her in the barn. She hung herself."

Gilbert was so startled that he couldn't think of a thing to say.

Fortunately, he was saved from carrying on his side of this conversation by a harried-looking serving girl who poked her head through the gap in the canvas curtains.

"You gents need a refill?" she asked, flourishing a clay pitcher.

"I'll have one," Nelonde said. He held out his cup.

"What about you?" the serving girl asked Gilbert.

"I'm fine," he said. "I don't remember seeing you here. Are you Gillian?" He suddenly recalled he had not questioned Gillian, which he should have done.

"She quit," the girl said. "She and Midge. So we're short-handed back here."

"Midge quit?" Gilbert asked. "Do you know why?"

"She took a job in town with her mother."

She started to withdraw, but Nelonde said, "Stay a moment."

"What more you want?"

"This fellow," Nelonde waved his cup at Gilbert, "claims that Sir Miles de Dinesley died here — in this very tub. Is that true?"

"That's what I heard," the serving girl said matter-of-factly. "You done?"

"I should say so." Nelonde drank deeply.

Gilbert wandered back to the hall, disturbed by what he had just learned.

Begilda was nowhere to be seen — likely still enjoying her bath — and Bill pulled at his leash at the sight of Gilbert, eager to be free. He spotted Hilde across the hall, arguing with a drunken customer over a bill. The customer swore that he had had only two pitchers, not three. Hilde settled the dispute by summoning Richard from behind the bar, who threw the customer to the ground and relieved him of the additional money for the third pitcher.

"You'll pay for that!" the customer shouted as Richard escorted him to the door, twisting an arm behind the customer's back. "Hey! You're hurting me!"

"I'll break it off if you keep it up," Richard growled before tossing the fellow through the door where he landed in a puddle.

"That was a bit rough," Gilbert said to Hilde.

"He's more trouble than he's worth," Hilde said. "Besides, it pays to set an example that we can't be cheated."

She stepped away, but Gilbert touched her arm.

"I have a question," Gilbert said.

Hilde crossed her arms and frowned. "I have a feeling this isn't about the state of the bathwater."

"Er, no. I recall you mentioning that Dinesley had a habit of being rough with women. Had he misbehaved with any of the girls here?"

Hilde paused before answering. She seemed to be trying to keep her face blank but there was an element of calculation in her eyes. "Miles was a bit rough with one of the girls. Knocked her about some. But he paid up, and handsomely. So it was water under the bridge."

"How could that be? Surely, you barred him after that."

Hilde shrugged. "If it had been anybody else, yes. But he spent too much money here." She licked her lip and added. "And I had a message from the town bailiffs that I ought not to do anything about it. Or they'd shut the place down."

"So you tried to have him barred."

"I gave the order, yeah. But, circumstances, you know?"

"When was this?"

"A couple of months ago?"

"And which girl was it?"

Hilde pointed to a thin blonde girl who was sitting on a burgher's lap. Strands of her hair had come undone from beneath her headscarf and wreathed her face. The left side of her jaw was bent, crooked. "Sara, there."

"Can I have a moment with her?"

"If you must. But don't take long."

Hilde caught Sara's attention and beckoned to her. Sara rose from the customer's lap.

"What's wanted, Hilde?"

"This little man is investigating the unfortunate accident that befell our client."

"You mean, Dinesley," Sara said, lips and eyes narrowing.

"The very same," Hilde said.

"What do you want then?" Sara asked Gilbert.

"I understand Dinesley roughed you up," Gilbert said, hesitantly. "I wondered if you would tell me about it."

Sara shrugged. "Not much to tell. He wanted to tie me up and have his way with me. I don't do that, no matter how much the client is willing to pay. When I refused, he smashed me jaw." She put a finger to the bent place. "Broke it clean. And did it anyway."

"Have you fully recovered?" Gilbert asked sympathetically.

"Do I look like I have?" Sara said with some heat. "I'll never be the same. I wasn't much to look at before — and now?"

She spun away and returned to the client's lap.

"I'm sorry," Gilbert said, although Sara was out of earshot.

"Sorry don't mean much," Hilde said.

Gilbert waited by Bill for Begilda to show up. The lift that the bath had given him seeped away, leaving him listless, tired, his mind filled with sludge. Slouched on a bench, he scratched

Bill's head and fed him an occasional scrap as his thoughts stuck in the mire. He learned quite a lot today, but he was still no closer to finding Dinesley's killer. His newest best suspect, Sara, had both a reason to kill Dinesley and perhaps the chance. Since she worked here, she could have slipped into Dinesley's alcove without anyone remarking on it. In fact, he could imagine Hilde conspiring with Sara for that very purpose. It brought revenge and ridded Hilde of a nasty client.

Begilda, meanwhile, emerged from the baths looking like a new person. She wore the same shabby clothes but wore an engaging smile that highlighted the freckles on her cheeks. She was freshly scrubbed, with clean nails and sopping hair from which no amount of wringing had dispelled all the water. At least I did some good today, Gilbert thought.

"You look well," Gilbert said.

"And you look like a cart ran over you," Begilda said. She felt Gilbert's forehead. "You're warm. We shouldn't have gone out today."

Gilbert stood up. This took more effort than he expected. His back creaked so that he thought the whole hall could hear it. "Don't worry. I won't die on your watch."

"I'm counting on it. I have no idea how to get to Ludlow. I doubt Lord Stephen will be back any time soon to show me the way."

"Lord Stephen," Gilbert muttered. He had not got used to thinking of Stephen as a lord, although he was entitled to be called one.

There was no reason why such a thought would lead to anything, but it was as if a bright light had suddenly burst in Gilbert's head. *Of course!*

"Come on," he said suddenly, marching toward the door. Well, it felt like a march in his mind, but was probably only a fast hobble.

He was gasping by the time they reached Little Gate, where he paused to catch his breath before hurrying up Saint Ebbe's Street. He swerved left onto Church Street, heading toward the massive barbican of Oxford Castle and stopped

A Curious Death

about halfway there. He counted the houses from the corner to be sure. The house in front of him was well-built with a ground floor of plastered stone capped by three upper floors of timber, the wood painted black and the wattle between it plastered white as well so that in full daylight the effect must be blinding. The house shone. It beamed with pride, and was clearly the residence of a wealthy gentleman, for no shop filled the space facing the street.

Gilbert stepped up to the door and knocked.

A young woman answered. It was Midge. She took one look at Gilbert and fled, leaving the door ajar.

"Midge!" said a woman out of sight inside the house. "What in the world!"

The elderly woman came to the door. She had deep lines on either side of her mouth running from eyes to chin.

"Yes?" she demanded. She glanced at Begilda and Bill. "Do you have some business here?"

"I'd like to speak with Lord Elias," Gilbert said.

"My lord is not home," the elderly woman said.

"Is he in town? Or in the country?" Gilbert asked.

"Mother!" Midge's muffled voice said from somewhere inside. "Send him away!"

"He is in the country," the elderly woman snapped. Her mouth tightened and Gilbert sensed what was coming next.

He threw his shoulder against the door as the woman pushed to close it. She was a slight woman, but stronger than she looked, and it took Gilbert a considerable effort to press the door open with his shoulder and step inside.

"You leave this instant or I shall call the bailiffs!" the elderly woman snarled.

"Call away," Gilbert said. "I am here on an official inquiry. The bailiffs will not interfere." He hoped they wouldn't, anyway.

"You have no official position!"

"I am the official representative of the earl of Arundel. That is enough."

Midge's mother snorted. "You look like you're not fit to be in charge of trimming hedges, let alone conduct some inquiry."

"Nevertheless, I am," Gilbert said.

There was a gap between the old woman and a wall. Gilbert took advantage of this gap by rushing into it and gaining the hall, although he had a perturbed and angry old woman at his heels, yapping protests.

He saw with relief that Midge was still in the hall, cowering by a post supporting an overhead passage from the rear first floor to the forward portion.

She looked worried, perhaps even frightened.

"What are you doing here, Midge?" Gilbert asked.

"I work here," she said.

"Yes, she does," Midge's mother said, now taking position between Gilbert and Midge as if to protect her. "She is my assistant."

"A new position, though, eh?" Gilbert said.

"What if it is," Midge said.

"It is a curious coincidence," Gilbert said. "This is your mother, but only suddenly, only now, do you find a position in this house. When before you were forced to work in a bathhouse for your upkeep."

"Circumstances change," Midge said.

"And a further coincidence that you found Miles de Dinesley dead in his tub and your present master ruled his death an accident."

"Sir Elias can be wrong, sometimes," the mother said. "He forms his opinions rather quicker than is sometimes prudent."

"Yes," Gilbert said. "Some men are like that. Too many, probably." He fished out the silver button and held out his palm.

The eyes of both women went wide and their mouths opened in shocked surprise. But only for an instant. Then the mother's face was a rigid mask, while Midge looked nervous.

"You have seen this before," Gilbert said.

A Curious Death

"No. We haven't," the mother said shortly.

"I say, what have you there?" said a male voice from the stairs. It was a stringy, balding man. "Where did you get that?"

"Go *away*, Benjamin!" the mother snapped. "I shall take care of this."

"No," Gilbert said, passing around the mother, who attempted to cut him off. He reached the foot of the stairs and held out the button. "You have seen this before."

Benjamin nodded, descending to the bottom of the stairs, where he bent over Gilbert's palm. "Yes, indeed. It looks like a button from a set my lord had commissioned in London. What is this about?"

"And Sir Elias lost just such a button recently," Gilbert said. It seemed more forceful and convincing to make this a statement rather than a question.

"He did, indeed. Fortunately, I was able to mend it easily. We have several spares. You know how buttons are always getting lost, and these are expensive and rare."

Gilbert held out the button again to the mother and Midge. "You know where I found this."

"I have no idea," the mother said with a shake of her head.

"I found it, or should I say my principle, Sir Stephen Attebrook, found it in the alcove at the moment Midge found Miles de Dinesley's body."

"What of it?" the mother said. "Someone could have found it and lost it there."

"Perhaps," Gilbert said. "But that's not what happened. You see, we, Sir Stephen and I, have puzzled over this from the start. Men — and women — need a reason to kill. And there seems to be a townful of people with reasons to hate Dinesley, reasons that could provoke many to murder.

"But you also need opportunity. And that's been the most difficult part. There is one other who had reason and the opportunity, yet I do not think it was her. So here is what I think happened. We know that Dinesley raped Lady Fanecurt and she took her own life as a result, unable to live with the shame."

Midge, her mother and Benjamin all drew breath sharply.

"You — you know about that?" Benjamin asked in a quavering voice. "No one knew! It was a secret! We promised to carry it to the grave!"

"One of the men with Dinesley confessed to the crime," Gilbert said. "Thus, giving Sir Elias the most powerful reason to want Dinesley dead. What could he do? He could appeal for murder against Dinesley. But Dinesley surely would demand trial by combat and act as his own champion, for he was a formidable fighter. Or he could hire one. Either way, Sir Elias, hobbled as he is, would have to hire a champion, and there was every reason to worry that the combat could go against him. He would hang as a false accuser if that happened.

"So what did he do? He was determined to kill Dinesley, and he wanted to do it himself. The insult was too grave to leave to another. So he enlisted Midge here to get him into the bathhouse when the coast was clear, and get him out again. She knows how easily that could be accomplished. There is a side door to the yard, where everyone's vision is obstructed by the woodpile. It would be a simple thing for Sir Elias to slip in, stab Dinesley in the neck as he rested unaware in his tub, and escape." Gilbert fingered the button. "I imagine Sir Elias put his weak arm around Dinesley's neck to hold him still for a moment and in the struggle to deliver the dagger blow, Dinesley tore this loose."

But then, it occurred to Gilbert that this was wrong. Dinesley's withered arm lacked the strength. He pointed a finger at Midge. "You made it possible! You held Dinesley's head so he could be slain! Confess it!"

The accusation hung in the air. Then Midge broke the silence with wracking sobs. She buried her face in her hands and nodded.

"You have no idea what he was like!" she cried through her fingers. "He was a monster! He preyed on women!"

A Curious Death

"And you," Gilbert said gently with sudden and uncomfortable insight. "What did he do to you?"

Midge straightened up. "I was a virgin. The working girls made fun of me because of it, and he overheard. After that, he was relentless. He pestered me to yield to him. He offered me incredible sums, but I refused. I am no whore. So, one evening, at one of their parties, he dragged me into an upper chamber and he took me. He forced me! Now I am soiled and no decent man will want me."

"Leave her alone!" the mother barked as she put her arms around Midge. "If someone hadn't acted, other women will have suffered the same fate as my Midge and darling Lady Fanecurt. Now, be off and make your appeal in court, and we will see what becomes of it!"

They reached the street before Begilda finally spoke.

"And you believe her?" Begilda asked.

Gilbert paused to think. "I do. I do believe her."

"That's good. So do I."

"So that makes the two of us. We can't be wrong, then, can we? It's a consensus."

"What's a consensus?"

"When people agree on what is right thinking. Come on. Let's get supper."

"There's nothing but old porridge back at camp."

"We'll see what the taverns have to offer. I think we've earned a reward."

They set off down Church Street in the gathering dark.

Chapter 28

The sun hurt Stephen's eyes. Its light fell hard on his face and when he opened them to see where he was, pain shot from his eyeballs clear to the back of his skull. When he raised a hand for the added shade it could provide, his fingers found a bandage wrapped around his head. The bandage was damp and crusty in spots, where he discovered the wound. Try as he might, he could not remember how he got it. The last thing he remembered was charging at the men in front of FitzSimmons.

It took a while to figure out where he was. The jolting, however, suggested that he was in a cart or wagon, and further investigation revealed that he was lying on a linen pallet filled with straw. There was no mistaking the occasional sharp pricks in the back and buttocks that were the hallmark of a straw mattress. His left thigh hurt, too, and his fingers found another bandage there. How had he got that wound? He had no memory of it, either.

He listened for voices, but there were no sounds but the creaking of the cart or wagon and of the harness of the horse, and horses' plodding steps. There was only one horse pulling the cart, and two others following; he was sure of it. So, this had to be a one-horse cart. He felt proud that he had figured this out before a wave of nausea swept over him and he dry wretched.

The cart stopped and a voice said, "My lord! You're awake! At last!"

"Barely," Stephen said, not daring to open his eyes. "Where are we, Wymar?"

"Almost to Oxford, sir!"

"How long have I been out?"

"Two days."

Two days! He felt lucky to be alive. He had seen men take a blow on the head as he must have done who never woke up.

"Did you get Oliver?"

"I did," Wymar said with pride. "I snatched his bridle while you kept them busy!"

A Curious Death

"My crafty plan worked, then," Stephen said, smiling wanly even though it hurt his face. "How is the boy doing?"

"He tried running away twice. I've had to tie him to a horse."

"Oliver!" Stephen croaked.

"Yes?" a child's sulky voice answered.

"Do you know why you're here?"

"That man said." That man being Wymar, no doubt.

"So you know I have . . . we have . . . been asked by your mother to return you home," Stephen said.

"That's what he said," Oliver replied.

Stephen sensed that Oliver did not believe this. So, he went on, "You can believe or not. Though you will when your mother takes custody of you. In the meantime, you understand that you are of gentle birth?"

"Yes," the boy said.

"And you know that certain rules apply to men of gentle birth when captured in battle?"

"Yes."

"Those rules apply to you as well as they do to grown men. You can consider yourself a prisoner of war being held for ransom. You understand that it is dishonorable to run away under such circumstances — especially if you have given an oath?"

"I've given no oath."

"But he can curse like a sailor," Wymar said under his breath.

"Do you want to be untied from that horse?" Stephen asked.

"Yes."

"Then you will swear that you will not leave us until your ransom is paid?"

There was silence.

"Is that satisfactory?" Stephen asked.

"Yes."

"Then give your oath."

Stephen was able to sit up by the time they reached Oxford in the late afternoon. The grass in the field north of town where the army had camped, normally the home to cows and horses, was still trampled down from the thousands of men who occupied it until a short time ago, which gave it a forlorn appearance. Not all had gone, however. There were four tents spread about and as many cooking fires. One of those tents, a blue one with yellow trim, Stephen had rented in Ludlow, and it was where he left it. He was tired of the tortures of the cart and was glad to see that respite lay at hand.

The dog Bill was the first to sense their appearance, and barked a challenge, which brought Gilbert and Begilda, who had been sitting by the fire, to their feet.

"Oh, dear Lord!" Gilbert exclaimed as the cart halted. "What happened to you?"

"I don't remember," Stephen said. "I seem to have taken a knock on the head. Don't have any idea how it got there."

"That must be some knock. Let me have a look at it."

Stephen could not climb over the cart's railings, however. It took Wymar lifting him and Gilbert and Begilda catching to get him out, and even then they failed in the catching so that Stephen landed in a huddle at their feet.

"Well, it took four men to get him in the cart," Wymar said, sympathetically. "Not a surprise that you'd drop him."

With Wymar on one side and Gilbert on the other, they managed to carry Stephen to the campfire, where he slumped gratefully onto a camp stool.

"What's for supper?" Stephen asked optimistically, eyeing the iron kettle hanging over the fire.

"The usual," Gilbert said. "But I think you'll need something more." He handed a few coins to Begilda. "See if you can fetch some broth for our lordship from the Rusty Nail."

As Begilda ran off toward town, Gilbert started unwinding the bandage about Stephen's head.

"Don't just stand there, Wymar," Gilbert said. "Get my linen sheet. We'll make a bandage out of that. Now, let's see here." He bent over Stephen's head. "Nasty cut, but it's closed up and doesn't look infected." He probed the skull on either side of the cut. "Nothing seems to be broken up there. I imagine you should be fine. I take it that's Oliver."

Stephen nodded.

"So, then, did we win the battle?" Gilbert asked. "By the look of you, I wouldn't be willing to bet on it."

Wymar returned with the sheet, which he handed to Gilbert, who began cutting strips from it with his small knife.

"Did we ever!" Wymar exclaimed.

"Ever what?" Gilbert asked.

"Win the battle, of course. You should have seen Sir Stephen! He knocked four men off their horses!"

"That many?" Stephen murmured.

"Maybe five!"

"Five," Gilbert said, with a false air of being impressed. "I've known Stephen to knock one or two off at once, but five!"

Gilbert finished rebandaging Stephen's head. "Let's have a look at that leg of yours." Before he attacked the leg bandage, he felt Stephen's head and frowned. As he cut through the bandage, he said, "You've a fever, you know."

"I am a little under the weather. I thought it was the knock on the head."

"It might be that, but I think this has something to do with it," Gilbert said, pointing to the leg wound. "It looks like you were speared in the thigh. And it's infected."

And it was. The wound, no more than two inches long, was open and seeping, with redness about it.

"Let's hope we can do something about that," Gilbert said. He entered the tent and returned with a leather flask. He poured the contents, which proved to be red wine, on the wound. "We'll let it air for a bit. That sometimes helps."

They were quiet while waiting for Begilda to return. Gilbert spooned out porridge for Wymar and Oliver, and then for himself and Stephen. They had to share the bowl, owing to a shortage of bowls.

Stephen ate his porridge without appetite, or any appreciation for the fact the barley and oats were well cooked and soft, and none of it was burnt. A cold fear had taken root in his stomach at the realization that his leg was infected. He had known infection in seemingly minor wounds to carry off many men.

"You know," Gilbert said, as if sensing Stephen's thoughts. "The wound's near the knee. If it gets really bad, you might be able to have the leg off."

"No," Stephen said, cupping the bowl. "I don't want to end up like Harry." Ending up like Harry, who had no legs above the knees, was the most terrifying prospect in the world.

"You might have a chance of surviving," Gilbert persisted.

"No need to think about that yet," Stephen said. "All I want to do now is go home."

"You should rest for a few days."

"We leave tomorrow."

A Curious Death

Chapter 29

Harry the legless woodcarver heard the creak of a cart outside his shop at the front of Stephen Attebrook's Ludlow townhouse. It stopped by the open window.

The stopping of carts outside the shop was not unknown, but it was not a daily occurrence. Usually, it meant the delivery of wood that Harry had ordered or a customer dropping off wood that he wanted worked. Curious that it might be a customer since he had made no orders, Harry pulled himself to the shelf at the window to see who it was.

It was not a customer. It was Gilbert and Wymar, looking exhausted, and a strange young girl and a sullen-faced small boy.

Then Harry saw what lay in the cart.

"Blessed Jesus!" Harry cried. "What happened?"

"A bit of bad luck," Gilbert said.

Harry's powerful arms were capable of projecting him some distance if the need arose — leaping up onto shelves was only a bit of what he could do. And he acted now. He threw himself across the considerable gap between the windowsill and the cart, where he caught the railing and pulled himself into the back. Harry and Wymar were used to such acrobatics, but the girl and boy gaped in mingled horror and astonishment.

"Pay no mind to Harry. You'll get used to him," Gilbert said tiredly to the boy and the girl.

Harry felt Stephen's cheek. "He's burning up!"

"He took a spear thrust in the leg," Gilbert said. "I thought it might heal, but it's got worse."

"What happened to his hair?" Harry exclaimed. "It's all cut off!" He actually could only see Stephen's head over his right ear, which wasn't covered by the bandage. There was stubble in place of Stephen's long black locks.

"It was part of a disguise," Gilbert said.

"What will Ida think of it? Stephen, bald as a bowling ball!"

"She's got more to worry about than Stephen's lack of hair."

"We need to get him in bed!" Harry turned toward the window. "Joan! Come quick! We need your help!"

It proved impossible to carry a limp, unconscious Stephen up the steep and narrow stairs to the bedchambers on the first floor. So, they put Stephen to bed on Harry and Joan's pallet in the hall.

They knelt about the pallet (except for Oliver, who slunk into a far corner and glanced at the door as if contemplating escape) while Joan cut up linen for new bandages and replaced the old ones. The head wound seemed to be healing nicely, but the one on the leg was swollen and bright red at the edges and there were filaments of crimson emanating from it.

"Do you think he'll make it?" Harry asked.

Gilbert shook his head. "I'm beginning to think not."

"Ida needs to be here," Harry said. "Wymar! Ride straightaway for Priors Halton. Bring Ida back."

"Should I fetch the priest as well?" asked Joan.

"Not yet," said a grim Harry. "Meanwhile, we'll pray and hope that makes a difference."

Ida arrived after dark. The horses had been slow, since they were tired from a full day on the road in addition to the six miles out and back to the manor.

She rushed into the hall while Wymar put up the horses in the Broken Shield Inn's stable.

She threw herself down by Stephen and took his face in her hands. Her eyes flicked to Oliver, still in his corner.

"That's him, eh?" Ida spat. "Thottenham's boy?"

"Yes," Gilbert said.

"And Stephen got this taking him back?" Ida asked.

"Yes."

"Oh, Stephen, you utter fool! Look what you've done!"

A Curious Death

Ida wiped tears from her eyes as Joan peeled back the bandage on Stephen's leg to show her what he was up against. She grimaced.

"It looks bad," she said miserably.

"I'm afraid it is," Joan said.

Meanwhile, Stephen stirred and muttered something. Ida leaned close to hear what it was.

"It sounded like 'Taresa, wait,'" she said. "Who is Taresa?"

"His dead wife," Gilbert said. "Christopher's mother."

"He never told me her name."

"It hurt him to speak of her," Gilbert said.

"Is there nothing we can do?" Ida asked.

"Call for a surgeon to cut of that leg?" Gilbert said.

"There isn't anyone in Ludlow skilled enough for that," Harry said.

Ida clasped shaking hands and forced herself to think. There was one physician in Ludlow, an elderly man living in Corve Street. She had heard he did not like his sleep disturbed and refused to make calls after sundown.

"Stephen told me once of an herb woman," Ida said. People with knowledge of herbs were often as good or better than a university-trained physician.

"Julia," Harry said.

"Where can she be found?"

"She lives in a shack in the woods off Upper Galdeford Road," Harry said.

"Do you know how to get there?"

"It's over there," Harry said, pointing across a dark field to a wood silhouetted against a starry sky and the light of a three-quarter moon. The orange light of a fire twinkled among the trees. "I think."

"You think?" Ida said impatiently.

"Only one way to find out," Harry said.

He turned his pony off the road, clambered down and up the sides of a ditch, holding precariously to the pony's mane since he was riding bareback.

Ida gave her borrowed horse her heels with a snap of a whip and jumped the ditch to catch up to him.

They picked up a path around the margins of the field, which was planted in winter wheat.

Presently, they reached the wood and ducked under low branches, the leaf buds rustling with their passage.

The hut was just within the wood under a huge oak.

A thin old woman wearing rags squatted before a fire over which a kettle was boiling.

"What have we here?" the old woman said. She did not seem the least bit fazed by the sudden appearance of mounted strangers. "You're Harry Carver, aren't you?"

He nodded.

"I've heard of you," the old woman said.

"I am Ida Attebrook," Ida said. "You know my husband, Stephen."

"We've met, yes."

"He's injured. His wound has festered, and he is in a bad way. Is there anything you can do?"

When Ida rode through Galdeford Gate to fetch Julia, the gate warden had assured her that he would stay up to let her back in. But when they returned, no amount of pounding on the gate, shouting, or cursing brought the warden to the window to see who it was.

Ida shot off a final string of curses promising death and retribution that made even the hardened Harry blanch. Still, there was no response from either of the gate towers.

She spun her horse, nearly losing Julia riding pillion who had never been aboard a horse before and had no idea what to expect, and thundered back across the drawbridge.

A Curious Death

"We'll try Broad Gate!" Ida shouted over her shoulder at Harry, who tried to keep up, but was only comfortable with a fast trot, for fear of falling off.

"Hold on!" Ida cried to Julia, and felt the old woman's hands tighten about her waist, as Ida asked the horse for a gallop.

It was not that far from Galdeford to Broad Street, but it seemed an eternity before Ida careered along a garden path of a house fronting on Broad Street and the great drum-shaped towers of the gate heaved into view, glowing silver in the moonlight.

She tried beating on the gate, but on horseback, she didn't make as much noise as she wanted. So, she dismounted, and, using the butt of her dagger, pounded as hard as she could, shrieking, "Gip! Get your lame-witted arse out of bed this instant!"

"Yeah, Gip," Harry gasped as he drew up, his pony's hooves drumming forlornly on the planks of the drawbridge which spanned the town ditch. "We're in a bit of a hurry!"

Ida's exertions, with their cloud of profanity, went on for several minutes before there was thumping and knocking behind the gate, and the little window at head height swung open.

"Now, now!" Gip's voice said, slurring due to his missing teeth, "what is this ruckus about? Don't you know it's long past curfew?"

"Gip, if you don't open the gate this instant, I will give you a piece of my mind in the morning that you will regret," Ida gasped, out of breath from all the shouting.

"Oh!" Gip exclaimed, poking his face through the window so he could be sure who it was. "Lady Ida! I had no idea such a lady as you even knew that kind of language. What are you doing out there? And you, too, Harry? How are you, lad?"

"Anxious to get in," Harry said. "It's important."

"And who is that with you?" Gip inquired.

"Julia, the herb woman," Ida said.

"Julia the witch, you mean," Gip grumbled.

"I am not a witch," Julia said.

"Witches are not the best judge of whether they are witches," Gip said.

"The next time one of your teeth gets an abscess, don't look for my help," Julia said. "It can rot in your head if you don't show some courtesy."

"I, ahem, well," Gip said and began to fumble with the gate's bar. "You'll have something for old Gip's bending the rules for you, won't you, my lady?"

"I will see you again in the morning," Ida said testily as she led her horse through the gate with Julia still aboard.

She remounted behind Julia this time, and kicked the horse, which bounded up Broad Street's steep hill.

At the townhouse, she slipped off, threw down the reins not caring what happened to the horse, pulled Julia off and dragged her inside.

Someone had fed the hearth fire, and it was blazing high when Ida and Julia entered the hall.

There was no mistaking the patient, who was out cold on his pallet with a damp rag on his forehead.

"Where is this wound?" Julia asked.

Ida cut the linen bandage away from Stephen's leg with her dagger.

Julia bent close. "Have you a candle or a rush light?"

"A candle, quickly!" Ida snapped.

When the candle was produced, Julia held it over the wound, which she probed with her fingers. "That is bad," she murmured. She held out the candle. "One of you take this. The rest of you, hold his arms and legs. This is going to hurt."

She drew a small knife from her pouch and examined it in the firelight, testing the edge with a thumb.

Ida passed the candle to Oliver. "Be useful for a change."

Then she grasped one of Stephen's arms while Gilbert clutched the other, and Wymar straddled his legs.

Julia then slid the point into the wound.

A Curious Death

Stephen could not sleep through this insult and he struggled to sit up, a cry rending his throat.

"Be still, boy," Julia said. "This is the only way."

She pressed the incision with her fingers, and a thick ribbon of puss spurted out and ran down Stephen's leg. She kept pressing until only blood flowed out, quite a lot of it.

"Ah, that's good," Julia said.

After Julia mopped up the mess, she produced a large clay pot that was stoppered with a piece of dry wood. She sniffed the contents and poured a dark liquid into Stephen's wound.

"What's that?" Ida asked. "It smells of onion — and garlic."

"It's that, and more," Julia said. "A tonic of onion, garlic, wine and bile. It's the only thing I know of that works against infections like this. And even then, not always."

She wrapped some more linen about Stephen's leg.

"Now, we'll just have to wait and see," she said.

By morning, when Julia inspected the wound in the wan light of sunrise, the redness and swelling had receded, and Stephen was able to sit up.

"If I was a betting woman, I'd wager you'll live after all," Julia said.

"I don't feel like betting on anything at the moment," Stephen croaked.

"You need to get some food and drink in you," she said. "If you can keep it down."

Julia handed the pot to Ida. "Put this on twice a day, and keep the wound clean."

She headed toward the door.

Ida caught up and said, "I haven't much money at the moment, but we will square up as soon as we can."

"Don't bother," Julia said. "Sir Stephen helped a good friend of mine, Beth Makepeese, out of a sticky situation a while back. We haven't had a chance to say a proper thank you."

"I see, well," Ida started to say thanks..

Julia cut her off, but with a smile. "Good day to you, then, my lady."

And she went out.

Gilbert crossed Bell Lane to see how Stephen was doing two days later. Harry was busy in his workshop, but the hall was deserted, except for Stephen, who was at the long table bent over a piece of parchment.

"What on earth are you doing!" Gilbert cried. "Get back in that bed!"

"I won't be long," Stephen said. "The women have taken the children to the market and this is likely to be my only chance for a while."

"For what?"

"To write to Margaret de Thottenham unhampered by reproaches."

"I think Lady Margaret can stand to wait a day or two."

Stephen shrugged. "Well, I'm almost finished, anyway."

Gilbert coughed to clear his throat. "There are more important things than letters to Lady Margaret."

Stephen twirled the pen in his fingers. "Like what?"

"Like what we are to do about Percival FitzAllan."

"What is there to do?"

"While you were riding about the countryside defending the king, I took up the investigation. I found out a few things about Dinesley's death."

When Gilbert finished, Stephen stared into a dark corner.

"You don't think it was robbery after all?" Stephen asked. "This Hilde — I remember seeing her in the alcove, near a pile of clothing. It could have concealed the money. And this claim that her betrothed came into an inheritance, it is obviously a lie. She had to have taken the money. More than reason enough for murder."

A Curious Death

"I agree. Hilde had the reason and the means. But I have Midge's confession."

"And you believed her," he said. "About her reasons."

"Begilda was there," Gilbert said. "She did as well. And there is the button to consider. It was clearly Fanecurt's. It had no reason to be there unless he was in the alcove before Dinesley's death. And how else to explain Fanecurt's slipshod examination of the body, but to cover up the real cause of death?"

Stephen's shoulders sagged. "You know what will happen to them, if we tell FitzAllan."

Gilbert nodded. "I've had some thoughts about that. None of them good."

"He won't accuse them publicly," Stephen said. "He won't want to bother with the law — too slow, too cumbersome, too unreliable. He'll simply have all of them murdered."

"I suspected as much. Which is why I thought I ought to talk to you first about it. FitzAllan promised you the return of Hafton Manor if you solved the case. It's up to you what happens now."

Stephen's mouth curled. "You could have kept silent and saved me the agony of temptation."

"I suppose so. But Begilda was there at the end. She would have said something eventually."

Stephen was quiet for a time. Then he blew on the letter to Margaret to ensure the ink had dried, and set it aside. He reached for a second sheet, and dipped his pen in the ink bottle.

"Who are you writing now?" Gilbert asked.

"FitzAllan," Stephen said.

"What ... what are you doing to say?"

"Midge got her justice, although she had to make it herself. So?" Stephen's shoulder lifted and fell. "I will send my regrets to FitzAllan, thanking him for his offer, but saying that due to my wounds I am unable to fulfill the commission. We will leave the matter where it lies."

Printed in Great Britain
by Amazon